IRON & VELVET

KATE KANE, PARANORMAL INVESTIGATOR

ALEXIS HALL

RIPTIDE
PUBLISHING

Riptide Publishing
PO Box 1537
Burnsville, NC 28714
www.riptidepublishing.com

Iron & Velvet (Kate Kane, Paranormal Investigator #1)
Copyright © 2013 by Alexis Hall

Cover art: Kanaxa, kanaxa.com
Editor: Sarah Lyons
Layout: L.C. Chase, lcchase.com/design.htm

ISBN: 978-1-62649-049-9

First edition
December, 2013

Also available in ebook:
ISBN: 978-1-62649-048-2

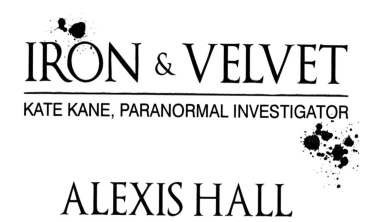

IRON & VELVET

KATE KANE, PARANORMAL INVESTIGATOR

ALEXIS HALL

RIPTIDE
PUBLISHING

To H.

TABLE OF
CONTENTS

CHAPTER ONE
WHISKEY & CIGARETTES

I woke to the taste of stale whiskey and the smell of stale cigarettes. Rolling over, I found a picture on the pillow—Patrick had been drawing me again. I stared into the face of the girl I used to be: someone young enough, pretty enough, and stupid enough to find that shit romantic. I'd dated a vampire when I was seventeen. It was a mistake I was still paying for.

The portrait wasn't quite up to his usual standard. Normally he shaded every eyelash. I'd given up hoping he'd get bored, so he must have been interrupted.

I tried to go back to sleep, but knowing somebody had been watching took all the fun out of being unconscious. Giving up, I crawled out of the covers and went to close the window. It wouldn't do any good, of course. I'd have to talk to Nimue about fixing the wards. But the last time I'd seen her, I'd been rebounding hard from Eve, so we'd been a bit busy for rituals.

I couldn't be arsed to shower, so I threw on what had been yesterday's clothes yesterday, and made myself a breakfast of reheated coffee and ibuprofen. The post was mainly bills. All right, entirely bills. And I hadn't paid my TV licence, which meant no more late night *Diagnosis Murder* marathons.

The truth was, since Archer'd died, since I'd *let* Archer die, work had been slow. Well, slower.

There was a voice mail from Dad on my laptop. I hadn't sent anything back for a while, but the messages still came in every month or so. And my mum, or rather my stepmum—as I'd discovered around the time I went through my dating vampires phase—had emailed a photograph of their new garden. They were standing in front of a shed, smiling and waving, Dad with that slightly off-kilter look that came from not being able to see the camera. It's weird to think of your parents having a life, but my dad was once the mortal consort of the Queen of the Wild Hunt. And by consort, I mean . . . yeah. Jenny—my stepmum—eventually got him out, but the Queen kept his eyes. They found me on the doorstep a few months later, wrapped in a wolf skin, in a basket made of briars. An honest-to-God faery princess. But since my mother's the immortal embodiment of an abstract concept, it's not like I'm going to inherit a magical kingdom anytime soon. And she'd never shown up at parent-teacher night.

My headache had eased just enough that I thought I could probably face daylight. It was Sunday, but I was supposed to be in the office working on the bottle of Famous Grouse in my bottom drawer. I was getting on with that, juggling my caseload of zero and reminding myself to take Archer's name off the door, when the incubus came in.

"Kate Kane?" His voice was sex and honey.

"Yeah?"

"The Prince of Cups commands your attendance."

I hadn't had much contact with the four princes who ruled the vampires of England. I knew they went by Cups, Swords, Coins, and Wands, and near as I could tell, Cups got people laid, Swords killed people, Coins bought people, and Wands kept the whole thing quiet.

"I don't work for vampires." I finished my drink and poured myself another.

His whiskey-gold eyes scanned my office. "It doesn't look like you work at all."

Zing.

There weren't many reformed sex demons working for vampire princes in this town. In fact, there was exactly one reformed sex demon working for a vampire prince. So, this had to be Ashriel, right-hand man to Julian Saint-Germain, Prince of Cups. The word on the street was that he'd gone celibate, which made him about half as dangerous as most other demons but still twice as dangerous as, say, me. And, as luck would have it, he and his boss were two of the city's supernatural power players I'd managed *not* to piss off. Probably because I hadn't met either of them.

I leaned back in my chair and gave him the once-over, which even I could admit was no chore. The promise of sex rolled off him like too much cologne. He was beautiful, and deadly, and thankfully not my type. "Sit down, then. Tell me what this is about."

He poured himself into a chair like bourbon over ice, hands folding primly in his lap. "I'm afraid I'm not at liberty to disclose any details. I'm simply here to escort you to the Prince."

"Escort?"

That could've meant anything from a polite drive to a bag over my head. I leaned forwards to pour myself a top-up, reaching with the other hand for the blade duct-taped to the bottom of my desk. I had a whole row of them: gold for vampires, silver for werewolves, iron for faeries, sanctified steel for demons. I hadn't worked out how to kill an angel yet, but I'd only had to try once.

"Escort," he repeated.

It wasn't a bag-over-the-head tone, so I left the knife. Kept the drink.

"I'll need more than that before I agree to anything."

"You don't have to agree to anything. You only have to come with me. And you will be compensated for your time."

"Eight hundred a day." I chinked my glass against the empty bottle. "Plus expenses."

"That's outrageous." He sounded almost amused.

"It's my 'I don't work for vampires' rate. Take it or leave it."

He stood, apparently taking it. "Shall we go?"

Not even an attempt to haggle. That meant one of two things. Either it was something pretty serious, or they were planning to kill me before payday. I went to one of my cupboards and slid back the false panel. The incubus drew in a soft breath. I had a lot of knives. Really, a lot of knives. And I liked people to know it.

Ashriel flicked up a brow. "There's caution, and then there's paranoia."

"I'm a big fan of alive." I took gold and sanctified steel. And a hip flask. "Where exactly will we be going?"

"The Velvet."

No surprises there. If you wanted to drink, dance, or fuck in London, chances were you'd pay the Prince of Cups for the privilege, and the Velvet on Brewer Street was the heart of Julian Saint-Germain's Empire of Sleaze.

"All right." I pulled my phone out of my pocket and traced a route on Google Maps. "But this is the way we're going."

He stood and leaned over me to peer at the map. He smelled of clean skin and sandalwood, with an underlying sweetness you might want to lick from his naked body. If you were into that. "What? No. That's ridiculous. We should go down Kingsway, not Drury Lane."

"It's my way or no way."

"Fine." He gave an exasperated sigh, but his orders probably involved getting me to Brewer Street, not bickering about the route.

It didn't seem like a trap, but that didn't mean it wasn't one. And anyway, there were tolls on Kingsway.

I locked up and followed Ashriel's taut little arse downstairs.

A metallic green Mini Roadster was parked on the double yellow lines outside my office. And here was me thinking that working for the prince of pleasure might actually involve some, y'know, pleasure. Where was the limo? The champagne? The twitchy-tailed bunny girls to drape themselves all over me? "Under-compensating for something?"

He grinned. All that and dimples too.

"Why me?" I asked, once I'd stuffed myself into the passenger seat, folding my legs up like reluctant concertinas.

Ashriel's eyes slid sideways and caught mine for a moment. "Discretion. Skills. You used to be the best."

"You used to shag your lovers to death. People change."

"Their behaviour, yes. In essentials, no."

He was still watching me, his eyes like pools of sunlight, drawing me onwards with promises of unimagined sexual ecstasy.

Been there, done that. I yawned.

"See." He dropped the demonic crap. "Useful skills."

I snorted.

Ashriel was texting one-handed with his phone pressed to the steering wheel. I reached instinctively for my knife, and he sighed. "I'm letting Julian know we're on our way. Not calling down an airstrike or marshalling my army of PI-eating demons."

It's all fun and games until someone gets stabbed in the back.

"Mind if I smoke?" he asked when he was done.

"Knock yourself out."

He pulled out a packet of unfiltered Camels and put one between his lips, and I reached my arm across the seats to light it for him, the flame from my Zippo defining the arch of his cheekbones in flickering gold. I should really get a new lighter. This one was a present from Eve and had the Serenity Prayer engraved on it. She always did have a cruel sense of humour. I used to find it pretty hot.

"Help yourself, by the way." Ashriel reduced the cigarette to a column of ash in a single inhalation.

"Yeah, right." Never take stuff from demons. Rule number obvious.

"Oscar Wilde," he drawled, "wrote that a cigarette is the perfect type of perfect pleasure. It is exquisite and leaves one unsatisfied." He paused. "Wanker."

About ten minutes later, we pulled up at the Velvet. It used to be a strip club in the sixties, a history it flaunted like a pair of nipple tassels. It was red and gold on the outside and red and gold on the inside; dirty, decadent, and smugly ironic, as though it was flashing you and winking at you at the same time.

Ashriel led me past mirrored walls and geometric Deco fountains, golden balustrades and plush velvet booths. It was what you'd call an intimate venue—full of nooks and crannies with no line of sight. I hated intimate venues. And I could have done without the low ceiling and the endless horizon of me reflected by the mirrors. Fuck, I'd let myself go a bit.

There was a gallery concealed behind suspicious-looking red velvet curtains and a corner stage still sparkling with glitter and lost sequins. Beyond the bar (more mirrors and gleaming racks of bottles), we passed a fire exit leading to the alley outside, and went through a set of swing doors opening onto a stone staircase. Each step was edged by a stripe of fading yellow paint, and the walls were covered with health and safety notices, fire drills, staff schedules, and hand-scribbled memos. I was glad to get away from all that shiny.

The next floor was a dressing area. One wall had been given over to yet more mirrors, each set into a frame of bare bulbs, while the rest of the room was a carnage of discarded glamour. I catalogued racks of costumes, ostrich feather fans tangled with wigs in every colour of the rainbow, silk stockings and feather boas, haphazard piles of makeup, and dodgy props, including a six-foot martini glass with its own inflatable olive.

The final staircase took us up to a much smaller admin area. There were a couple of office workers here, tapping away at their keyboards and answering phones. But as soon as Ashriel stepped through the door, they stopped whatever they were doing and stared at him. He was standing close enough to me that I felt his body tense.

Demons can't feel pleasure unless they steal it from someone else, which means they're basically out-of-control junkies. And their hit of choice is people, the only drug that actually jumps up and down shouting, "Pick me, pick me!" I'd have felt sorry for him if I hadn't seen how badly demons can fuck you over. And the more damage they do, the stronger they get and the harder it is to kick them back to Hell where they belong. It sounds harsh, but demons hurt people just by existing. I'd never met one that was trying to stop. If he really wasn't feeding on anyone, Ashriel had chosen to make his own life a living hell. Poor fucker.

I offered him an alternative temptation. "Smoke?"

He pulled a cigarette from the packet with a crackle of paper that made me want one too. "Marlboro Lights," he sighed. "Barely a peck on the cheek of destruction."

"I'm commitment phobic."

He bit off the filter. "Julian is waiting for you. Straight through there. I'll be downstairs."

Once he departed, office life slowly resumed with a clacking of keyboards. There was only one other door in the room. "Julian Saint-Germain – Manager" was embossed on it in gleaming gold. And just like that we were back in Shinyland. I went inside, only mildly reassured by all the knives I'd brought. Vampire Princes being what they were, I could have been stepping into anything.

But it was quite nice in there.

No orgies of androgynous bonk demons. No blood-slaves chained to the furniture. Instead, accents of gold on walls the colour of a really good merlot, lots of gleaming, honey-coloured wood, and the sort of heavy antique furniture you're not allowed to make anymore because trees, conservation, blah. Between the exposed ceiling beams, a vast skylight framed the rooftops and towers of the London horizon against a sweep of grey morning sky. That was just showing off. Even though it didn't physically hurt them, most vampires avoided direct sunlight because it weakened their powers. You'd only hold court under a giant window well after dawn if you were crazy powerful or crazy reckless. I was guessing the Prince of Cups was both.

Julian Saint-Germain was sprawled in a chair that was basically a throne, one leg hooked casually over the arm for maximum possible louche.

"Well," she purred, her Bette Davis eyes sweeping me up and down, "you're not quite what I was expecting."

Huh.

That made two of us.

CHAPTER TWO
PRINCES & CORPSES

She was wearing the traditional uniform of *that* sort of vampire: tight leather trousers, knee-high boots, a plum velvet frock coat, and a sleazy grin. Her ridiculously ruffly shirt had slipped from one shoulder to reveal ivory skin and a hint of black lace. And I was staring.

There was no point wishing I'd showered this morning, but I wished I'd showered this morning.

"Well, you're just what I was expecting, Ms. Saint-Germain." I folded my arms and pointedly neglected her title.

"Call me Julian, sweeting. Let's be intimate."

"Let's not. And don't call me sweeting."

She pulled her leg from its rest and leaned forwards on her throne, elbows propped on her knees as she studied me. I dug through what little I knew about Julian Saint-Germain: vampire (obviously), probably about eight hundred years old, powerful, ruthless, and . . . hot? Really, really hot. She was giving me a use for words I'd never thought I'd need. Gamine. Sylph-like. Exquisite. Damn it. Damn it all to hell.

"You," she said suddenly, "have extraordinary eyes."

I do. They're purple. Thanks, Mum.

But Julian's voice came over me like a rush of silk, and it took me a long moment to remember that I was done with vampire bullshit. I turned to leave. It was mid-morning, so I was spared a full-on vamp-bamf, but she darted past me anyway, an inhuman blur.

One day, a vampire will do that to someone and they'll just keep walking. One day.

But not today.

I stopped just before we collided. We were so close that I'd have felt her breathing except she, well, wasn't. She was shorter than me—most people are—but that just meant she had to turn her face up to mine as if she was expecting a kiss. Damn it. Damn it.

"You didn't invite me here to practice cheap pickup lines."

She grinned. "No, but I'm willing to be flexible if you are."

"I'm armed, you know."

"I do know." She took a step forwards, her body aligning itself to mine, cold but yielding in all the right places. "I enjoy dangerous women in fedoras." She danced her fingers down my forearm, outlining the shape of my knife through my sleeve.

I sidestepped, and she followed as though we were dancing.

"Oh my," she murmured. "Your heart is beating so fast. I can almost taste it."

I leaned away from her. "Do you actually need a PI?"

She moved back and ran a hand through her hair, which was short and dark and looked like it would be as soft as feathers beneath my fingers. Which I wasn't thinking. Not at all. "You distracted me," she complained, as though it was somehow my fault that she'd jumped all over me. "There's a dead body in the alley outside."

"And it just slipped your mind?"

"No, I just decided to seduce you first."

"Corpse first."

"He's dead, he's not going anywhere."

"*You're* dead."

"Yes, but I'm better in bed." She waggled her eyebrows.

I growled. "Tell me about the goddamn murder."

"And Ash said you wouldn't take the case."

"Wait, what? I . . . haven't taken the case."

She smiled brilliantly, snow white teeth and cherry red lips. "Then why are you asking me about it?"

Well. Damn it. Damn it *again*. She had me there.

She sauntered off and took a seat on the edge of her desk, one leg drawn up to her chest, the other swinging idly. Lethal had never been so cute. "Obviously I'm paying for your discretion as well as your . . . services." She did the eyebrow thing again. "I really don't need the mortal authorities to start poking into my business, or for the press to get hold of this. 'Man Horribly Killed While Trying to Have a Good Time' is not going to sell out my venues." Her expression turned momentarily thoughtful. "Or maybe it would, I don't know. People can be so macabre. Anyway, find out who did it so I can stop them doing it again." Her fangs flashed. "By killing them."

"What makes you think it's connected to you?"

"Sweeting, I'm a motherfucking vampire prince. Everything is connected to me."

"Any actual evidence for that?"

"Killing on my premises is personally insulting." Her eyes met mine. So very very blue. *Ngh.* "Take the case, Kate."

I knew it would be nothing but trouble. I knew *she* would be nothing but trouble.

But.

Eight hundred a day plus expenses would make a change from zero a day and expenses.

And there was no denying it. Julian Saint-Germain was my kind of trouble.

I nodded.

Julian grinned. "Fabulous. Shall we shag to seal the deal?" She put her hands behind her and rested her weight on them, her body arching beneath the spill of lace and velvet like a cat's.

"Dead body. Downstairs."

She looked disappointed. "Well, I'll be here if you change your mind."

"I'm not going to sleep with you."

"Not now."

"Not ever."

"Ever is a long time, sweeting. I should know."

I left the room with great dignity, her laughter following me like smoke from a cigarette. Cigarette. I put one to my lips but thought better of lighting it indoors and made my way downstairs, telling myself I could have it after I'd seen the body. I'd forgotten how work could get in the way of your lifestyle.

Ashriel was leaning against the bar, hands in his pockets.

"Tell me what you know."

He could have been a dick about me taking the case, but he let it pass, and I allowed myself to feel pleasantly surprised. Perhaps this was the start of a beautiful indifference.

"The body was found this morning by a delivery man. No witnesses, but we spoke to a homeless guy who said he was woken up by strange noises coming from the alley at about four this morning."

"I'll want to talk to both of them." I reached into my inside pocket for a pair of latex gloves and tugged them on.

"That will not be possible." A different voice from right behind me. I wheeled round.

Patrick was standing far too close and was glaring intently. Acting like he hated me was how he showed he cared. My dad's favourite joke was that Patrick turned me gay. He didn't. He was just a phase I went through, a phase I'd have really liked to leave behind. Sometimes I hoped he'd find some new faery-blooded, purple-eyed teenager to fall for, but I wouldn't wish Patrick on anybody.

He was still gorgeous, in a boy-band kind of way: pale and sculpted, with glowing, tawny eyes and copper-touched hair that was always slightly tousled. But even though he hadn't changed, I had, and I couldn't find anything to like in him anymore, let alone love. I mean, the first couple of years were fine because there'd been plenty to get in the way of us actually being together. His profound self-loathing, people trying to kill me, and the Queen of the Wild Hunt trying to kill him. And then he went through a cycle of leaving me for my own good, until I finally realised we didn't have anything in common and the sex did nothing for me, so I dumped him. Of course while all this was going on, I was also coming to terms with being half faery, which meant I'd flunked all my A-levels and blown my chances of getting into a decent university.

So here we were. Me, one vocational qualification, ten years, two demon invasions, and three thousand cigarettes older. And Patrick, still the sort of Class A wanker who spouted ominous bullshit while standing directly behind you.

"For fuck's sake, Patrick. You shouldn't have blanked them until I was done." There was absolutely no point arguing with him, but I couldn't seem to stop doing it.

"They had nothing of value to say."

"That's my call, not yours."

He looked very grave. "The preservation of vampire society is my responsibility, Katharine."

Patrick is an agent for the Prince of Wands, which is kind of big deal for a vampire less than two hundred years old. Wands is basically head of vampire MI5. His business is secrets, which includes keeping the ones that have to be kept. Like pretty much everything about the existence of vampires. He didn't always succeed, and people tended to find out about this shit because it was kind of massive, but there was still technically a no-witnesses policy.

Patrick was involved in a mix of PR and recon. He fed information to the press to cover up supernatural snafus, monitored mortal institutions like the police and the government, and occasionally infiltrated high schools to keep an eye on teenage girls with otherworldly heritage. Which was what he'd been doing in my A-level biology class. His job was actually one of his few interesting features. Of course, when we'd been going out, he wouldn't tell me anything about it. For my own protection.

The annoying thing was, he was probably right on this one. Eyewitnesses are notoriously unreliable, especially when the supernatural is involved. But I hated being forced to rely on Patrick. He'd always been big on the sort of trust that only went one way.

I went to look at the body instead.

It was lying just beyond the fire escape in a contorted pose. Male, mid-twenties, attractive in an engineered-hair, dead kind of way. His clothing, the regulation club wear of dark-wash jeans and a dress shirt, was rumpled and probably designer. He had the sleek look of privilege about him and defensive wounds on his hands and wrists. From his colour, he'd most likely been exsanguinated.

Ashriel joined me. Patrick had probably gone to brood in a corner somewhere.

"Someone freak out and nom a patron?" I asked. The simplest solution and all that.

"No."

"You're that certain?"

"You met Julian. She doesn't react well to being crossed."

Do any of us? But he had a point.

I crouched down and carefully turned the head so I could take a look at the neck wounds. Normally I'd have been more careful about contaminating the crime scene, but nobody calls me in for a mundane kill. The skin here was a mass of mottled bruising and burst blood vessels, which didn't look like a vampire bite. Then again, I've known vampires to tear a victim's throat out to cover up the marks. Classy, right?

I leaned in to get a better look at the body, my senses sharpening. It was a reflex, as unconscious as blinking, and another unwanted inheritance. My mother's power is the strength of wild things, the hunter's hunger, the taste of blood and fear. Some of it is inherent in what I am, and the rest of it I keep locked up tight in a box marked No Fucking Way. Faery magic is ancient and abstract. It's about being and becoming. And, frankly, the idea of turning into my mother would be frightening enough if it wasn't a literal possibility.

With my new unwanted super-smell, the mingled scents of blood, death, cigarette butts, vomit, back-alley action, and—oh joy of joys—a nearby sewer grate washed over me in a fetid, chaotic tide before I managed to block it out again. You'd think super-senses would be useful for a PI, but I'd learned pretty quickly that the world got ugly if you stared at it too hard. And you can't concentrate when everything stinks.

Up close, I could see that the marks on the neck were concentric rings of tears and scratches, each with a deep puncture wound in the middle. Not a clean sort of puncture, either. The skin was puckered up like when you stick your tongue into an orange. If I hadn't been dragged so mysteriously out of my office, I'd have brought my camera, but as it was, I had to make do with my phone. I snapped a few pictures and made sure not to socially network them. Not that I was in many social networks—not after Eve—but I didn't want to accidentally invite my family to Like my Gruesomely Deceased album.

What I'd initially thought were defensive wounds on his hands and arms turned out to be the same as the marks on the neck. I took out a nail file and scraped under his fingernails, transferring the grey-brown gack I found there into one of my handy ziplock drug bags.

I was rapidly coming to the conclusion that whatever had killed this guy was icky.

Possibly even squamous.

That was it for the body. I went through his pockets and assembled the usual jigsaw of personal effects. There wasn't much: a bank card, a money clip holding two crisp twenties, a single Yale key, a condom (Kimono MicroThin Ultra lubricated), a small quantity of recreational drugs, and an iPhone. He probably couldn't have carried any more without ruining the line of his jeans.

I flipped over the bank card—the familiar green of Coutts of London, in the name of Mr. Andrew J. H. Vane-Tempest.

Well, fuck.

That was a corpse of a different colour.

The Vane-Tempests were the biggest werewolf family in the Southeast. And they probably wouldn't be too thrilled about one of their own turning up dead on a vampire's doorstep. This was worse than murder. It was politics.

And it meant I was going to have to voluntarily talk to Patrick.

I called his name, and he stepped out of the shadows. The alley was gloomy, but it didn't take much to make Patrick's skin shine like a pearlescent light bulb. I knew his oh-so-sexy roofie bite was a mark of his bloodline, but the stupid glittering was all his own.

"Bad news." I stood up. "You've got yourself a dead woofle."

"That is unfortunate." His eyes flicked to the corpse. He didn't exactly sneer, but he added dismissively, "A mere cousin."

Lycanthropy is sex-linked, like haemophilia, so unless he had an extra X chromosome, Andrew Vane-Tempest could only have been a partial shifter, able to sprout a few fangs or claws or maybe even do the full wolf-man deal, but not transform completely. Though, since there wasn't much sign of a struggle, he probably wasn't even that.

"I don't think that's going to be much consolation to his family."

Werewolves protected their own. Vampires protected their own. Mages protected their own. Faeries were just bat-shit crazy and dumped their kids on people's doorsteps. It was a funny old world.

Cousins were technically the lowest rank of the werewolf hierarchy, but if you asked me, it was probably the best deal going. No responsibilities whatsoever, but a lifelong allowance. If it wasn't for werewolf cousins, there'd be far fewer fashion interns, It boys, graphic novelists, bespoke shoe boutiques, and sushi-haggis fusion restaurants in the world. And what a loss that would be. Or perhaps I was just jealous.

"I will take care of this." Patrick paused. "If," he added with what was clearly a tremendous effort, "you are done."

Sometimes he tried. It would have been endearing if he wasn't such an arse.

"I'm done."

"Katharine . . ." He stared at me.

"Oh, not now."

"Katharine, this could be dangerous, especially for a mortal. You should not be involved."

I sighed. Here we were again. "Not your problem."

"I love you. That makes it my problem."

"Always the romantic."

"I will not allow you to do this."

We'd had this argument. We'd been having it for ten years. And breaking up with him made no damn difference. At this stage, it was either punch him or ignore him. Punching him would be more satisfying, but ignoring him would be more effective. Decisions, decisions.

I turned to go back into the Velvet. I was so Zen.

"And you should stay away from Julian Saint-Germain," he added. "She is dangerous."

"Yeah, yeah."

"I mean it, Katharine. You cannot begin to imagine the acts she has committed or the secrets she holds."

"Now you're just trying to turn me on."

"Katharine!" His hand closed round my upper arm.

I turned into his grip and pulled myself free. "Don't touch me, Patrick. Don't ever touch me."

He looked deeply pained. Or faintly constipated. "You should listen to me. I warned you about that witch. And I warned you about Eve—"

I hit him.

My mother's strength roared out of me, unintended and uncontrolled. Patrick's head snapped back and he toppled over, landing in a pool of stale vomit. I heard his skull crack against the concrete.

I wondered how bad I should feel. But he was a vampire. He'd be fine.

Inside the Velvet, I unlocked Andrew's iPhone and looked through the contents. I should probably have been grateful for social networking. Those Sam Spade days of creeping through someone's apartment looking for clues were over. All you needed was their smartphone. And, wow, this was a man who liked his apps. Grindr, huh? I looked at his Facebook page and his Twitter feed and dug through his favourites. Party party party party. Real *Made in Chelsea* stuff.

A lot of his recent photos had been taken here. Just your usual drunken club shots of people getting hammered or getting off with each other. He had a whole collection of blurry arm's-length self-portraits, grinning like an idiot, his head resting against the electric-purple wig of a truly fabulous drag queen. She looked oddly familiar, but I could count how many truly fabulous drag queens I knew on the fingers of no hands.

Huh.

I swiped through the photographs, trying to make the connection click into place.

And then I recognised her. She was only on the walls of the damn club. I must have been getting rusty. Miss Parma Violet, compere of the Velvet's Friday burlesque club, Cabaret Baudelaire, and Saturday's rather more direct Dragaganza. I made a mental note to follow up that lead later, then looked through Andrew's recent calls. He'd made eight on the night he'd been killed, between two and four, to someone called Kauri.

Time for an awkward telephone call.

I pulled out my own phone and dialled the number. It's received wisdom that you do this sort of thing from the victim's phone because you might get A Clue from the way the person reacts, but since I've never yet had anyone answer with, "Hey, didn't I just murder you in the billiard room with the candlestick?" it just seemed an unnecessarily shitty thing to do to someone who might genuinely care for the victim.

I'm cynical, not a complete dick.

It took a while for someone to pick up, but eventually a sleepy voice said, "Uh-huh?"

"My name's Kate Kane, I'm a private investigator. Are you acquainted with a Mr. Andrew Vane-Tempest?"

There was a moment of silence. This was probably going to be complicated. As far as either of us knew, the other could have been any sort of psychopath, an assassin, an inland revue inspector, anyone.

And then, less sleepily, with a trace of a New Zealand accent: "What's this about?"

"What's your relationship to Mr. Vane-Tempest?"

Another measuring silence. At this stage, it had come down to a game of arsehole chicken over who was going to hold out longest. Kauri lost.

"He's my boyfriend. Now what's this about?"

Oh dear. I was sorry for his loss, but most people are murdered by their nearest and dearest.

"I'm afraid I have some bad news. Would you like to meet, or would you rather talk over the phone?"

"I'll be there. Where should I come to?"

"I'm at the Velvet on Brewer Street. Have you been there?"

He gave a huff of laughter. "You could say that." And hung up.

Huh.

I looked again at the posters on the wall. You didn't keep that many photos of someone on your phone unless you really liked them. Or you really liked stalking them. As far as I knew, I was still Patrick's wallpaper.

Ashriel was waiting by the bar. "What's the deal with this dame?" I asked, jerking my thumb at Miss Parma Violet.

"Professionally, personally, or supernaturally?" His voice rolled over me again, warm and sweet as an Irish coffee, without too much of the coffee.

"Supernaturally?" This could be bad, very bad.

"When she isn't working, his name's Kauri. He's one of Julian's descendants. His *philetor* is Jasper Glyde, who is Julian's third *parastatheis.*"

My eyes glazed over. Vampire family trees were practically fractal, and I always got the terminology muddled up. It didn't help that no two bloodlines seemed to have the same name for anything. "Wait, rewind. Kauri's a vampire?"

"A fairly young one. I think he's dating one of the Vane-Tempests."

"*Was* dating."

Ashriel's brow twitched upwards.

You'd think vampires and werewolves would hate each other, but, assuming nobody gets murdered on anyone else's doorstep, they're actually on fairly cordial terms. That said, werewolves think they have this sacred mandate to police the other supernatural races, which meant that even if Andrew didn't have enemies, his family probably did.

"Anyone here have a problem with the Vane-Tempests?"

"Not as far as I know." He shrugged. "And besides, why would anyone waste hate on werewolves when there are so many mages running around summoning things that shouldn't be summoned?"

"There's genuinely nobody who would object to one of Julian's, uh, grandkids getting it on with a woof?"

"Not that I would know about. I try to keep away from other people's sex lives."

"What about Kauri, then?"

"His too."

"Ha-ha. No, I meant what sort of person is he?"

"Oh, you mean did he randomly murder his boyfriend in a fit of crazy vampire bloodlust?" Ashriel looked thoughtful. "In my estimation, no. Julian's very careful about who she turns and who she lets people turn. And if something had gone wrong, he'd probably have come to us directly."

And who in their right mind would kill their lover on their boss's turf and then leave the body right outside?

At that moment, someone came running in. He was wearing black jeans and a black vest and the traces of last night's makeup. Even without the glitter and glamour, he was striking, hard muscles standing out on his bare arms. Cultivated stubble framed the red smear of his lips, and there were dark smudges beneath his gold- and blue-painted eyes. This was probably Kauri.

He glanced between Ashriel and me. "What's happened to Andy?"

"Take a seat." I hated this part.

"People only ever tell you to sit down when it's really fucking bad." But he slipped onto a barstool.

"It's Mr. Vane-Tempest." I tried to pause in a sensitive sort of way. "I'm afraid he was killed last night."

Kauri's eyelashes swept across his eyes, but his expression didn't change. I wasn't really telling him anything he hadn't already guessed.

"Was killed?" he repeated softly.

"That's what I'm investigating. We think you were the last person he spoke to before he died."

"Yeah . . ." Kauri looked bleak. "I was telling him to fuck right off." I gave him a moment or two, and he went on. "We'd had this fight. One of his jealous freak-outs. And, hello, he hasn't even deleted Grindr. Oh fuck, he's *dead*."

I gave him another moment or two. But this time he was silent, looking down at his painted nails.

"Any idea what he might have been doing in the alley?" I asked.

"He waits for me after the show. But I left him hanging for being a dickhead."

He probably felt fifty shades of shit. I wanted to say something comforting, but I'm crap at that. "Did he have any enemies?"

"No way. He was a complete fluff-bucket."

"Do you have any enemies?"

He pulled back his drooping shoulders and indicated himself with a sweep of his finger. "Who'd have a problem with this?"

Unexpectedly, I remembered Julian grinning at me. *I'm a motherfucking vampire prince.* I guess it ran in the family.

"Good point, well made." That won a wan smile from him. Vampires tend to be pretty proud of their enemies, so I didn't have any particular reason to disbelieve him. I guess not everybody shared my talent for pissing people off.

Everything about this murder said opportunistic. Unless the killer knew that Andrew would have a fight with his boyfriend, and that this would make him wait in an alley until four in the morning. I wasn't ruling anything out, but that's a lot of fuss for somebody completely unimportant. As much as I hated to admit it, Julian was right. It probably *was* all about her.

"What's going to happen to him?" Kauri asked.

Ashriel answered for me. "The body will be returned to the family. What happens next is up to them."

When I was a teenager, I'd hung out with this posh girl called Heather from the private school up the road. A little while after Patrick had shown up, I'd found out she was a werewolf. And a little while after that, I'd found out she had a crush on me, which I hadn't really known how to handle. When her granddad had died, she'd had to go on some kind of sacred hunt thing to protect the body, but I was vague on the details. I didn't think saying to Kauri, "Well, actually, I think something nasty might come out of the woods and eat him," would help with his grieving process.

I'd learned just about everything I could here. Andrew had no enemies of his own and a boyfriend who didn't look good for it, which meant it was either vampire stuff or werewolf stuff. Time to talk to Julian and let her know the score. My body remembered her in a flare of heat that travelled all across my skin.

Plan B.

"Ashriel," I said, "tell Julian what's going on. I'm going to speak to the werewolves."

CHAPTER THREE
WEREWOLVES & LINGERIE

Back at the office, I made several unsuccessful attempts to get an appointment with Tara Vane-Tempest, the local alpha woofle. She must have had a lot of fans who rang her publicist claiming to be private investigators, because they kept me on hold for three hours. So I hung up and read her Twitter feed instead: *Tallyho darlings, getting ready for La Perla at The Dorchester tomoz. So busy. See you at the launch partay #mwah*

Oh, dear God.

I spent that evening and the next morning getting my ducks in a row. I needed to do some fairly basic grunt work on everyone involved, and that meant making appointments, ordering files from records offices, poking around the internet because it's amazing what people will put in the public domain, and doing a lot of other banal shit. After lunch, by which I mean a packet of salt and vinegar crisps and a glass of whiskey, I took my camera and my fake press pass and headed for the Dorchester.

The Mayfair-situated, inherently British, five-star Dorchester hotel combines 1930s glamour with a contemporary edge. I know because the website told me. It also currently contained a crazy powerful werewolf doing a lingerie shoot. And she was about to learn that a member of her family had been offed outside a vampire's nightclub.

It wasn't the sort of place where I was likely to fit in, but the trick to getting anywhere you're not supposed to be is Just Go For It. I strode through the main doors and was halfway across the lobby before someone finally plucked up the courage to try and stop me.

"Excuse me, Madam . . ."

I flashed the pass. "I'm here for the shoot." And kept moving.

Nobody dared chase me down. Tally-fucking-ho.

It's usually fairly straightforward to locate the big events at these sorts of places. Edging out of the Bar Mitzvah in the Crystal Suite,

I followed the bustle and the air of excitement all the way to the penthouse on the eighth floor. They were still mid-shoot, so I was able to stuff myself discreetly into the small crowd.

I was in the sort of room that had a statue of a naked dude over the fireplace. Full-length mirrors decorated with green swirly shit took up one whole wall, and the other walls were hung with red floor-to-ceiling curtains. And they say red and green should never be seen. I guess if you spend enough money, it doesn't matter. Enormous French windows opened onto a balcony bigger than my flat.

A balcony with a fountain on it.

A fountain with a statue of a naked woman and a swan.

I shit you not.

The room had been cleared to make way for lights, cameras, and those big umbrella things. There was a mound of bright silk cushions on the floor. And on the cushions sprawled Tara Vane-Tempest, wearing a red basque, matching knickers, and a pair of shiny black riding boots. The boots were climbing a pair of supple golden legs that went on forever and ever. I knew because I checked. Thoroughly.

I stood there dazed as they finished the shoot, Tara obligingly adopting a series of interesting positions.

She was rather flexible.

When they were done, she shook out her long blonde mane and slipped into a silk dressing gown that came all the way down to her ankles and covered precisely nothing.

My professionalism was hanging by a thread.

She was immediately surrounded by a gaggle of flunkies and flatterers, and I stepped forwards, looking for a way to draw her aside.

Her eyes lit up when she saw the press pass stuck in the band of my hat. "Oh, marvellous," she cried. I'd expected her to have one of those terrible cut-glass accents that came directly out of the nose, but instead her voice was rich, dark, and smooth like a perfect cup of Jamaican Blue Mountain. "You're from *Horse & Hound*, yah?"

Well, never look a gift horse (or hound) in the mouth. "Yes," I said. "Yes, I am."

She wafted her dressing gown vaguely around her limbs. *Ngh.* "Let's go onto the terrace, yah, so we can have some privacy. I adore horses and hounds. In fact, the thrill of the hunt inspired this whole collection. You hunt, of course, Miss . . .?"

"Kane. Kate Kane."

"How charming. It makes you sound like a private investigator."

We stepped onto the balcony, and I closed the doors behind us. "That's because I am a private investigator."

Suddenly I noticed that Tara Vane-Tempest was taller than me. It had been too swift and subtle a transformation for me to really track, but I'd come outside with a lingerie model, and now I was face-to-face with an alpha werewolf. She stared at me with bright amber eyes, distant and predatory. And it took all my willpower not to flinch.

She leaned in and inhaled deeply. "You smell like death. Which of them sent you?"

"I'm working for Julian Saint-Germain."

"And what does the Prince of Cups want with me?"

"I'm investigating a murder," I explained. "I'm afraid the victim was a member of your family. Andrew Vane-Tempest. His body was found outside the Velvet this morning."

Tara turned away from me and stalked across the balcony. It seemed a lot smaller now I was stuck on it with a pissed-off lycanthrope. "I was under the impression," she snarled when she came back, "that the Velvet was a safe haven. How did she allow this to happen?"

Defending Julian was not part of my job. But all the same . . . "It actually happened outside."

"It's still her territory. If she can't defend it, then it should pass to someone who can."

"I'm here to solve a murder, not discuss politics."

She smiled, the wolf fading from her eyes. "You're talking to an alpha werewolf on behalf of a vampire prince, and you don't think it's about politics?"

Huh.

"Go on then," I sighed. "Politics me."

"Well, we wouldn't have hurt one of our own, yah." She tossed back her hair in a ripple of gold and sunlight. "And the vampires don't shit where they eat, which suggests to me that somebody wants to start a war."

"Or someone has a personal grudge against woof— er, werewolves, and is lashing out at whoever they can."

Tara sat down on the edge of the naked-woman-swan-fountain thing, crossing one leg over the other. "Anyone with a grudge against werewolves has been dealt with. I can protect what's mine. It must be the Witch Queen."

I really hoped it wasn't. That would be embarrassing. And it didn't seem her style. I admit I've made some bad dating choices, but last I checked, Nim wasn't a complete psycho.

"I'm not sure what the mages would get out of it," I said carefully.

"Power. Chaos. Opportunity. New hoodies. Who knows what those wretched little upstarts want."

I blinked. This was way above my pay grade. "They probably just want to be left alone."

"Well in that case, they shouldn't dabble with powers beyond their understanding."

"Do you have any other suspicions?" I asked, trying to salvage the conversation.

"Demons find people too valuable to kill, and faeries don't do politics."

"But they hold grudges, don't they?" I knew that from experience. "And your people have been hunting basically everything for like a thousand years."

Tara's head snapped round, and she glared at me. It wasn't a happy experience. "We watch the edges of this world, yah, because no one else can. If it wasn't for us, you'd all have been slaughtered or enslaved centuries ago."

"Which means you must have made some powerful enemies."

"My enemies are my business, Kate Kane. They have no part in this."

Bully for her, but I couldn't take that on trust alone. "What makes you so sure?"

Her lips curled back, revealing a lot of sharp, white teeth. "I'm sure."

There was definitely something here, but there was no way I was getting it out of her, at least not without risking a mauling. I made the traditional *don't eat me* gesture. "Just doing my job."

Tara smiled faintly, the tip of her tongue tracing the full arch of her upper lip. I guess she liked displays of submission. Maybe that would come in handy one day. Well, a girl could hope. Then she sighed, her breath stirring a lock of hair that had fallen across her face. "Poor old Andy. What rotten luck. When you find out who did this, I'll expect to hear from you."

Unfortunately, I'm not very good at being submissive. "I'm working for Julian Saint-Germain."

To my surprise, she didn't freak out and throw me off the balcony. Her eyes swept across my body. "People don't usually say no to me, Kate Kane."

"In that outfit, I'm not surprised."

Her eyes gleamed. "I'm a werewolf, yah. For me this is overdressed."

I cleared my throat.

"So, Kate Kane"—a playful little breeze twitched the edges of her robe apart—"is there anything else you want to say no to?"

I swallowed. "Not on a balcony at the Dorchester."

"Some other time, then?"

I made my escape. The worst thing about this job, apart from the shitty working hours and the constant risk of death, was that it was basically impossible to get anyone to tell you anything about anything. Maybe Tara was right and it was totally impossible for one of her family's enemies to have come after Andrew in that alley, but I was fucked if I was taking her word for it. I'd look like a right knob if I spent the next week unpicking vampire politics, only to find that it was some spirit with a grudge all along.

Yesterday's grunt work had revealed that the Vane-Tempests had about eight houses in London and a spooky ancestral seat in the wilds of Oxfordshire. I'd visited Heather's family holdings up by Hadrian's Wall, and it had been haunted as shit. If I was going to look for greebly monsters that might want to kill a werewolf, it was the best place to start. And the best time to do that was while the pack alpha was knocking back champagne at a lingerie shoot after-party.

Archer would have told me this was a mistake, and I had no idea what I was getting into. But he was dead, so what could he do?

I took the Tube home, grabbed my iron dagger, then got in the car, stuck on some Tom Waits, and floored it to Oxfordshire. I was headed for Safernoc Hall, a place so hard-core posh it wasn't even on Google Maps, and my route plan petered out somewhere around Aylesbury. I had to stop and ask for directions in places with names like Ickford, Worminghall, and Shabbington, and although nobody did the full Transylvanian peasant routine, they still looked at me a bit funny. I knew I'd found the place when my mobile phone went dead and I was suddenly alone on a narrow forest road in deepening darkness.

There was probably some god-awful Gothic pile somewhere around here, but I didn't want to just drive right up and be like, "Hey guys, mind if I stick my fingers in your birthright?" On a rational level, I was aware that wandering around an unknown haunted wood after dark looking for clues was not one of my Top Ten Most Sensible Plans ever, but I hadn't got where I was by being sensible.

Of course, where I was wasn't that great. But fuck it, I had cold iron and a Maglite, and I was going monster hunting. Thanks to mummy dearest, I have quite a good instinct for otherworldly shit, and a pretty good sense of direction. All I had to do was stick close to the road and see if I could pick up the trail of something evil and bloodsucking. As recon went, it was pretty basic, but it was better than sitting around in a library.

I let my senses sharpen and set off.

The woods smelled of late summer, leaf mould, and wet dogs. It could almost have been a nice place for a walk, but not enough light got through the trees, and it was colder than it should have been for the time of year.

Yep, haunted as shit. Just like Heather's place.

A light glimmered in the distance, pale as a star and, to use a technical term, wibbly. I hadn't been the sort of kid who ran around in the woods a lot, but I was pretty sure chasing after weird lights in the dark was a one-way ticket to drowned in a marsh.

I ignored it and kept walking. Dust caught at the back of my throat. A few more lights danced at the edges of my vision, like they were trying to get my attention.

No, thanks. Not playing that game.

A ghostly sobbing drifted out of the forest.

Nope. Not playing that one either.

I trudged on, realising I was in a bit of a bind. There was clearly something dodgy going on here, but I couldn't find out what it was without letting it lure me into a trap. I figured the trick was to hold out for better quality bait.

After a while, the lights and weeping faded. Then I saw a flash of silver in the distance. I froze, my hand tightening on the iron dagger. This time, there was definitely something out there. I waited, and there it was again. A gleam through the trees, and a huge white stag stood in the darkness watching me.

Huh.

I had no idea if this was what I was looking for, but I got a sense of its power, its age, and its anger. It didn't seem like the sort of thing that would command an army of bloodsucking monsters. Then again, I'm not sure what somebody who *did* command an army of bloodsucking monsters would look like.

I inched towards it. Moonlight spilled down the many points of its antlers.

If you shot this guy's mum, you'd seriously regret it.

When I got closer, it bolted. My mother's instincts flared hot, and before I knew what I was doing, I was chasing the thing.

I was dimly aware it was a really bad idea, but I just couldn't stop.

Faery magic: fucking with people's heads since ten million BC.

Okay Kate, stop running now. It's a faery, it's a trap, you're going down. Seriously, stop running. Now. Any minute now.

The trees rushed past in a blur, and I thought I saw glimpses of ghostly figures in the shadows. I heard the crunch of withered leaves under my feet. This was not good.

All right, Kate. One last try.

I stopped. The forest was noticeably deader here. And I could hear an eerie singing coming from everywhere at once. Logically, if I turned round and walked back the way I'd come, I'd eventually find my car.

So I tried it.

I got about ten paces, and then there were wolves in my way. They slunk out of the forest, surrounding me.

Here lies Kate Kane. Eaten by big bad werewolves. Beloved daughter. Sorely missed.

I did the gesture Tara had liked so much. "I'm a PI, I'm investigating a murder. I'm not carrying silver."

A sandy-brown wolf, slightly larger than the rest of them, padded forwards and shook itself. There was a fluid shift of skin and fur, and then I was staring at a naked dude, which was the last thing I'd expected. I nearly blurted out something stupid about men not being full shifters, but then I wised up. I guess it was about genetics, not gender identity.

"Uh, hi," I tried instead.

"You're trespassing." He was tall and muscular, with a strong jaw and very chiselled cheekbones. Reminded me a bit of Tara.

"I'm investigating the murder of a member of your family."

"Oh, you're *her*. We thought you might try something like this."

I'd been on a balcony with Tara for less than fifteen minutes, and she already knew me so well. I was almost touched. "Well, your alpha wouldn't tell me anything, and I couldn't rule out the possibility that something you'd already pissed off was coming after your family."

Unlike Tara, this guy didn't immediately freak out, but he didn't look exactly thrilled either. "I'd probably do the same if I were you, but this is family business. We take care of our own."

I was hearing that a lot lately. "Look, I get the fact you've got the big pack loyalty thing going on, but somebody was killed by some weird-arse monster, and you're living in a forest full of weird-arse monsters."

"Hmm." He stroked his chin thoughtfully. I'd never realised how much I took fully clothed witnesses for granted. Finally he frowned, looked me in the eye, and asked, "How did he die?"

Oh, God. We were here again. It was like a game of poker where nobody wanted to call. If I told him about the bloodsucking thing, there was a very good chance he'd leap to the obvious conclusion. But if I didn't tell him, I'd get nothing, and this whole picnic would have been a giant waste of time. "Okay. He was sort of, well, exsanguinated. But I'm pretty sure it wasn't a vampire. There were these bruisy-sucky bite marks all over the body. Right now I'm thinking demon or faery or general creepy monster."

There was a long silence.

"Okay." His eyes were still steady on mine. "We do not share our secrets with outsiders, but I will tell you that nothing in this forest could have done what you describe."

There was another long silence.

"No offence, but why should I take your word for that?"

He put a hand on his chest, and a faint smile touched the corners of his lips. "You doubt the word of an English gentleman?"

"My line of work, you doubt the word of your own nan. But I guess I don't have a choice." Well, I did have a choice. My choice was believe the werewolf, or spend the rest of the night in a haunted forest, searching for something that might not even exist.

"You're very slightly more reasonable than Tara led me to believe."

I've never been good with compliments, but I didn't think that was one. "Thanks."

I got a full wolf escort back to the road. I'd like to think it was for my safety, but by the way they chased my car halfway back to town, they probably just wanted to make sure I left.

I got back to my flat close to midnight, which left me a couple of hours to look over the case notes and drink heavily. I hadn't learned anything definite, but it looked like the werewolf connection was a non-starter for the time being.

I laid out the evidence I did have. Archer'd had this whiteboard he liked to use, but I had a coffee table. I pulled the crime scene photos out of the file and stared at them. Still a dead guy, still missing eight pints of blood, still covered in those weird circular bruises. Further examination of the ziplock bag confirmed my initial suspicions: it was icky. The whole thing was icky. The weird goo. The marks on the body. Those alone almost ruled out the major powers. Vampires and werewolves are many things, but they're not generally slimy. And the things at Safernoc hadn't been slimy either.

It could have been a random act of monster, but somehow it didn't feel random.

I laid out a mind map of the case with the contents of my drinks cabinet. Vermouth for Julian. Tequila for Tara. Tonic water for Andrew, poor bastard. Goldschläger for Kauri. I wasn't sure how Nim fit into this yet, but I poured myself a shot of Drambuie to represent her.

I spent half an hour moving everything about, until I realised I was sitting in front of a table of empty bottles with no idea what any of it meant.

CHAPTER FOUR

BISCUITS & MEMORIES

I woke to the taste of stale whiskey and the smell of stale cigarettes. Patrick was busy, so my pillow was mercifully picture-less. That called for a celebration, so I had a shower and poached an egg. Then I headed for the office to finish off my background checks. Julian turned out to be complicated, Ashriel even more so. Julian owned a vast network of businesses through a variety of shell companies, the most prominent of which was the Calix Group. Ashriel just plain didn't exist. I dug deeper into Tara and Andrew, only to find I had the opposite problem. If I wanted, I could have got their family history going back to the Crusades, and a basic public records search crashed my browser. Once I'd filtered out some of the noise, checking on Andrew only confirmed my suspicions that, family connections aside, nobody would have any reason to murder him unless it was deeply, deeply personal. But deeply, deeply personal and bloodsucking ick monster didn't exactly go together.

I checked into Kauri fairly extensively because, not counting butlers, it's the partner nine times out of ten. I couldn't let myself forget the fact that, although he seemed to be a nice guy, he was still a vampire. Miss Parma Violet had an excellent reputation on the boylesque scene, but the only information I could find connected to the name Kauri Kallili was a missing person's report from 2001, which I assumed was when he'd been turned.

I chucked it in at half five, with no leads and no patience. Supernatural crimes are always a real bugger. None of the suspects officially exist, there's never any physical evidence because magic, and everybody's motivated by thousand-year-old blood feuds, ancient debts of honour, or perverse occult master plans. And most of the time everyone blames the mages anyway.

On the subject of which, I realised I'd better find out their alibi, because Tara seemed pretty convinced by the "let's have a war" theory, and right now it was the best lead I had. Normally after a full day of getting nowhere, me and Archer would go round the corner to the Coach and Horses and have an overpriced beer. It was a bit touristy in there, but it was the closest thing we had to a local. Seeing as he was dead, I just went home and illegally watched a rerun of *Lark Rise to Candleford*.

The next day, I went in search of Nimue.

Ashriel had called me paranoid but, compared to the mages, I'm practically careless. Magicians are mostly self-taught, so they make a lot of mistakes and a lot of enemies, and the ones who don't know how to protect themselves end up very dead very quickly. Nimue's court moves around a lot, but she showed me how to find it years ago. It's a complicated ritual and it only works if she wants it to, but she's never turned me away when I've needed her.

Once I'd washed and chased away the worst of my hangover, I made my way to the Southbank. The area under the National Theatre is the trendy hang-out of aspiring skater punks and posh kids who think they're Banksy. From floor to ceiling, on the slopes, the pillars, and the arches, it's an anarchic riot of colours and styles, the kind of graffiti that gets sold as Urban Art in respectable galleries. It's also conveniently close to Waterloo tube station for your congestion-charge-averse PI.

On the way, I'd picked up a copy of the *Metro* that someone had left on the seat opposite, borrowed a pen from the guy next to me, and scribbled Nim's calling name into the crossword on the back page. And then I returned the pen. Like a good citizen.

Huddled behind one of the pillars, I surreptitiously tried to burn the paper with my Zippo. The graffiti is legal, but starting fires in public isn't. I gathered the ashes from the floor as best I could, hoping nobody had pissed there recently, and smeared them across my eyelids.

There was a sudden shift in my perception. Everything was still the same, but I was looking at it differently. It was like one of those magic eye pictures. Or like I always imagined magic eye pictures were supposed to be, because I could never do the damn things. I stared dizzily at the graffiti, the colours writhing together like snakes. And then I adjusted, and everything popped back into focus, except one particular image was standing out from the rest. It was a drawing of a policeman with the head of Ronald McDonald, in a tank, pointing an AK-47 in the direction of Waterloo Bridge.

Off I went.

I headed south, away from the river, stomping along as the traffic roared past until I came to the IMAX. There was a huge billboard behind the circular glass walls, flicking between adverts for Samsung and Apple. I stared at them like a lost time traveller until the words "Stamford Street" flashed up.

I took the first left off the roundabout and walked on, keeping an eye on the buildings and billboards for any further messages. I was starting to think I'd missed one when I passed a Pret a Manger with a scattering of steel café tables outside. Suddenly my world went monochrome, except for an abandoned cardboard coffee cup.

This was the second part of the ritual. Sometimes it's a pond, sometimes it's a dustbin lid full of rainwater. Today it was half a cup of cold Americano. I lifted it to my lips and whispered Nim's calling name three times. The oily sheen on the surface of the coffee stirred sluggishly and formed a sepia-toned image of a squat, square building at the corner of a terraced street. The sign outside read "Siddons Road Community Centre."

I made my way back to Waterloo and hopped on the Jubilee line to Green Park before taking the Victoria line to Seven Sisters.

Tottenham, huh. Nim really knew how to show a girl a good time.

Siddons Road Community Centre didn't look much better outside the coffee cup. It was a plain, yellow brick building. The double doors were standing open, so I went in. Inside, it looked like every community centre I'd ever visited. The walls were painted in peeling cream and the carpet tiles were a faded blue. There were pinboards in the hallway, studded with typical community centre notices: yoga on Thursday, please wash up your cups, I have lost my umbrella.

To the left was a tiny kitchenette area, where a curvy redhead was diligently washing a large pile of cups. There was a sign over the sink reading "This water is hot," and an industrial-sized bottle of Robinson's

Orange Squash standing on the side. To the right was a decent-sized hall with plastic orange chairs stacked up against the walls.

Nim and a couple of kids were hammering away at a foosball table near the back. It was obviously a quiet day. Two mages I hadn't met before were playing Scrabble (one of them had managed to get "quixotic" on a triple-word score) and Gabriel, the court seer and Guardian of the Watchtower of the North, was feeding a baby. I regularly forget the birthdays of people I really care about, so I'm hopeless at keeping up with other people's children, but I could vaguely remember that Gabriel and his wife had been trying for a third when Nim and I were last on-again.

He was the only one of Nim's four advisors I'd actually met. They had kind of an elemental theme going on, so Gabriel was all about wibbly watery prophecy stuff. Someone called Rachel apparently did strange stuff with the airwaves, and a guy called Jacob talked to the dead on the Underground. I'd known a Guardian of the Watchtower of the South—a big-up fire channeler—but she'd been killed in a really nasty mage war six years ago.

"Hi, Kate." Nim surrendered the game and crossed the room towards me. She was wearing faded jeans and a grey hoodie. She'd grown out her hair so it fell past her shoulders in loose, dark coils.

It must have something to do with her magic, and I've never worked out whether it's deliberate or not, but Nimue slips out of my memory like mist. It's only when I see her again that it all comes flooding back, a rush of tangled images. Burying my hands in her hair, kisses that taste of cold mornings and deep midnights. Meeting all over London. The glittering terraces of Kensington, the muddled suburbs of Uxbridge, the concrete temple of a multi-storey car park in Peckham, the motley patchwork of stalls at Portobello Market. The city through Nimue's eyes.

The night she took me to the Eye, the barriers standing open for her, the lights coming on one by one, blue and gold and silver. Slowly, silently, the wheel beginning to turn, carrying us into a sky so dark and full of stars, like a reflection of the city shining below. That was the first time I kissed her. The first time I really understood who she was and the power in her. The city beneath her skin, a living landscape, as beautiful and terrible as the wilds of Faerie. Dawn breaking over a steamed-up capsule high over an oblivious London. The rising sun falling over us like a blanket, painting Nim's body in shades of burnished copper, and gilding her black hair with fire.

"Kate?" Nim waved a hand in front of my face. "Earth to Kate?"

I snapped out of it, the memories scattering like pigeons. "Uh, yeah, hi."

"You remember Gabriel, right? I don't think you've met Maeve, she's on kitchen duty at the moment."

A disembodied voice called out a greeting in a faint Irish brogue.

"And that's Ector, and the other one's Dinaden." They looked up from the game long enough to wave.

"I'm actually working a case," I said.

"Oh, so you're here on business?" I couldn't tell whether she was pleased I was working, or disappointed I was working an angle.

"Somebody murdered a werewolf on the doorstep of the Velvet. Nim, I kind of have to ask. Are you trying to start a war?"

She laughed. "No. Duh."

"Okay, just checking."

"So what happened?" she asked.

"I'm not sure—there were odd marks on the body. My best guess at this stage is somebody summoned something. And it looks like they were specifically trying to attack Julian's holdings."

"Julian's?" Nim tilted her head curiously. "When did you get on first-name terms with the Prince of Cups?"

I cleared my throat.

"I thought you didn't work for vampires."

"It turns out that not working for vampires pays really badly. Look, I was hoping you'd be able to tell what killed the guy."

Nim folded her arms. "Sorry, Kate, I *really* don't work for vampires."

I should probably have thought of that before I tried hitting her up for a favour. "The thing is—" I paused. "—it looks like magework. I don't want to give them any excuse to come after you."

Ector glanced up from the game. "Let 'em try. Tottenham's locked down."

"Oh, please," I snapped. "You're only safe because nobody cares enough to come and kill you."

He stood, knocked over the Scrabble board, and got all up in my face. "Where the fuck d'you get off?"

I was really tempted to say *Seven Sisters* but I didn't think that would help. God give me the serenity to accept angry young men being dickheads. Especially when they're ginger. "Do you have any idea how much shit an angry vampire prince can throw at you?"

"We can give as good as we get."

"Sure you can. You might even survive. But what about your family? What about your mates? What about the school down the road? Vampires don't fight fair."

Nim put a hand on my shoulder. "Cut it out. You don't come to my court for help and start a pissing contest. And, Ector, stop making an arse of yourself. Move the chairs."

Ector and Dinaden dragged six chairs into a circle while Gabriel gently ushered his older kids out of the room. Maeve came in with a tea tray, and while they set up I got myself a cup of Sainsbury's Red Label and a custard cream. I twisted the top off and scraped the dusty yellow paste from the inside with my teeth. The familiar taste of sugar and sawdust reminded me of my grandfather—Jenny's dad.

"Din ate all the bourbons." Maeve grinned. "Fecker."

I'd never seen the court in session before, but I assumed the empty seat was for me.

It wasn't.

Ector sniggered. Apparently trying to sit in the wrong chair is a major fucking faux pas.

"That chair waits for the one who will fill it," explained Nim.

Well, that cleared that up. I took my place, standing in the centre of the circle.

Nim spoke first. "I, Nimue, hereby convene this court to hear the petition of Katharine Kane of Consett. Let those here present make themselves known."

And then the others spoke in turn:

"I, Gabriel, Guardian of the Watchtower of the North, recognise the petitioner."

"I, Maeve, Priestess of the Quiet Gods, recognise the petitioner."

"I, Ector, Knight of the Watchtower of the South, Keeper of the Nine Keys, Pilgrim on the Burning Path, recognise the petitioner."

"I, Dinaden, some guy who works in a shop, recognise the petitioner."

Nim smiled encouragingly. "Over to you, Kate."

"Uh, right. I was wondering if any of you knew what would leave marks like this on a body." I fished out my phone with the photos, and the ziplock bag with the goo in it, and passed them both around. "It appeared in an alley on Brewer Street around 4 a.m. on Sunday, exsanguinated a fully grown man, and vanished without leaving a trace."

Ector shrugged. "Not my bag, not my problem."

"The trouble is," said Maeve softly, "it could be one of a dozen things. It probably didn't come out the river, but there are creatures you can call down from the stars if you know how."

"How many of you have that kind of power?" I asked.

Nimue met my eyes. "You know I won't answer that."

"Well, if wasn't a mage, what else could it have been?"

"Something from Faerie," she suggested. "It's not common, but it's possible."

"Or something demonic," added Dinaden. "Hell is full of oogly things that suck stuff out of people."

Gabriel had popped his kid in a baby carrier and was now cradling my smartphone in the palm of his hand, his eyes unfocused. "This creature came from below. It serves a power that is ancient and fallen, something that is not what it was."

I'm not really a fan of vague prophecy, but that seemed to be pointing demonwards. In my line of work you don't have to worry about things standing up in court, and a lead is a lead, but it wasn't like I could go back to Julian and say, "Well, I know it's not the mages, because they told me so."

Nimue took the phone from Gabriel and handed it back to me. "Is there anything else?"

I couldn't think of anything, since there's only so many times you can ask somebody if they're guilty as fuck. I got the rest of my stuff back and thanked them for their time. Nimue pronounced the court dissolved, and walked me to the door.

I stuck my hands in my pockets and tried to sound casual. "So how've you been?"

"I'm fine," she said. "But I'm not the one working for a vampire prince. I'm not going to tell you to be careful, but I hope you know what you're doing."

"Do I ever?"

Nim's fingers brushed lightly over a strand of my hair. "You do okay. I don't know how."

"Blind luck, bloody-mindedness, and dashing good looks."

That made her smile. "You know what they say about people who fight with monsters."

"They have really good sex?"

"Safe journey, Kate."

There was excellent service on all lines from Seven Sisters.

CHAPTER FIVE

BLUES & BAD IDEAS

W hen I got home that evening, Julian was lounging on my sofa with her booted feet resting on the coffee table.

"You don't call," she drawled. "You don't write."

"You don't knock."

She grinned. "I know. Aren't I terribly spontaneous and exciting?"

It was Patrick all over again. "Get the fuck out of my house."

She raised an eyebrow. Her expression seemed to suggest it was completely unreasonable of me to expect a bit of privacy in my own damn home. "It's been four days. And it didn't seem like you had any intention of coming to me."

"It's been three days and I was waiting 'til I had something to report." It wasn't exactly a lie.

She pulled her feet off the coffee table and sat up. "You spoke to the werewolves without consulting me."

"I do lots of things without consulting you."

"You used my name."

"You broke into my house."

"You should get better locks."

"You should give clearer instructions."

She grinned suddenly. "Well, you should stop distracting me with your purple eyes and your come-hither scowl."

Under very *very* different circumstances, I might almost have found her charming. As it was, I was just pissed the fuck off. "You need to stop flirting with me, and you need to get out my house."

I'd never seen anyone look genuinely crestfallen before, but Julian's crest fell pretty damn hard. "Okay," she said, in a small voice. "I can see I've fucked this up really badly. I was going to ask you out for dinner but . . ." She ran a hand through her hair. "Yeah, that's probably not going to work now, is it? Wow, I haven't blown anything this badly since I tried to shag Catherine of Aragon."

I pointed to the door.

"Look." She spread her hands in an *I give up* sort of way. "I really like you. I didn't mean to come here and freak you out. Well. Not in a bad way. I've got a booth at the Forty-Four. You could come join me. I'll wait for you."

I pointed to the door.

She peeped up at me through her lashes. "I'll wait all night if I have to."

I pointed to the door.

"I'm going, I'm going."

She unravelled into shadow and was gone like smoke from a cigarette. It was a cute trick, but I was still too angry to be impressed.

I slumped onto the sofa and put my head in my hands. Fucking vampires. She bloody well *would* be waiting all night. There was no way I was going.

I sorted miserably through the bottles on my coffee table until I found one that still had liquid in it and poured myself a drink. I wasn't really in the mood to think about the case, and dodging the TV licence fee had lost its thrill. So I watched the last of the light leaking out of the sky until I was sitting in the dark like the moody loner I am.

This sort of behaviour comes across way better in movies where you can have a convenient montage and get the whole thing over with in about three minutes.

I picked up my phone and fiddled with it. Archer was still on speed dial. I rang him.

"This is Archer, leave a message after the beep. Beep."

Then the evil robot woman told me the mailbox was full and that my message may not reach the recipient.

Well, no shit.

I hung up.

What would I have said anyway? I'm sorry you're dead. I'm sorry I had sex with the woman who shot you. I'm sorry I seriously considered letting her go. I'm sorry I didn't even find that statue thing you were supposed to be looking for.

So that'd killed a good ten seconds.

What the fuck had happened to me? I was sitting alone in my flat at ten past eight on a Wednesday evening, with nothing to do except ring my dead partner and play Teeter, which I suck at even when I'm sober. I cast around for something to distract myself with. When Eve had been living with me, there'd been a bunch of game consoles, but during the division of assets we agreed that we'd each take away what we brought with us. So Eve got the Xbox, the PlayStation, and most of our friends. And I got the Tom Waits CDs and the mortgage. She tried to pay it off when she turned into the lesbian Mark Zuckerberg, but I wouldn't let her. The Tom Waits CDs, the mortgage, and my pride. And at least I'm not picking her socks off the floor and wiping cheesy wotsit dust off the furniture anymore.

I never thought I'd miss that.

Fuck it, I was going out.

I went into the bedroom to change my shirt. I had no idea what trendy young lesbians were wearing these days, but it was almost certainly not something they'd already slept in more than once. I shuffled through my work clothes, trying to remember who I used to be, and finally dug out a pair of skinny jeans, a soft cotton V-neck, and a fitted blazer, in which I could conceal at least three knives.

I am such a catch.

I was halfway to the Candy Bar when I realised that Julian probably owned it.

I told myself I didn't care. And twenty minutes later I was in a basement full of drunk, badly karaokeing lesbians.

Well, fuck.

No wonder it had been free entry.

I squeezed through the crowd, trying to find someone who didn't look twelve. I must've got old when I wasn't looking. I somehow reached the bar, and was evaluating their fine selection of Sourz, when somebody beside me put their lips to my ear and bellowed "HI!" over a terrifyingly sincere rendition of "Sometimes When We Touch."

"HI, YOURSELF," I replied. Suave.

"YOU KNOW," she yelled confidingly, "I KNOW ALL THE WORDS TO THIS SONG!"

"SO DO I."

"GREAT. WE'RE FAIL-MATES."

I took a deep breath. It was really hard to be pithy at this volume. "SOMETIMES WHEN WE TOUCH, THE IRONY'S TOO MUCH."

"LOL."

"DID YOU ACTUALLY JUST SAY LOL?"

"TOTES."

Could I really sleep with someone who said LOL in cold blood? Could I really *not* sleep with someone who said LOL in cold blood?

We took a moment to appreciate the music.

"I LOVE," said the girl, "THE WAY IT RHYMES 'DIE' WITH 'CRY.'"

"I LIKE 'WRITER' AND 'PRIZE FIGHTER.'"

"OH YEAH, THAT'S GOOD SHIT." There was a pause. "SO WHAT DO YOU DO?"

"I'M A PRIVATE INVESTIGATOR."

"THAT'S HOT." My pullee was not uncute. Tomboyish. Gelled hair. Tattoos. Knew all the words to "Sometimes When We Touch."

It was too loud to offer any penetrating insights into my surprisingly unglamorous profession. "YES," I said. "YES, IT IS. YOU?"

"I'M HOT, TOO!"

Oh help. I couldn't think of a single thing to say except *How does that pay?* which made it sound like I thought she was a prostitute. I fell back on old reliable. "BUY YOU A DRINK?"

"I'LL HAVE A J2O."

"A WHAT?"

She pointed at the soft drinks fridge. "I DON'T DRINK."

"I'M SORRY."

I bought her a ludicrously overpriced bottle of orange juice.

"I HAVE OTHER VICES." She grinned.

She was a demon, wasn't she? I have the worst taste in women.

"OH YEAH?" I said, with a mounting sense of dread.

"YEAH, BUT IT'LL TAKE MORE THAN ONE DRINK."

Okay, she was probably wasn't a demon, and I moved my hand away from my sanctified knife. My love life was so fucked.

"HOW ABOUT TWO DRINKS?" I asked, to get things back on track.

"IT'S A START. I'M TASH."

Tash the Teetotal Lesbian. I guess I wouldn't forget that in the morning.

"KANE, KATE KANE."

"SING ME SOMETHING KANE KATE KANE."

"OH, HELL NO."

She kitten-smiled up at me. "IT'LL BE WORTH IT."

So this was what it took to pull human women these days. Fine. I hustled round the tiny stage. There seemed to be a queue for the public humiliation, but I caught the eye of the cute drag king in the bowler hat, and the next thing I knew I was clinging to the mic and belting out a surprisingly girly rendition of "Little Drop of Poison." About halfway through, I realised it was a fucking weird song choice. And probably hit a bit too close to home. Although Eve had actually left in late summer, and I'd never been one for keeping pictures.

I finished to confused applause and slunk back to Tash the Teetotal Lesbian.

"YOU'RE REALLY GOOD," she lied. There was a pause. "NOT WHAT I WAS EXPECTING." There was another pause. "DO YOU WANT TO GET OUT OF HERE?"

Wait. That had worked? Unless she meant *because I'm sick of the sight of you.*

"SURE."

We spilled out onto Carlisle Street, kissing clumsily while the queue yelled at us to get a room. Her tongue was sharp with overpriced citrus, and she smelled strongly of hair product and faintly of sweat. We zigzagged, liplocked, her hands roving and groping. And then we crashed into the window of a Pizza Express. Her palm slid under my shirt and zoomed upwards like a breast-seeking missile.

Ah, to be young and horny.

This was probably a bad idea. I could tell because I really wanted to go with it.

"You're so fucking hot," whispered Tash the Teetotal Lesbian.

Okay, Kate, be strong. Tell this nice young lady you're fucked up and walk away. And don't wait until you've shagged her first, because that would be wrong.

She gave me an enthusiastic squeeze and popped the button on my jeans. Well, this was going faster than I expected.

"Easy, tiger." I covered her hand with mine. "I'm thirty-three. If I have sex in a doorway I'll feel it in the morning."

"Okay," she said cheerfully, "do you want to come back to my place? My roommate's at her parents' and it's only fifty minutes on the Tube."

"I can see why you prefer doorways."

"Shall we go to yours, then?" She wriggled against me and turned her face up to mine. She was really very pretty in a pixie-ish sort of way. And there was something just a bit familiar about that cat-who-got-the-cream look.

I'd got all dressed up and gone to all this trouble, only to go home with a twenty-year-old girl who looked a bit like the eight-hundred-year-old vampire I was trying not to think about. Wow, that was pathetic. There was no way I could shag her now. Not even a little bit round the edges.

"Look, Tash." I tried unsuccessfully to disentangle myself. "I don't think this is going to work."

"It's fine, we can get the night bus." She stood on tiptoes and kissed the edge of my jaw and started working her way downwards.

"No, no, I mean *this*," I flailed. "I'm just—" Kiss. "—in a bit of a weird—" Lick. "—place right now." Nibble. "It wouldn't be—" Kiss. "—fair on you."

Tash the Teetotal Lesbian left my neck alone, took a step back, and put a wrist to her forehead. "Oh noes. The hot older woman wants to take me home and use me for sex. Who will save me from this terrible fate?"

"Seriously, Tash, I'm in a bad place. The love of my life left me for a tech startup, and I had to send my rebound girl to prison for murdering my partner. That's not the cool kind of fucked up."

"Whoa." She blinked at me. "Is that true? Because you could've just said if you didn't fancy me."

"It's true."

"And in what way was that supposed to make me *not* want to sleep with you?"

"Tash, I'm as surprised as anyone about this, but it turns out I'm not looking for a random hook-up. You're great and, under different circumstances, you'd totally be my type." Too much my type, that was the problem.

"Okay, okay." That was the second time this evening I'd seen somebody's crest fall. "I get it." She pouted. "I was really looking forward to fucking a PI. I bet you've got handcuffs and everything."

"I'm a detective, not a dominatrix."

"A girl can dream, can't she? Give me your phone."

"Promise you won't smash it or steal it?"

"Just gimme." I handed it over. She faffed with it a moment and then snapped a picture of herself, grinning cheesily and throwing devil horns. "There's my number. In case you change your mind and buy some handcuffs."

I gave her my card. "Fine. There's mine."

"Oh wow!" she cried. "You've got a card and everything. I'll call you the next time I want something private investigated."

She blew me a kiss and headed back towards the club.

I ran away.

I got the Tube home, and sat slumped in a corner seat feeling confused, but mildly less shitty than I had when I went out. I stared at the picture of Tash the Teetotal Lesbian and wondered if I'd been a complete idiot. Had I really just turned down a night of erotic gymnastics with a hot twenty-something for an empty flat and a cup of Bovril? Had Julian really screwed with my head that much? I'd only spoken about two hundred words to her, and most of those had been *fuck off*.

I made it back to the flat and was shocked to discover that no vampires had broken in while I was out. I was starting to wonder if I'd overreacted earlier. I was about to take nearly two and a half grand of Julian's money, and she had no idea what I was doing for it. Way to be professional, Kate.

There was nothing for it but to go to bed. And I'd finished all the Bovril, so I had to go alone.

I lay staring at the ceiling.

I seriously considered calling Tash and telling her I'd changed my mind. I was pretty sure if I phrased it right, I could get it to sound sexy and impulsive, instead of lonely and fucking pathetic. I pulled out my phone and looked at her picture. She really reminded me of Julian. And so did everything else.

Well, fuck.

There was no way I was going there again. Blood loss and mind control are not a good basis for a relationship. But to give Julian her due, when I told her to fuck off, she did, at least, fuck off. And I couldn't remember Patrick ever apologising for anything.

How long was she going to wait for me, anyway? She'd said all night. It had already been about six hours. I think Eve camped outside Game at midnight to get *Wrath of the Lich King*, but I've never waited six hours for anything in my life. True, I'm not immortal, but Julian looked like she got bored easily.

I just couldn't imagine her waiting for me. It wasn't like she could order a shot of blood and ask the bartender to keep it coming. She was probably shagging the waitresses by now. I was tempted to go over there to see what the hell was going on. There was no way she'd still be there.

Wait. No. I wasn't going to give her the satisfaction.

I was going to sleep.

Two hours later, I was in a cab heading for the Forty-Four.

Well, fuck.

The Forty-Four was an all-night blues and pudding bar—the sort of place that had invested in a hazer when the smoking ban came in. Truthfully, it was my kind of joint, full of miserable, lonely people drinking whiskey and singing about it. It was owned by an MP's son following his dream. A pretty specific dream.

I stepped through the door into the smoky darkness. Mournful growling emanated from the stage. Julian was sitting in a booth near the back, her chin propped on her palm.

It was three in the morning, it was drizzling outside, I'd paid off my cab, and I honestly hadn't planned past this point.

Backing out seemed too much like hard work, so I went over and sat down.

"I bought you a drink," she said, "but I'm afraid it's warm."

"As long as it's still wet."

Julian gave me a mischievous look. "You make it too easy."

I lifted the glass and took a sip. The whiskey was smooth and rich, and probably expensive. Truthfully, I'm not that much of a connoisseur. I just like to get drunk. "Yep, that's alcohol. I recognise it right off."

There was a pause. On the stage, the singer started on one of those classic blues songs where a guy shoots his wife and is sad about it.

After a long silence, Julian looked up at me. "I didn't think you'd come."

"Neither did I."

"I'm really sorry about earlier." I'd expected the apology to involve big blue kitten eyes, but it didn't.

"Just don't do it again."

"People usually enjoy it when I show up unexpectedly."

"I don't like surprises. And I'm not most people."

Finally, she grinned. "I noticed."

I took another drink to stop myself from smiling back. "So," I said into the awkward, "what are we doing here?"

"We're having a good time." Lounging in the booth, with her arms stretched over the back of the seat, Julian looked like she actually was.

"Oh great, nice of you to tell me."

She shrugged. "I thought it might be your kind of place."

"You mean weird and trying too hard?"

"I kind of like it. It's just what it is, you know?"

"Deep."

She leaned forwards like she had when we first met, watching me like I was the most fascinating thing she'd ever seen. "Are you always this cagey?"

"With vampires, yes."

"Did we torch your village and eat your family?"

"That's not funny."

"It's a little bit funny." In the dim light, her eyes glinted like glass. "Come on, what've you got against us?"

"You mean apart from the fact you're all a bunch of amoral, bloodthirsty megalomaniacs?"

She laughed. "And I thought you didn't like me."

"Cute."

"I could find out for myself, you know." She shrugged. "It'd be less trouble. And probably cheaper."

"That would really piss me off."

"So you'd better save yourself the aggravation and tell me everything I want to know."

I finished my drink. "That's the worst logic I've ever heard."

She leaned in a little closer. Beneath the familiar burn of whiskey, I caught a faint and dusty sweetness, like a swirl of roseleaves. "Let me buy you a dessert. Maybe it'll sweeten you up."

What the hell? Was she planning on seducing me or eating me? "I don't want a pudding."

"Oh, go on," she purred. "Everybody wants dessert."

"What the fuck is wrong with you?"

"It's an escalation thing, sweeting. One minute I'm watching you eat a delicious sugary nothing and the next . . ."

"Do not go there."

Julian gestured in the smoky air, and within seconds, a waiter was at her elbow. "What's on the menu tonight?" she asked, sitting up eagerly.

"Well, Madam, we have an Eton Mess—"

"Oh, what's that?"

"It's a mixture of strawberries, meringue, and cream."

She closed her eyes blissfully. "That sounds wonderful. Does it melt in the mouth? Describe it for me."

The waiter looked a bit panicky. "It's, uh, nice?"

"You can do better than that." She poked him lightly in the ribs.

"Well it's . . . it's . . ."

"Does the tart flavour of the strawberries perfectly complement the dry sweetness of the meringue, like dust motes dancing on an April morning?"

"Absolutely, Madam."

She clapped her hands excitedly. "Excellent. All right, what's next?"

I had the feeling this could go on a long time. "I'll take the Mess."

He thanked us and withdrew hastily.

Julian sighed. "Some people have no soul."

"What was that about?"

"What was what about?" She gave a dismissive little wave. "Have you ever had an Eton Mess before?"

I wasn't letting it go that easily. "No. But I've also never asked a waiter for an oral rendition."

"Maybe not," she said plaintively, "but you haven't spent eight hundred years on an all-blood diet."

"Boo hoo."

"You're so mean." She pouted. "I'm bad with things I can't have."

"No shit."

"And, besides, when I was alive the desserts were shit. Have you ever had a white rose pudding?"

"Doesn't sound that bad."

"Hah. I'll make you one someday. It's flower-flavoured goop in a bowl. And I wasn't even allowed it very often—sins of the flesh and all that."

"Aren't you all about sins of the flesh?"

There was a pause. "I used to be a nun."

I nearly choked on the dregs of my whiskey.

Julian made a face. "Well, career opportunities were pretty limited for women in the late twelfth century. Can I get you another drink?"

"No, but I could stand to hear the adventures of Sister Julian, Pudding Nun."

"Could you now?" She smirked. "How about you tell me what you've got against vampires, sweeting, and I'll lingeringly assuage all of your curiosities."

I sighed. "I dated one, okay? Move on."

"We've all have bad relationships. And anyway, I heard you used to be with Eve Locke. Does that mean you've sworn off humans too?"

"So you did have me checked out?"

"Hah, no, checking you out is a pleasure I reserve for myself. But Locke is dangerous, and I make it my business to know her business."

"Don't you start."

She widened her eyes, flashing a million miles of blue. "Now what have I done?"

"I'm just sick of being told how dangerous everyone is."

"Sweeting, we're all dangerous, even you."

That was the nicest thing anyone had ever said to me.

At that moment my pudding arrived. It kind of lived up to its name, being a mess of strawberries, cream, and meringue muddled into a tall glass.

"Oh, wow!" cried Julian. "That looks amazing. Like fresh blood on new snow. What does it taste like?"

I dug out a spoonful. "Like dust motes dancing on an April morning."

"Get your own simile." Julian scowled. "And eat it slowly. Savour it. Roll the flavours across your tongue."

"Are you getting off on this?"

"Of course I am."

"I'll eat at whatever damn speed I choose." To prove the point, I stuffed down an enormous mouthful.

"That's so sexy," said Julian dryly. "Hamster cheeks totally do it for me."

"Mrmff you."

And then she leaned over and swiped a smudge of cream from my lip with one cool fingertip. I tried not to dissolve into spun sugar.

"So, come on," she pressed. "Who put you off vampires?"

"Patrick Knight," I mumbled.

She cackled delightedly. "Oh my God, that was you? Weren't you seventeen?"

I ate my pudding.

"Didn't you nearly start a war between two werewolf families?"

I ate my pudding.

"Didn't the Queen of the Wild Hunt attack your school?"

I ate my pudding.

"Didn't he think you were dead and come back to London to petition the Prince of Swords to execute him?"

"Look." I pushed away the pudding. "I know it's probably this enormous joke to you but it was fucking awful, okay? He took my entire life and cut out everything that wasn't about him. Because he—" I did sarcastic air quotes. "—loved me."

At least she'd stopped laughing. "Sweeting, that's awful. Shall I have him killed for you?"

"That's exactly what Patrick would have said."

She looked crushed. "But I was joking. Sort of."

"You'd still have done it, though."

Julian pondered. "No, I don't think I would. I don't want to get into your pants so badly I'd risk pissing off the Prince of Wands." She was silent a moment. "I get it," she said eventually. "And you're even basically right. I enjoy power. I enjoy control. As previously established, I'm a motherfucking vampire prince. But I've also been around for eight hundred years, and I'm kind of over it. I've got enough going on in my unlife that I don't need you to be the centre of it."

"Huh." This was new.

"I won't break into your house again unless you say I can. I won't try to kill myself if you leave me. I don't care who your friends are, and I don't think it's my job to look after you. I'm also a hedonistic, bloodsucking narcissist with nearly a thousand years' worth of enemies but—" She flashed her fangs at me. "—I'm never dull."

"Maybe I like dull."

"I don't believe that for a heartbeat. Not that I have one."

It was quite a sales pitch. There was just one snag. "I don't date vampires."

"Sweeting, you're dating one right now."

"This isn't a date."

"Oh, it's just a late-night meeting where I buy you pudding and try to seduce you?"

Okay, so I was on *a* date with *a* vampire. But I still didn't date vampires. *Keep telling yourself that, Kate.*

I suddenly realised I'd stopped staring at my drink and was staring at Julian instead. No wonder I hadn't sounded very convincing. It's kind of hard to pretend it's not a date when you're gazing longingly into someone's eyes.

For a dead woman, she seemed more alive than anyone I'd met in a long time. I wasn't sure I'd have said she was beautiful, and she certainly wasn't pretty. She was too vivid and complicated for that. There was something about her face that made me want to keep looking at her. It was like watching the sky or the sea, never changing but never the same. I wanted to inscribe the arch of her cheekbones with my thumbs, shape her mouth beneath my mouth.

"This is such a bad idea."

Julian's eyebrows waggled. "All the best ideas are."

"Your place or mine?"

"That was sudden."

"What, you're changing your mind now?"

"No, no, God, no. You just surprised me."

"Well. Sorry."

"Don't apologise, I like being surprised." She smirked at me. "I'm an eight-hundred-year-old vampire prince. It doesn't happen very often."

"Your life is so hard. No pudding, no surprises."

"Come back to my place and console me in my dreary immortality."

This was a really, really bad idea. I could tell because I really, really wanted to go with it.

CHAPTER SIX

SEX & VIOLENCE

J ulian had a ground floor flat in Lennox Gardens—the sort of place so damn swanky it was probably technically an "apartment." We stumbled through the front door, kissing.

"You taste of strawberries," mumbled Julian happily. "And meringue."

Her tongue slipped eagerly into the warm corners of my mouth. I tried to press her up against the nearest wall, but there wasn't one, just an archway leading into a bijou kitchenette. We careened, entangled, into the pristine white fridge. Julian made a slightly surprised noise against my lips, and we went sliding sideways across the fitted cabinets, knocking over a really expensive coffee grinder and a stainless steel toaster that looked like it had never been used.

"What are you doing?" asked Julian, as I hoisted her into the sink.

"No fucking clue." I smothered her words in a deeper kiss. Her mouth yielded eagerly to the contours of mine, and she tasted of wine and roseleaves, madness and power, red velvet rooms and centuries of forbidden indulgence. She made my blood dance.

She braced herself on the taps and twined sinuous legs around my waist, pulling me closer. "You know I have a bedroom, right? Just down there."

"You mean you're not hot for the kitchen?"

"Well." She squeezed me gently with her knees. "I've never been in here before, so it's a novelty."

"God, this is such a vampire shag pad. I bet there's no food in the fridge."

Julian ran her tongue over the tips of her fangs. "I ordered in."

I kissed her very carefully. What can I say? I've had practice kissing vampires. I liked the danger of it, the promise of softness behind her wickedly sharp teeth, a prize in a castle ringed by briars. Beneath mine, I could feel her lips curving into a smile, and I claimed that too. It's not like I've had masses of experience getting it on with supernatural beings, but there was something about Julian. It was five in the morning and I should have been barely conscious, but I felt more awake—hell, more alive—than I had in a long time.

Everything was brighter and sharper and clearer. I could have lingered a lifetime on the pearl-pale curve of her cheekbones. Her eyes were as endless and shifting as the sea, the blue as rich as lapis lazuli. Between my fingers, her hair was cool as silk and soft as feathers. Her face was fascinating, as though she was a puzzle I couldn't quite solve. Time's cryptic crossword, ageless and ancient, fragile and eternal . . .

Oh, whatever. She was hot. And she wanted me. And I was high on wanting her.

But maybe not in the sink.

I swung her back onto her feet. It was totally suave.

Her lips touched the edge of my jaw, tooth-edged kisses tumbling here and there against my throat. "You know," she murmured, "I have twelve houses. You can have your pick of weird rooms. Coal cellars. Pantries. Airing cupboards."

"Oh, shut up."

I pulled off my blazer and slipped the frockcoat from Julian's shoulders, half-tripping over the pile I'd made as we staggered back into the hallway. That never happens in the movies.

Julian was staring. "Wow, you really are armed." She unstrapped my knives and cast them to the floor. And then: "Ow. Fuck."

"Sharp things tend to be sharp."

"You are a walking deathtrap, lady." She put her finger to her lips and sucked away the blood.

"Wait, aren't I the one who's supposed to cut herself, and aren't you supposed to freak out over it?"

"I'm sure you're delicious, sweeting, but I'm not the Cookie Monster."

I reached for her hand. "Here, give me that."

"Are you going to kiss it better?"

"I'll kiss whatever you like."

"Promises, promises."

"Shouldn't this have healed by now?" I lightly kissed the nick on her fingertip.

"It's too close to dawn."

"It's tiny."

"It really stings." She pouted.

"Then I'd better take your mind off it."

I tore off the ridiculously ruffly shirt, which I'd been wanting to do since I first saw her. Maybe just because I hated it. She was moon pale against the black lace of her lingerie, her skin so delicate I could see the frail hollows of her collarbones and a lace-like tracery of blue veins at her pulse points. I put my mouth against her silent flesh and breathed heat. Julian gave an unabashed whimper.

A few more steps and we were in the bedroom. At least I assumed it was supposed to be a bedroom. It was showroom tidy, with wooden floors, French windows, a king-sized bed and, for some reason, a bath in the corner. I gaped at it.

"What?" Julian blinked innocently at me. "I enjoy bathing, especially in company. Why restrict it to the worst room in the house?"

I tossed her onto the bed and pulled my T-shirt over my head. Julian propped herself on her elbows and grinned at me. This was turning out to be pretty decent evening.

And then the French windows burst open. In came a rush of cold air, a wash of grey morning light, and an honest-to-God tentacle monster. It was a ball of pulsating, translucent viscera, covered in twitching mouths and sucking orifices, and it went straight for Julian.

Way to kill the mood.

What happened next happened fast.

I didn't see Julian move. She was on her feet, hissing like an angry viper, all bared fangs and burning eyes. The creature erupted towards her with a speed I hadn't expected from something so . . . gooey, but she'd already gone. I looked up and saw her clinging to the ceiling, out of reach.

So Mr. Squidgy went for the closer target.

I dropped to one knee, going for the dagger strapped to my left calf. It was at this point that I really *really* regretted wearing my pulling jeans. Unable to get at the damn thing, I looked up and got a faceful of monster.

I'd thought it was ugly before. Up close it was even worse. A fetid pile of discarded organs and stretched ligaments. It was enough to put you off everything. Forever. It lashed out at me with distended cords of flesh. I threw myself backwards, but one of its pulpy tendrils latched onto my arm and I could feel things that weren't quite teeth scraping at my skin as it began to suck. For one sickly fascinated moment I watched as my blood seeped up its feeding tubes, staining them a dull red.

Then I yanked my arm away, trying to break its grip, but it just clenched harder with its mouthparts. Worst kisser ever. Grabbing the tentacle with both hands, I tried to rip it in two. It felt rubbery, lumpy, and slightly wet, like a condom full of vomit. Worst stress ball ever.

When another tentacle whipped out and latched onto my biceps, I realised that, tight jeans or not, I had to get a knife or I was fucking dead.

Unfortunately I was kind of attached to a flying squelch monster and couldn't reach. I hooked my knee up to my chest and started to work my trouser leg upwards, while trying not to overbalance and present my head as a deliciously available target. Least dignified escape ever.

Finally, I got my dagger free. It wasn't particularly sharp—there's a reason we wanted to get out of the Iron Age—but you can run somebody through with a poker if you put enough weight behind it. I put enough weight behind it.

I drove the dagger through the monster's skin and gouged. There was a spray of ick and the tentacle flopped to the floor. The end still stuck to my arm went on suckling, my blood trickling uselessly into a puddle. Well, great. And then two more tentacles hit me, pulling me into a squirming embrace.

Well, fuck.

Here lies Kate Kane, killed by a bloodsucking monster in the Knightsbridge flat of a far more attractive bloodsucking monster. Beloved daughter. Sorely missed.

There was a horrific rending noise and an explosion of offal. I found myself face-to-face with Julian. She was grinning and holding in her outstretched hands the flaccid, dripping remnants of Mr. Squidgy. The rest of him was spattered across the walls. And the floor. On the bed. In the bath.

"Honestly," she said, "the lengths some people will go to for a threeway."

I pried off the still twitching tentacles. I was starting to feel lightheaded from loss of blood and lack of sleep. "Just so you know, I'm not shagging you in here."

"Any excuse to get me back in the sink. Are you all right?"

"Fine."

Julian took me by the wrist and checked the marks. "You've lost quite a bit of blood."

"Yeah, it's on the floor."

"Do I need to get you to hospital?"

"No, I'll be okay. I just need a shower."

"Great." She grinned. "I can languorously soap monster guts off your heaving bosom."

"My bosom does not heave."

"Well, I'll need to make an independent assessment."

We had a utilitarian shower in which we did, in fact, just shower. Mr. Squidgy had sort of taken the edge off. Whatever I might have told Julian, I was actually feeling a bit shit, and I probably wasn't doing a very good job of hiding it. I ended up leaning in a corner while Julian gently sponged me down in a thoroughly non-erotic manner. And then she wrapped me in a big fluffy towel, gathered me into her arms, and carried me to the spare room. I was too knackered to object or to fully appreciate how weird it was to be picked up and carted about by a woman nearly a foot shorter than me. I just crawled gratefully under the duvet. To my surprise, Julian snuck in beside me.

"Um, I'm kind of wiped out."

Julian gave an immense yawn. "Look, just because I'm Prince of Sex, that doesn't make it a constant obligation. It's after sunrise and I just kicked the arse, well, the flagella, of a killer tentacle monster. I'm pretty tired too. I'll sex you later."

"I didn't know vampires slept."

"Only if we get hurt or kick the arses of killer tentacle monsters."

She buried deep into the covers and curled into my back with a murmur of pleasure. At least she wasn't watching me sleep.

"Hey," I said groggily, "you promised me pudding nun."

"Well, aren't you tenacious, sweeting." Her hand came to rest lightly on my hip. "A bedtime story it is. Once upon a time, in Colchester, there was an oysterer's daughter."

"Oysterer?"

"A man who catches oysters. Stay with it. And this oysterer's daughter was—"

"Was she hot?" I let my hand rest on hers, and her fingers laced through mine.

"Yes. She was super-hot."

"It's for my mind's eye," I explained.

Julian made a put-upon noise. "She was *ful gracios wyth*, um, hotness, okay? Anyway. This oysterer's daughter was cursed, for the Devil had come to her and anointed her eyes with his iniquity, such that she found no beauty in mankind."

The last bedtime story I remembered had involved elephants and balloons. In my current state that was about my level. "She what?"

"She became vain in her imagination." Julian's lips brushed against my shoulder. "Her foolish heart was darkened." She wriggled a little bit closer, sliding our bodies sweetly together. "She dreamed of Bathsheba in the moonlight." There was a long silence. "She was a lesbian, sweeting."

"Oh, right."

"Wracked with guilt at her . . ." Julian's hand slipped out from under mine and snaked up to my breast ". . . unnatural yearnings, she surrendered herself to a convent. Needless to say, thrusting herself into cloisters full of nubile young novices did not alleviate her condition. Such was her fervour for redemption that she soon came to the notice of the Order of St. Agrippina."

"The who?"

"A holy sisterhood devoted to protecting the world from evil spirits."

I perked up a bit. "You mean demon-fighting ninja nuns?"

"Basically, yes."

"Kill anything interesting?"

"You're so bloodthirsty, sweeting. Quite a lot of vampires, actually, a couple of werewolf packs, a faery lord, and the occasional demon." There was a pause, and Julian's hand found mine again. "But the darkest and the deadliest creature that the Order faced was Anacletus the Corruptor, an ancient vampire of unimaginable power and unspeakable appetites. They pursued him across half of Europe and slew scores of his progeny, and, in vengeance, he took one of the sisters for his own."

"Did you get her back?"

She burst out laughing. "Are you unconscious? It was me, you goose."

"Sorry."

"He took her and turned her and kept her. For decades it was his mission to make her as corrupt as he. Anacletus had long since withered past material pleasures, so his only joy was in witnessing the debasement of others. He subjected the oysterer's daughter—"

"You mean, you?"

"The oysterer's daughter. It's my story and I'll tell it how I want. He subjected her to every temptation imaginable."

"Is this where the pudding comes in?"

"Alas, the luscious world of puddings was already lost to the oysterer's daughter."

"Alas."

"But," Julian went on doggedly, "it was to no avail. She resisted all enticements and finally, in disgust, he gave her to his incubus, a wretched creature who had been bound to his will for untold centuries."

"Is this a recurring character?"

"Will you shut up? The oysterer's daughter told the demon about mercy and forgiveness and the eternal hope of redemption. And the demon's black heart melted and he fell to his knees before her—"

"Seriously?"

"Oh, all right." She nuzzled into the back of my neck, her teeth nipping lightly at the skin. "The demon realised it was his chance to get the hell out of there. And together they escaped, setting their captor's palace on fire, as is traditional. The pair fled to London, where they parted ways, not to meet again for many years. And the oysterer's daughter, believing all that had happened to be the Devil's curse for her inversion, wallowed in darkness and misery, drinking the blood of vermin, and praying to a God who wouldn't answer for a death that wouldn't come."

I rolled over to face her. "That's really sad. What happened next?"

"She got over it."

"Is that it?"

I caught the glint of Julian's teeth as she smiled. "Yep."

"I thought you were going to be redeemed by the love of a good woman."

"There's still time, sweeting."

CHAPTER SEVEN
BLOOD & VIKINGS

I woke to the taste of wine and roseleaves. Something was wrong. Perhaps it was the unfamiliar ceiling. The sheets with a thread count so high it felt like being wrapped in clouds. Or the vampire prince nuzzled into the crook of my arm. But mainly it was the fact I didn't have a hangover.

Huh.

We'd slept through most of the morning. There was a sheen of noonday light seeping through the thin curtains. I was bad at getting up even when I wasn't entangled with a hot chick but, after a few minutes, necessity demanded, and I realised I was going to have to find a bathroom that wasn't full of monster splatter.

Julian made a sleepy sound as I eased out of the covers. "Mmmf, five more minutes."

And when I came back she'd sneakily annexed my side of the bed and was rolled in a sausage of duvet. Her hair was all tousled. She looked, frankly, adorable. I leaned over to kiss her and, quick as a snake, she hooked her arms round my neck and pulled me down on top of her.

"Gotcha."

"I knew it was a trap."

I reached up and closed my hands over her wrists, stroking the cool, tender skin of her forearms. Even in full daylight, she could easily have resisted, but she let me break her hold. I pinned her hands to the pillow and smirked down at her.

"Gotcha back."

She stirred beneath me and I felt the languorous stretch of her body even through the duvet. I fit my fingers to hers, tracing my thumbs over the pale lines that crossed and re-crossed her palms until I felt a shiver in her skin, an answer to the needle sparks of desire that flashed inside me. She seemed absurdly fragile. But her eyes were as endless and as ancient as the sky. Her strength, as undeniable as steel, yielded to me without hesitation.

I bent to kiss her, slipping my tongue between her fangs into the velvet softness of her mouth. The same rush of madness. She tasted of promises and secrets. Although I was holding her down, I felt like I was falling. We shed the duvet, falling together, skin to skin. She was as smooth as silk and marble, but her mouth was a spill of heat under mine. Her liberated hands traced the curve of my spine, pleasure igniting like stars wherever she touched me.

I tasted the hollow at the base of her throat and the fragile ridges of her collarbones, the softness of her breasts, and the sleek valley that led across her unbeating heart. Julian's fingers tangled in my hair, her body twisting against mine, her lips opening on a deep, rich sound of desire. I've always been pretty quiet, so the intensity of her response caught me by surprise. Even more surprising was how much I liked it. Her passion and her ease in it heated my skin like lovers' breath.

I tend to think of myself as focused. I get the job done (though I don't charge expenses). Maybe I'm just a naturally wary person. Or maybe it's because people keep trying to kill me. But this was different somehow. It was Julian. She pursued her pleasure like it was her prey. She was fearless, relentless, and shameless. And I was out of my depth.

My head was spinning again. She sparkled in my mouth like champagne. My kisses landed on her skin as vivid as butterflies. The idle play of her fingertips glittered over me like dew across a spider's web. The world had collapsed into nothing but this. Tangled sheets, tangled bodies, and Julian.

A wave of cold air suddenly swept the room, and a gravelly voice came from the doorway: "I seek audience with the Prince of Cups."

I rolled away from Julian. There were two knives in the hall and one in the master bedroom covered in monster. I was fucked. But, unfortunately, only metaphorically. In the absence of weapons, I scrabbled for a sheet and pulled it over myself.

"One moment, Your Highness." Julian rose from the bed and pulled on a robe. Standing at the foot of the bed were four vampires, which was exactly four vampires more than I'd want to watch me having sex. They were the Prince of Swords, two of his progeny, and—oh hurrah—Patrick, wearing an expression of utter betrayal.

Aeglica Thrice-Risen, the Prince of Swords, looked exactly like what he was: a one-armed giant who basically refused to die, from a time when beards, long hair, and furry boots were all the rage. Right now, what with it being the twenty-first century, he was wearing a surprisingly well-tailored suit and an overcoat with a fur collar, although he still had coarse shoulder-length hair in warrior's braids and a beard like the drummer from a Norwegian death metal group.

I'd met him once before, the first time I came to London, back when I was seventeen and pleading for Patrick's life. At least I'd been dressed then. His job was to kill things that the Council wanted killed. Anything from inconvenient mortals, to monsters from beyond the stars, to whiny pillocks who thought suicide was a great way to tell your girlfriend how much you cared. I'd only met the others briefly, but I was pretty sure the Edwardian widow with the claws and the veil was probably Mercy, and the Aryan poster boy was Sir Caradoc.

Between the bloodsucking tentacle monster, the mob of vampire enforcers, and my dickhead ex-boyfriend, I was really beginning to miss Tash the Teetotal Lesbian.

"I don't normally discuss business in my bedroom, Aeglica," said Julian, with a smile.

"I've heard otherwise." Sir Caradoc sneered.

Julian shot him a contemptuous glance. "Your dog needs a muzzle," she told Aeglica.

"Be silent, Caradoc." Aeglica raised his hand. "That is not how you address a Prince."

"My apologies, Lady." Caradoc bowed his head, but he didn't look particularly sorry.

"Highness," corrected Julian.

Caradoc glanced at the Prince of Swords and found no support. "My apologies, Highness."

"So," continued Julian, "to what do I owe the pleasure of this visit?"

"You have been attacked." I'd say this for Aeglica: he got straight to the point.

"I'm flattered, but I'm fine. How did you even find out?"

Mercy stepped forwards. "There is a large hole in your back wall and the dismembered corpse of a void-beast lying in plain view of your patio. The police were alerted, and Patrick brought the matter to us."

Julian did her best to look innocent. "Whoops."

"This was the second attack," said Aeglica. "This must be stopped."

"I've got someone looking into it."

Aeglica regarded me for what felt like a long time. One of his eyes was blue, the other brown, and his attention would have been intense even if I hadn't been dressed only in a bed sheet. "Is this her?"

"Yep." Julian grinned.

He thought about it. "It does not seem," he concluded, "that she is being very useful."

I normally don't stand for people telling me how to do my job. But then I don't normally try to fuck the client in the middle of a murder investigation. I knew there was a reason I didn't work for vampires. "Shall I just leave?"

Julian patted my knee. "No. You stay right there, sweeting."

Patrick chose this moment to defend my honour. "Don't tell her what to do," he snarled. He had never liked other people ordering me around.

Aeglica turned slowly, and the weight of his gaze fell on Patrick. "Mr. Knight. Have you not duties to perform?"

I was pretty sure that Patrick thought cockblocking me was his most important duty, but he probably wasn't going to be able to convince the Prince of Swords. He cast one last smouldering glance in my direction and left.

"Look, I'm handling it," said Julian.

Aeglica turned his attention back to her. "With respect, you are not."

"You know, I wouldn't take that from anybody else."

"Yes." He paused. "We must not show weakness, Julian. If you do not act, I must."

"It's fine, it's only been five days."

"Five days," said Mercy coldly, "in which you have failed to execute the most basic duties of your position. One of the wolfkin was murdered on your territory and you sent a mortal to tell the family. Then you allowed yourself to be attacked by a monster of the void and left its dismembered corpse lying in your ground floor apartment in clear view of the patio."

In Julian's defence, she hadn't exactly sent a mortal to tell the werewolves their cousin had been murdered. The mortal had gone on her own. But I didn't particularly want a room full of vampires getting interested in the way I do my job.

"Enough, Mercy." Aeglica's voice was unusually gentle.

"Really don't need to be lectured by a minion," Julian snapped. "I've been ruling this domain since you were giving handjobs in Venice. Don't fuck with me."

Sir Caradoc smirked. There's only one thing worse than vampire politics, and that's vampire family politics.

Aeglica blinked slowly. "Do not threaten my *aeth-sweord*. It is not your place."

"Then keep them out my face."

He nodded. "Be careful, Julian." And then turned to me. "I did not expect to see you again, Miss Kane."

This could be bad. Very bad. "I didn't think you'd remember me."

"I had never before been defied by a seventeen-year-old girl."

"Yeah, sorry about that. I was in a weird place."

"You may continue your investigations."

"We'll keep you informed," offered Julian. "But this was supposed to be a private party, so do you think you could leave us to it?"

They all left. Thank fuck.

"Well, that was a buzzkill." Julian huffed out a sigh. "Now, where were we, sweeting?"

I scrambled out of bed and began looking for my pants. "We're at the point where I remember I have a job to do."

She pouted. "Are you sure we weren't at the point where you were lying on top of me? I liked that point."

"I liked it too, but it was followed by the point where an immortal Viking, a killer school mistress, Fabio, and my ex-boyfriend walked in on me naked."

"Geat," said Julian.

"Geat to you, too."

"No, he's a Geat, sweeting. Not a Viking."

I'd achieved about thirty percent dressed, though most of my clothes weren't in great shape. I sat back on the edge of the bed and began pulling on my socks. "Are you making this up?"

"Believe me, I could not have made Aeglica Thrice-Risen up. He was a hero, then an outcast, then a monster, then a vampire."

"Fun times. Anyway, he's kind of right. You hired me to investigate a murder, not to fuck you, and I should get on with it before anything else happens."

She slithered up behind me and put her arms round my waist. "I'm not going to be attacked again today, and the corpse isn't going anywhere."

"You said that about the last corpse."

"Well, fine. I could just fire you."

"Then I'd definitely be too pissed off to fuck you."

Julian gave a woeful little shrug. "Then do what you have to do."

I left the gorgeous, nearly naked vampire prince and went to hunt down the rest of my clothes and sort through monster innards. Professional pride is so overrated.

Mr. Squidgy was where we'd left him—pretty much everywhere. I took some photos and scraped some of him into a ziplock bag. This was getting to be a theme. Still, a personal attack on Julian pretty much squashed the werewolf hypothesis. So I put my game face on and went back to her. She was still lounging around in bed, and she'd ditched the robe. I was starting to see why the Prince of Swords had made a personal visit.

"Forget something?" she asked, raising her brows hopefully.

"We need to work out who wants you dead."

"I've been around for eight hundred years. Nearly everyone wants me dead."

I sat down on the edge of the bed, trying to ignore all the nakedness and lounging. "Then let's narrow it down. Whoever it is, they're summoning monsters, and they know where you live. Or, at least, how to track you."

Julian yawned. "Well, that limits it to mages, anyone who can hire a mage, or anyone who can dig up a second-hand grimoire."

Be firm, Kate. Don't look at her. Don't think about her skin or her eyes or—shit. "We'll start with mages."

"What, do you want a list of every mage I've pissed off in eight centuries?"

"Actually. Yes. Start with the ones that you know are definitely still alive."

"That could take a while." She sighed. "I'll email you."

"Mages aside, how bad could this be?"

She was so quiet, I turned around. For a brief, uncharacteristic moment, she looked serious. Naked and gorgeous and fuckable, but serious. "Absolute worst-case scenario," she said slowly, "it's Anacletus."

"Is that likely?"

"No idea. He's been gone for centuries."

"Well . . . what's the *second* worst-case scenario?"

"Not sure. It could be one of the other princes making a power grab."

To be honest, at this stage, it could have been anyone. The politics of the undead were absurdly complicated. For that matter, it could have been Julian, playing some kind of completely batshit shell game. She didn't really seem the master manipulator sort, but then, if you really were a master manipulator, you wouldn't.

"It's too indirect for Aeglica," she went on. "If he wants you dead, you know it. Briefly. I suppose it could Mercy or Caradoc, but I don't know what they'd get out of it. On the other hand, it's too blatant for Sebastian."

Sebastian Douglas was the Prince of Wands—the guy Patrick worked for. That was basically all I knew about him. He lived in Oxford, which meant I'd never really had any run-ins with him.

"So that just leaves Mr. Pryce, the puritan bean counter."

"Is it his style?"

"He has no style. He's an accountant."

"Can you please be serious for five seconds?"

Julian pulled her knees up to her chest and wrapped her arms round them. "If anyone was going to hire a wizard to mess up my business, it would be him. He's a greedy little rodent, and he's tried to buy me out before."

"I'll look into it," I said. "But I don't think this was business, I think it was personal. It was showy and aimed right at you, but it was also sloppy. Would another prince really send something you could tear apart in six seconds?"

"Maybe he was just trying to ruin my reputation and devalue my properties. Someone called the health inspectors on one of my restaurants a while ago."

"The summoning still probably means mages. And there aren't many stupid enough to work for vampires. No offence."

"Hey, we can be very charming. Well. I can."

"Whatever happened, somebody sent that thing after you. We might as well start with mages who hate you. Send me that list."

She grinned at me over her interlaced fingers. "Do I get a reward?"

"Yes. You get to catch the bad guy."

"Cute. I usually am the bad guy."

I went home to shower again and swap my monster-gack jeans for a nice generic suit. And then to the office to dig out Archer's whiteboard, because my drinks cabinet wasn't going to cut it anymore, and deal with the mounds of paperwork I'd been resolutely ignoring. I checked the post box for the first time in a fortnight, and it vomited a heap of envelopes onto my shoes. On the top was a tastefully expensive square of cream-coloured card with a gold crest and a black border. It invited me to join the family in commemorating the passing of Andrew Vane-Tempest this coming Sunday.

I'd never been invited to a werewolf funeral before.

I couldn't tell if it was an insult, a trap, or a come-on. From what little I knew of Tara, it was probably all three. Given the way things had gone at Safernoc, maybe they figured I'd crash it anyway. I'd more or less ruled out the werewolf connection, but it would be a useful opportunity to double-check. Besides, I kind of felt it was the least I could do for the poor fucker.

Of course it also meant I had to RSVP to the email address on the back. This took me the best part of an hour, because it's hard to phrase that kind of thing. It's not like you can say you'd be delighted. In the end I settled for: "I am writing to confirm my attendance."

By the time I'd dealt with that, Julian's email had come through. It was a list of about fifty names in no particular order, with scrappy notes indicating the time and nature of the disagreement. Most of them didn't seem like reasonable suspects. They were either too long ago or too far away or, in one extreme case, a head in a box. Google and I were nearly at the end of the list when a name and a note jumped out at me: "Blood-witch called Maeve, short disastrous relationship, don't ask."

Well, that was motive and means, and being able to summon greebly shit meant opportunity was a given. And even though Julian was an immortal bloodsucking fiend at the heart of an ancient and terrifying supernatural conspiracy, when you got right down it, most crimes were committed by people close to the victim. Until Mr. Squidgy, Andrew was the only victim I had, but the direct attack on the flat confirmed that Julian had been the target all along. Maybe I was jumping to conclusions, but Maeve was the most solid lead I'd found, and truthfully, pissed-off ex was a far more likely scenario than obscure vampire politics.

Still, I had to play it carefully. If I was wrong and I went to Julian, I'd get an innocent woman killed by an angry vampire. And if I was right and I went to Julian, I'd probably start a war.

So I went to Nim.

The court wouldn't have moved since yesterday, so I jumped on the Tube back to Tottenham. Right in the middle of the rush hour. I pegged it to the community centre and burst into the middle of a karate club for ten- to sixteen-year-olds. They were all lined up in a row, punching and shouting.

I made a sheepish retreat.

Nim was in the back room folding newsletters for distribution. Occasionally she would stop and make a small discreet mark on one of the corners. She was wearing faded jeans and a grey hoodie. She'd grown out her hair so it fell past her shoulders in loose, dark coils.

"Hi, Kate." She looked up with a smile. "Come to volunteer?"

Nim had been helping out at places like this for as long as I'd known her. I'm wary of reading too much into the actions of people with unimaginable power, and I know this stuff is partly a cover for magic shit I don't understand, but I think Nim might be a genuinely nice person. That's what made this so difficult. "I need to see Maeve."

There was a pause.

"I'll need more than that," she said softly.

"There was another attack last night, this time on Julian personally. Somebody's summoning these things. It's got to be someone local, and it's got to be someone connected to Julian. It might be nothing, but Maeve fits the bill."

"What's the connection?"

I let silence do the talking.

"Oh, she didn't? Not with the Prince of Cups."

Nimue stood up. The light bulbs flickered and the newsletters swirled upwards and scattered.

"Nim," I blurted out, "I haven't said anything yet. To Julian, I mean."

"It's too late, Kate. Maeve was part of the warding ritual. If Julian drank from her, then she has power over her, and we've as good as invited the Prince of Cups into our sanctuary. Until we get the wards back up, we're completely defenceless. I need to summon the others, and I need to do it now."

She slipped past me, out of the community centre and into the street. I trailed after her. It was a still suburban evening, the sun hanging low in a clear blue-grey sky. Where Nimue walked, the streetlights crackled, lighting up one by one like beads on a necklace. Sparrows and pigeons lined the gutters, fences and rooftops, as if waiting for orders.

"Call the court," she whispered.

The lights snapped out. And the birds lifted into the air in a whirling of wings.

I'd seen Nimue send up the bat signal before. In an hour or so, Tottenham would be swarming with wizards.

She turned to me. "Thank you. For coming to me first."

I'm not very good with gratitude, so I ignored it. "If we act quickly, we can fix this. If Maeve's guilty, and we bring her in, Julian will have no reason to come after you."

Her eyes held mine, dark and steady. "You said yourself, vampires don't fight fair. And I won't hand one of my people over to one of them."

"One of your people might have tried to kill the Prince of Cups."

"But she might not."

I stuffed my hands in my pockets. "And either way, I'll know for certain when I find her."

"I won't let you hurt her, Kate." A wind picked up from nowhere, stirring spirals of litter and old leaves.

"I'm an investigator," I said, "not an enforcer. I'm just paid to find things out."

"And you aren't responsible for what happens next?"

I had no answer, so I glared at her. "I think we're getting away from the fact that one of your wizards probably summoned a tentacle monster, and it tried to eat my face."

Her expression didn't change. She didn't seem angry, but I felt weirdly like I'd let her down. "Then you should be more careful where you put your face."

I had no answer for that either, so I glared again. There was a long silence.

Nim tucked her hands into her sleeves. The streetlights were crackling again. "This could end badly for a lot of people."

"It'll definitely end badly if one of your people attacked a vampire and you don't do anything about it." I sighed. "Julian's not stupid. If I can figure it out, she will too."

"I'll do something about it." The glow of streetlamps crowned Nim's hair in gold. "If Maeve attacked a member of the Council, she broke our codes, and she'll be punished. Will the Prince of Cups be satisfied with that?"

"It's going to be a tough sell."

"So sell it."

"I've got to find Maeve first."

"I know. And I won't try to stop you. But if you won't walk away from this, bring her to me. If you deliver her to Julian, I'll have to act." There was a pause. "Kate, don't mess this up."

"There goes Plan A."

"Really. We can't protect ourselves from this. If the Prince of Cups moves against us . . ."

"I'm on it, Nim." I would have promised not to let her down, but I have a bad track record. "You know, this whole thing would be resolved slightly faster if you just told me where she was."

She shrugged. "I don't know where she is."

"She's a member of your court. You could find her for me in a second."

"You know that isn't going to happen." She looked genuinely sad, and I felt like a total shit. "While you're working for Julian Saint-Germain, I can't interfere, but I won't help you either."

"Can't blame a girl for trying."

Nim went back into the community centre, leaving me totally screwed on a street in Tottenham. It took a lot of time and patience to track someone down, particularly if they could do magic, but I was low on time and I've never been big on patience. Unless I could find Maeve, and find her quickly, everything was going to Hell. I've been a couple of times. It's not great.

I went over the facts. I basically had none. About the only thing I knew for certain about Maeve was that we had similar taste in women.

My vocational qualification hadn't covered this.

Which left me only one option.

I went into the centre's kitchen and closed my eyes, trying to block out the karate class, and conjure an image of Maeve as best I could remember. This would have been way easier if I'd known her real name or paid any attention to her at all. If I had to, I could track anything as long as I had a reasonably clear idea of what it was. Of all my unwanted gifts, this was the one I tried hardest not to use. It made me lose myself, which wouldn't be a problem on its own, but it turned me into something I liked even less.

It always starts with scent. The smell of weak lemon Fairy liquid and dusty custard creams. And underneath, traces of damp earth, fresh blood, and cold starlit nights. This was who I was. A hunter. I unleashed my mother's power. And, somewhere in the Deepwild, she watched. I felt the cool leaves beneath her bare feet and the skin-smooth stone of the knife she held in her hand.

Back in the kitchen, an image came together. A fire-and-ice redhead, cold eyes, tumbling tresses, and curves just where I like them. How could I have missed that? It must have been Nim. She tends to make me forget the rest of the world.

I had her. Scent and memory and instinct.

My head snapped up.

The world was grey. The trail was bright.

I followed.

Through a tangled spool of suburban streets. Past square-block houses and cars hunched like metal toads. Past iron trees and chain-link briars. Past the markers of a world that was fast losing its meaning. To the stone stream with its swift steel currents. I did not stop or slow, and warhorns echoed in my wake.

I followed.

More winding paths. Brick-lined. Glass-lined. And then a place of grass in an iron prison.

I followed.

A bridge where the stream joined the river in a rush of bright light and a roar of strange waters.

I jumped.

Landed on metal, which buckled beneath me. The river swept me to its banks and threw me to the grass.

I ran. North.

The world fell to my footsteps.

In darkness, I came to the end of the trail. My quarry had fled behind blue walls to a warren of windows and doors. A voice tried to stop me. But I did not stop. A lock tried to stop me. But I did not stop.

Inside, she waited, back to the wall, knife in hand. I sprang forwards. She put the blade to her leg and slashed. My flesh tore open, the air sweetening with the scent of blood. But I was on her now. I wrenched the knife from her grip. Pinned her down. Heart fast-beating under mine. Her pulse beneath my fingertips. Ragged breath against my cheek. I bared her throat for the blade. In the Deepwild, my mother watched and smiled.

I paused. There was something else.

This . . .

This wasn't what I'd come for.

I struggled to think. I tried to remember.

Every time it was harder to come back. The blood will claim me if I let it. I fought for myself, fought for control. And slowly, the world came back. The room. Maeve. The knife in my hand. I threw it away. My body was shaking. There was dull, deep fire in my leg.

"What the feck are you?" gasped Maeve.

I let her go and fell back. I'd been so close to killing her. It would have been so easy. The most natural thing in the world. A thin red line.

Maeve pulled herself into a sitting position. Her breathing was quick and shallow, her face waxen, her eyes shadowed.

There was blood soaking through my trouser leg and I had no idea where I was.

Well, fuck.

I applied pressure to the wound—I'd worry about it later—and limped over to the bed, sitting on the edge of it like I hadn't just been about to rip someone's throat out. Maeve was in no state to make a run for it, which was good because I was in no state to follow. She had long, straight cuts running along the top and bottom of both forearms. I'd known a few blood mages in my time, and I recognised summoning marks when I saw them. She'd called something down from the sky, and she'd done it in the last couple of days.

"You tried to kill the Prince of Cups."

"And so now you've come to kill me." It wasn't a question.

I shook my head. "I'm just an investigator."

Maeve gave a funny sort of laugh. The sort of laugh that says *I'm not amused and I'm not convinced.*

"Who are you working for?" I asked. I had no evidence she was working for anybody, but you get better answers if it seems like you know more than you do.

She eyed me suspiciously. "Nimue had nothing to do with this. I fucked up and I'm trying to fix it." She was silent a moment. "So what happens now?"

I tried to stand up, then decided to give myself a minute. Falling flat on your face in front of the suspect isn't very professional. "I'm here to take you back to Nimue."

"I thought you worked for Julian Saint-Germain."

"I do."

There was that sort of silence you get when you're both knackered.

Maeve climbed painfully to her feet. "I don't suppose I can persuade you to let me go?"

"No," I said, "but at least I'm not giving you over to the vampires."

Maeve huffed out another gloomy laugh. "I think I'd rather take my chances with Julian."

"She'll probably kill you."

"Only probably—she's fickle. But Nimue . . . she'll imprison me for a hundred years or turn me into seafoam."

"It's still better than being dead." I'm a look-on-the-bright-side kind of girl.

"You've never seen a mages' prison."

"I don't think Julian's in a forgiving mood, and I don't want your death on my conscience. I'm going to call us a cab."

I checked my phone. It turned out we were in a Travelodge in Enfield. Shit. I'd run about twenty miles. I was going to feel that in the morning. The wound in my leg was getting a head start—I was feeling that now.

We waited exhaustedly for the taxi. If the cabbie was surprised to turn up at a Travelodge and pick up a couple of women who looked like they'd been in a knife fight, he didn't say anything.

"You should really get to A&E," Maeve said, once we were on the road.

"Nice try."

"No, I mean it, that looks really bad."

"What is this, early-onset Stockholm?"

"I'm not a psychopath." She huddled into her seat, resting her head against the window. "I wouldn't have attacked you if you hadn't attacked me."

"I bet you say that to all the girls."

I leaned back and carefully stretched out my leg. I was feeling pretty shitty, but there was no way I was taking my eyes off Maeve. Attempted murder aside, she seemed like a fairly decent person, but you didn't have to be a crazy super-villain to get out of a taxi because the PI who'd caught you had fallen asleep.

"I couldn't trust Julian," said Maeve suddenly. "She would have come for us eventually."

"Not until you gave her a reason."

"Vampires don't need reasons. They take because they can."

"You seemed happy to give it."

"Well." Maeve flushed. "She can be very disarming. I thought I knew what I was doing."

She was either right or playing me. Or both. The thing to do now was just to let it go, hand her over, and close the damn case. But something was still bugging me.

"I get why you went for Julian, but why some random werewolf?"

She lifted her head wearily off the window. "That wasn't me."

Suspects you've just caught are not what you'd call reliable witnesses, and I had no reason on Earth to believe her. She'd already told me she was terrified of what Nim would do to her, so she was probably just covering herself, but then why admit to anything?

It was late, I was tired, I'd had my mother in my head, and I couldn't think straight. She'd attacked Julian. There had to be consequences for that.

The taxi rolled on through the night.

CHAPTER EIGHT

IRON & VELVET

There was a gang waiting for us outside the community centre. Half a dozen bikers in various flavours of scary. Their leader was leaning against her motorbike, an FLSTF Fat Boy with a custom paintjob. What can I say? I went through a biker chick phase. And by *biker chick phase*, I mean I slept with a lot of biker chicks.

I asked the cabbie to wait on the other side of the street and climbed out after Maeve. There was definite attention from the bikers.

"Are they on your side?" I asked as the leader came towards us.

"That's Michelle," whispered Maeve. "Guardian of the Watchtower of the South."

Well, that explained all the flame decals.

"You look like shit," said the Guardian of the Watchtower of the South.

She was a little shorter than me, but still looked like she could dribble me like a basketball without breaking a sweat. I couldn't see much beneath all the leather, but I could see on her neck and the backs of her hands the tips of what was clearly a large and complicated tattoo. She had a spill of dark braids and a *do not fuck with me* expression. I had no intention of fucking with her.

"Me or her?"

She put a hand on Maeve's shoulder, firm but not aggressive. "Come on, Maeve. What a fucking mess, you silly cow." Her eyes flicked briefly to me. "And you can fuck off as well."

She didn't wait for an answer and, as they turned away, I saw the back of her jacket was emblazoned with the image of an angel brandishing a flaming sword.

I fucked off to A&E.

St. Ann's was only ten minutes away—just long enough, in fact, for me to pull out my phone to call Julian and then think better of it. The news that I'd found the killer, who had turned out to be her ex-girlfriend, and promptly handed her over to my ex-girlfriend, would probably sound better in person. Also, my leg was really hurting.

I got to the top of the triage queue pretty quickly because I was dripping blood everywhere, but that meant I was completely stumped when the guy in blue pyjamas asked me what I'd done to myself. *Got in a fight with a blood-witch* was obviously out, and my old standby of *cooking accident* wasn't going to cut it either. So I said I'd fallen into my dishwater and landed on a carving knife. They mopped up the mess and gave me some painkillers, then left me sitting around for three hours, which I spent wishing I had a book or, better still, a drink.

Well, at least I was out the house.

Eventually I was shown into a cubicle between a bloke who'd been shoved through a shop window and another bloke who'd broken his hand punching someone in the face. Fun times. A doctor stopped by to confirm that we had, indeed, broken our hands, cut our legs, and gone through plate glass windows. And then a medical student came by to see what it looked like. I related my Dishwasher Carving Knife Adventure to three other people and informed each of them that yes, I did smoke, yes, I did drink, but no, I wasn't allergic to anything or taking prescription medications. After another hour, a nurse I hadn't seen before stuck me with a local anaesthetic and sewed me up in five minutes. I waited another half hour for a doctor to come and give me permission to go home, before I thought fuck it and discharged myself.

I smoked a quick fag in the hospital car park under the cheerful blue banner that read *This is a smoke-free site* while I waited for a cab to come and take me to Brewer Street. I arrived in the middle of Section 28, the Velvet's official gay night, as opposed to all of its other really-quite-gay nights. Ashriel was on the door, wearing a tight T-shirt and tighter jeans. Every boy in the queue was staring at him in awe.

"You look like shit," he greeted me.

"Thanks. I get that a lot. You look like a gay pin-up."

He grinned. "Thanks. I get that a lot."

"Hah. I see what you did there. Seriously, though, are you on the pull? I thought you didn't do that anymore."

"I don't, and even if I did, I'm not a big fan of cock."

I put my hands up. "Preaching to the choir. But I thought demons did anything with a soul."

"That doesn't mean we don't have preferences."

"Are you saying," I smirked, "that you're gay for pay?"

"If by 'for pay' you mean 'in order to suck the soul, essence, and very capacity for joy from my victims,' then yeah, kind of. But not lately."

"No offence, but what's with that?"

"I saw someone make a choice, and I made a choice of my own."

"Wow, cryptic."

He gave me a look. "I'm standing on Brewer Street in a shirt you can see my nipples through. How personal do you want this to get?"

"But they're such good nipples."

"Incubus." He gave an illustrative gesture.

"It's just," I went on, "I've never met a demon who was able to make that choice."

"There are a few of us around. And working for Julian takes the edge off. It's a vampire sex power thing."

"Speaking of, I need to see her."

Ashriel waved me through. "She's in the gallery."

It was packed in there, the air thick with sweat, sex, and other fun stuff. The dance floor was alive with writhing bodies. They were playing some kind of disco-infused tech house that was way too trendy for me to recognise. But it did make me want to dance and promote a homosexual lifestyle, so I guess it was doing its job. The gallery was curtained off and accessible only by the slightly rickety spiral staircase near the bar. There was a burly bouncer type at the bottom, but Ashriel had obviously told her I was coming because she unhooked the little velvet rope and let me through.

I went up. So this was the vampire sex room. Everything was blood-red velvet or gleaming gold, the sort of exquisite bad taste you could only get away with if you really were an eight-hundred-year-old immortal hedonist. Julian sprawled on a *chaise longue*, yet another ruffly shirt hanging half off one shoulder, a long cigarette holder dangling from between her fingers. As I picked my way through a pile of languidly entwined female bodies, she drew one of her groupies gently towards her, brushed a fall of hair from the woman's neck and bit her. A rush of pleasure seemed to engulf the room. Julian's victim? Partner? Mid-evening snack? Whatever, she was writhing in blatant orgasmic ecstasy.

I felt like a total eleventh wheel.

I thought about coughing politely, but then realised it probably wouldn't do any good and searched around for something to look at. I was technically still at work, and this was definitely NSFW. I fixed my eyes on an ornate silver chalice standing on a pedestal next to the *shag longue*.

After what seemed even longer than the wait at A&E, Julian let the woman go, and she crumpled to the ground, spent. Julian wiped blood from her face and licked it from her fingers with the sensuous relish of an actress in a chocolate advert.

"Oh, good evening, Kate," she purred.

I was quipless. "Hi."

Julian addressed her orgy. "All right, my kittens. Run along and play."

There was a brief delay while clothes were gathered up, and then we were alone.

"You've got a little something . . ." I brushed my face in the universal gesture for *you're covered in blood*.

Julian retrieved a white silk handkerchief, dipped it into the chalice, which turned out to be full of pure, clear water, and dabbed at the mess on her face. "All gone?"

I nodded.

"Soooo . . ." She fell back onto the *chaise longue*. "Are you here for business or pleasure?" She grinned. "Please say pleasure."

"Business."

She looked disappointed and gave me big eyes.

"I caught somebody."

"Great, can we fuck now?"

"It was your ex-girlfriend. She was definitely behind the attack last night. I can't be so sure about the werewolf."

There was a pause.

She blinked. "Sorry, which ex-girlfriend?"

"Maeve."

Julian looked blank.

"The blood-witch."

"Oh, *her*," she drawled. "Well, where is she? I take attempts to kill me pretty personally."

"I left her with Nimue. She'll handle it."

And the next thing I knew Julian was right in my face, teeth bared. I'd thought she moved quickly in daylight, but this was a full-on vamp-bamf. She could have torn my heart out and I wouldn't even have seen it coming. Instinctively I stepped back, and she was already behind me. I turned to face her.

"That was not the deal."

People had kept telling me Julian was dangerous. I thought it was because they didn't want me to sleep with her, but I was starting to realise it was because she could rip me to fucking pieces. And probably would if I pissed her off or showed her I was scared.

"We didn't have a deal," I said, trying to keep my voice from cracking. "You gave me a job. I never said I'd help you kill anybody."

"I don't need your help to kill anybody."

Dating Patrick had given me a fair amount of experience with vampires losing their rag. You know you've totally blown it when they get so angry they forget to pretend they're alive. They don't move, they don't twitch, they don't even blink. Right now, Julian was so still and so cold and so about to kill me, it was like staring down the barrel of a gun.

"I was trying to avoid starting a war."

"I hired you to find a killer, not play diplomat."

"Well, I did what I did, and I did find the killer." I took a deep breath, just in case it was the last one I ever had. "Either kill me for it, or get the fuck out my face."

She stared at me with pale, empty eyes. "I should kill you."

"Then do it, just do it, just fucking do it."

I found myself unexpectedly alive.

She stroked a sharp fingertip down the line of my throat, right along my carotid artery. "God, you're sexy when you're being an idiot."

"You are fucking impossible," I growled. "I thought you were going to kill me."

"I was."

I had no idea what to say to that, so I kissed her. It was rough and messy, and Julian's hands closed round my forearms hard enough to bruise, so I wasn't sure whether she was trying to pull me close or shove me away. I forced her lips apart and pressed myself into her mouth. It was like slipping into silk, though the rest of her was ice and steel. I caught my tongue on the edge of her fangs, drowning everything in a rush of heat and iron.

Julian made an unimaginable sound, lust, fury, and pure feral hunger. And the next thing I knew, I was flat on my back and pinned breathless on the *chaise longue*. Julian reared up, fangs bared, a few drops of my blood clinging to her lips.

Here lies Kate Kane. Killed in a foreplay accident. Beloved daughter. Sorely missed.

And then she hesitated. I was stuck staring into the face of a predator, but somewhere in her eyes I thought I could see Julian. And Julian bought me puddings and—usually—didn't want me dead. I pulled her on top of me and rolled sideways. We tumbled gracelessly onto the floor. She lay underneath me like an unexploded grenade.

Well, this was fun.

Actually, it kind of was. My leg was aching, my mouth was bleeding, I'd barely slept, but I felt so fucking alive.

I tore her stupid frilly shirt open again to reveal white skin and red silk. A flimsy nothing of a bra held together by a ribbon I pulled open with my teeth. Julian shifted, a breathless sound catching at the back of her throat. Heat was gathering under her skin. She stretched her arms over her head, her fingers twisting around the legs of the *chaise longue*. Her breasts lifted like they wanted attention. So I got on with that, and slipped a hand between her legs. Julian's hands tightened on the *chaise longue* until the wood splintered, and her hips arched under mine.

"Kate," she gasped, her head tipping back to expose her throat. "Fuck me."

She didn't have to tell me twice.

Or maybe she did. She had just tried to kill me.

"Ask me nicely." I traced the underside of her breast with my tongue.

She let go of the *chaise longue* and propped herself on her elbows, shaking me free. "Make me," she said, glinting a toothy grin.

"Oh, it's like that, huh?" I braced myself on a knee and ran the nails of my free hand down her side. She shivered but her expression didn't change.

I slipped the steel dagger from its sheath on my forearm and passed it to my right hand.

"I do like a girl who comes with her own toys," sighed Julian.

I ran the point of the blade lightly down her neck. I wouldn't do this to somebody with a pulse, but there's something kind of liberating about being with someone you can't hurt.

Julian raised an eyebrow.

I kissed her steel-touched skin. She was as warm as me now. I moved the knife to her hip and drew a new path up her body, between her breasts.

Julian watched me, playing it cool.

I pressed a little harder and made a shallow cut just beneath her collarbone. She gave a surprised yelp that turned into a low moan as I put my mouth to the already healing wound and gently tasted her. I don't know what I was expecting, but pleasure rolled through me like a good single malt. Julian fell back, holding me to her, fingers buried in my hair, legs coming up to embrace me. I had just enough wherewithal to spin the knife away from us.

"Oh, Kate," she whispered. "Kate."

I kissed my name from her lips, my mouth wet with the last traces of her blood. There was nothing but the moment. The taste of wine and roseleaves.

I worked a hand down her trousers, beneath the velvet and the silk of her underwear to warm, wet skin. Julian clung to me, cried out, and I couldn't quite repress an answering moan. She felt so good. I slid my fingers into her and circled her with my thumb. It was an awkward angle and I wasn't going to win any prizes for technique but, just then, it didn't seem to matter. Julian's back arched, and she pressed herself against my hand, an incoherent litany of pleasure spilling from her lips. She convulsed under me, came on my fingers, snapped forwards and bit me.

I had a brief moment to be pissed off.

There was a fleeting spark of pain, and then an endless, incapacitating ecstasy.

"Oops, sorry," came Julian's voice sometime later. "Instinctive response."

I felt battered and wrung out and kind of awesome and really in need of a cigarette. Maybe later I'd be embarrassed. Normally people have to touch my cunt before I come. And, somewhere at the back of my mind, I was vaguely aware that letting vampires get their teeth into you made you more vulnerable to their mind control bullshit. Still, right now, I was thinking it was probably worth it. And besides, Julian knew where I lived and could kill me without blinking, so we were basically already playing trust games here.

I blinked up at her. "You could have warned me."

Julian yawned and stretched like a cat. "Did you mind?"

"Well, I'm not going to look a gift orgasm in the mouth. I just wasn't expecting it."

"I'm the vampire prince of pleasure, sweeting. What *were* you expecting?"

She had a point.

"So I suppose I won't be needing your services anymore." She grinned. "Not your professional services, anyway."

"I'm still not sure about the first attack."

"Somebody attacked me, someone is being punished for it. I'd rather do it myself, but I've decided to let it slide because I like you."

"I'm not sure that works for me. You hired me to solve a murder, not find a scapegoat."

Julian nuzzled into the side of my neck, her legs still holding me tight. "Whatever happened to the customer always being right? It already goes against my instincts to leave this in the hands of the Witch Queen. Frankly, I'd like to put this whole thing behind me. I won't be hiring you again." She kissed the tip of my nose. "Your loyalties are too conflicted and your rates are exorbitant."

"You're not Miss Easy To Work For, either. You keep trying to shag your employees." Her teeth grazed my earlobe. "I don't like mixing business with pleasure."

"Sweeting, my business is pleasure."

I sighed. "Do we have to be fucking for you to call me Kate?"

"You'll have to work that out for yourself."

CHAPTER NINE
GUNS & MONEY

I did the stagger of shame back to my flat at about seven o' clock in the morning and face-planted into my pillow. I woke up around noon with that strangely hollow feeling that always comes at the end of a case. It'd be great if everything tied up in neat little bows like in an episode of *Poirot*, but in my line of work there are no easy answers. You can't put all the suspects in a room until one of them confesses. You just do what you can with the evidence, and try to make sure you don't get too many people killed. If you're lucky, you're left with something that makes some sort of sense. If you're not, there's just a bunch of stuff that happened and the nagging feeling that you're missing something. Like when you put up a piece of flat-pack furniture.

I thought about calling Julian, but it wasn't like I had anything to report, and she'd been pretty clear about where she stood. I was off the books. The case was closed. I'd fucked the client. And right now, all I was doing was lying around in bed, picking at loose ends and feeling vaguely unsettled.

I didn't even think I'd got it wrong, just that I hadn't got it right enough. If Archer had been here (not in my bed, obviously), he'd have told me to either let it go or do something about it.

I think his exact words would have been *Shit or get off the pot*.

Besides, how needy would it look if I rang her up saying, "Hey Jules, you know that murder you don't care about anymore? Can we still investigate it together anyway?" Shagging the prince of pleasure was probably a one-time deal, but I'd known that going in.

I went for a shower to clear my head. Gently rinsed the gash on my thigh. Sponged the vampire bite on my neck. Tended to the puncture wounds on my arm. Wow, I was a mess. At least Mr. Squidgy hadn't left anything permanent. I know chicks dig scars, but they draw the line at tentacle monster love bites.

Huh.

Now I was looking closely, these weren't the same marks that I'd found on Andrew. Sure, they looked similar, but, if you wanted to get technical about it, mine were more bruisy and less rippy, and the stabby bit was cleaner. It didn't mean much by itself, because mages can summon all kinds of shit, but it was something else that didn't add up and something else that suggested that I was looking for two attackers. Surely if it had been Maeve both times, she'd have used the same monster twice because it was easier, or completely different ones to cover her tracks. There's no reason to make your second crime look like a bad copy of the first.

Unless that's exactly what it was. Just like she'd claimed.

Perhaps I was grasping at straws, but it was starting to look a lot like there was something else going on here. The problem was, with only two attacks, I couldn't tell what fit the pattern and what didn't. You can always draw a straight line between two points, but it doesn't actually mean they're connected. Maybe Maeve had tried to attack the Velvet, then tried to attack Julian. Or maybe someone had hired Maeve to attack the Velvet, then she'd decided to attack Julian on her own. Or maybe someone else had attacked the Velvet and Maeve had jumped on the bandwagon. Or maybe someone else was behind both attacks, and Maeve was just covering for them. Or maybe it was Ashriel. Maybe he was Keyser Söze. With the information available, I had no way of knowing.

Fuck. I had to get back on the case. On my own time. For no money. Fuck.

I knew there was a reason I didn't work for vampires.

I still didn't have what we in the detective business call "evidence," but at least I had something I could point at and say "that right there doesn't make sense." And sometimes that's all it takes. First thing to do was call Julian. Well, first thing to do was get out the shower, and then call Julian.

I dialled the Velvet with one hand and pulled on my trousers with the other. I got through to the back office, and bounced around a couple of promoters, before being told that Miss Saint-Germain was in Brighton on business, and nobody knew when she'd be back or how to contact her. I'd have said this was another reason I didn't work for vampires, but I had a feeling Julian would have been exactly the same if she was human.

So where did this leave me? With similar but potentially unrelated monster summonings, a suspect who was good for at least one of them, a victim nobody wanted dead, and an eight-hundred-year-old vampire prince in the middle of it all. If Maeve had been working alone, then it was a slightly weird crime of passion and I'd solved it, so there was nothing to worry about. But if she hadn't been working alone, then it was complicated. And complicated almost certainly meant politics. And politics almost certainly meant vampires. And that meant there was another prince involved somewhere, because a vampire can't brush his fangs in this town without a prince knowing about it. If vampires do brush their fangs. Well, they have to get the blood off somehow, right?

The Prince of Cups was the target, and the Prince of Swords was a crazy Viking in UGG boots, which left Wands and Coins. Julian had suspected the Prince of Coins, and it seemed as good a place to start as any. Besides, when in doubt, follow the money.

Thomas Pryce operated out of a big, shiny building in the heart of the financial district. He had one of those companies with the words "fund" and "capital" in the name, and he'd spent the last six hundred years moving other people's money in circles. It wasn't just that he was wealthy—he commanded wealth. And, unlike Julian, he was one of London's supernatural power players I *had* managed to piss off.

A couple of years back, I was hired to solve this murder that turned out to be the work of a serial killer who turned out be a dashing young vampire with a thing for chopping up women. Something he'd been doing, off and on, for the best part of a century. I stopped him. Hard. Only later discovering that he was Thomas Pryce's pet sociopath, and that the Prince of Coins did not appreciate people tampering with his property. Still, it'd been a few years, and he hadn't gone out of his way to murder me, so maybe he was over it.

I set out for the headquarters of PCM Capital Fund Management. It was a vast glass seashell curved around an open plaza paved in cool grey stone. In the middle of the plaza stood one of those modern sculptures that look like absolutely nothing. I'd probably have thought it was a pile of girders if I hadn't been on Lime Street. I was braced for corporate cockwaving and marble pillars, but the reception area turned out to be pretty normal for a more-money-than-God kind of place. I mean, yes, the floors were still marble, but they weren't in your face about it.

I went up to the main desk, which sat beneath a tastefully understated sign that read "Pryce, Cromwell, Moore." So that's what it stood for. I had no idea who Cromwell and Moore were, but knowing vampire princes, they were probably all the same person.

"I'm here to see Mr. Pryce." I didn't think *Horse & Hound* was going to cut it this time.

The receptionist was a fresh-faced young man in a Savile Row suit. "Do you have an appointment?"

"Well, here's the thing," I said. "No."

"I'm very sorry, but I'm afraid Mr. Pryce is in meetings all day and never sees anyone without an appointment."

I guess I should have seen that coming. "Okay." I gave what I hoped was a charming smile. "Can I make an appointment?"

There was a very slight pause, and I realised he had one of those spirally FBI earpieces.

"No, Miss Kane."

It was going to be like that, was it?

I decided to pull out the big guns. "I'm working for Julian Saint-Germain. And I'd like to make that appointment."

"I'm afraid that will not be possible. Mr. Pryce's diary is full for the foreseeable future."

So much for him being over it. Honestly, you take out one little serial killer and you never hear the end of it.

"It's kind of important," I tried. "There's been a murder."

"I'm sorry, but Mr. Pryce is in a meeting."

Right. Time for Plan B.

"Thank you for your time."

I turned and pegged it up the corridor as fast I could. Within seconds I'd been trapped between two pairs of steel security doors and ejected from the premises by a squad of armed guards.

Right. Time for Plan C.

There was no Plan C. I'd forgotten how hard it was to get access to a vampire prince who doesn't want to get in your pants. Thomas Pryce was a paranoid, immortal zillionaire who hated me. I had precisely zero leverage. In fact, with my latest stunt, I was probably in negative equity.

I sat on a bit of the abstract art and had a cigarette. The only people vampire princes have to listen to are other vampire princes. And even if Julian had been in town, you can't get the client to interrogate your suspects. It just looks unprofessional. That left Sebastian and Aeglica. I'd never met Sebastian, and besides, he was in Oxford. But, as luck would have it, I'd dug up the Prince of Swords's address back when I was seventeen, and I was glad I'd finally get to use it for something other than saving Patrick's annoying arse. I really hate begging favours from vampires, but it didn't look like I had much choice. And he had asked to be kept informed. Okay, so there's a bit of a difference between "informed" and "involved," but maybe he wouldn't mind. He seemed like a pretty hands-on kind of guy.

Fifteen years ago, Aeglica had lived in this spooky, walled-off mansion just up from Holland Park, and he hadn't moved since. So it was back on the Tube and halfway across London. I felt like a guerrilla marketing campaign for the Oyster card.

The mansion hadn't changed in a decade and a half. It was still straight out of *Beauty and the Beast*, complete with overgrown rose garden. No talking clocks, though. I scrambled over the wall, which did not look at all suspicious at three o' clock on a Friday afternoon, landing on the other side in a tangle of tall grass and weeds. I made for the front door, which was unlocked, just like last time, and slipped inside. The entrance hall would have been majestic, but two hundred years of neglect had turned it into the set of a Christopher Lee film. Thick shadows spilled down the stairways and cobwebs smothered the chandeliers. Dust clung to the rotten curtains, covered the floors, and gathered on the gigantic skull that sat on a plinth in the middle of the hall. The last time I'd, uh, visited, Aeglica had told me it had belonged to one of the last dragons in Mercia.

I wandered through dark and empty rooms until, finally, I found Aeglica. He was sitting on a low wooden stool, his hand resting on the pommel of an impractically large sword.

"Um, hi," I said.

He nodded. "Miss Kane."

"I need to talk to—" Suddenly I noticed that hanging on the wall behind him was an enormous portrait of a naked chick, like the picture Leonardo DiCaprio does of Kate Winslet in *Titanic*. It was the only thing in the whole place not covered in dust. "Whoa. I did not see that last time."

Aeglica came to his feet and turned slowly. "It is a portrait of the most beautiful woman in Venice, painted by a great master."

She was definitely a hottie, milk-pale skin, and fire-red hair, and dark eyes that seemed to look right through you. "It's very nice. And you have it . . . why?"

"I admire her. Can I help you, Miss Kane?"

"Maybe. There are some loose ends I'd like to tie up. I'm pretty sure I've got one of the people responsible for the attacks on Julian, but I think there might be more to it."

"How?"

"I don't think the two attacks were connected, and I'd like to eliminate the Prince of Coins as a suspect, but he's not making it easy."

Aeglica's head moved very slightly. "He would not. He is young and fears for his position."

"Do you think you could get me an appointment?"

"Yes. Come with me." He laid his sword on a bench that seemed to have been designed for the purpose, and I saw that there was a shard of brownish pottery set into the hilt instead of a jewel. I filed that little detail away under Weird Vampire Shit.

"You could just phone." I offered him my mobile.

"I am more persuasive in person."

Well, fuck. I had a feeling this was going to end badly for someone, probably me.

I'd been following Aeglica for about ten minutes when I realised he was actually intending to walk to Lime Street.

"We could get a cab," I suggested.

"That will not be necessary." He didn't slow down.

"There's a Tube station two minutes that way."

"That will not be necessary."

"Bus? They're bendy now."

"I do not like buses."

He had a point. But I bet he never had to put up with creepy guys standing next to him.

Two hours later, the sun was setting, and we had just arrived. Aeglica strode through the front doors of PCM Capital Fund Management, with me trailing behind him like a school kid whose mum was determined to speak to the headmaster.

He went up to the reception desk. "Tell the Prince of Coins I am coming."

"M-M-Mr. Pryce is in a meeting," replied the clearly suicidal receptionist.

Aeglica ignored him and made for the stairs, breaking through a series of security doors that slammed into his path.

Well, if the Prince of Coins didn't hate me before . . .

There were guys with guns on the stairwell.

There was a brief explosion of gunfire.

Then there weren't guys with guns on the stairwell.

Then there were more guys with guns on the stairwell.

Holy shit. I ducked back into the corridor and kept my head down. I had an invulnerable escort but, once again, I'd brought knives to a gunfight, and getting caught in the crossfire would seriously ruin my day. When I was very *very* certain that nobody was shooting at anything anymore, I crept after Aeglica. The staircase was littered with crumpled bodies and spent shell casings, the walls were pitted with bullet marks, and the air was white with plaster dust.

Looking back on it, Plan B had been pretty fucking stupid. But, to be fair, the security guards in most city firms don't have actual guns on account of how it's massively illegal. I guess you can get away with a lot when you're immortal and richer than most countries.

The chaos continued up twenty-five flights of stairs and, at the top, I caught up with Aeglica. His clothes were in tatters, but he seemed otherwise entirely unfazed. I, on the other hand, felt really quite fazed. We stepped out into a corridor. There were two large boardrooms on either side of us, fronted by smoky glass windows etched with the name of the company, and, at the very end, an office door marked "Thomas Pryce – Chief Executive."

I half expected Aeglica to kick the door down, but he just pushed it gently open and went in. I followed cautiously. Thomas Pryce's office was an expensive mixture of the vintage and the cutting-edge. He had a hardwood desk covered in papers, with an hourglass and an actual quill pen resting next to a sleek, ultra-thin laptop. One wall was entirely taken up by a bank of flat-panel monitors, flicking endlessly and apparently randomly through footage, figures, and those wiggly stock market charts like you get in cartoons. The other walls were hung with glass-fronted cases, containing a metric crap tonne of what I thought were probably antique coins. Not exactly subtle, Mr. Pryce. The floor-to-ceiling windows looked out over a city scattered like a child's Lego set.

The Prince of Coins was sitting at his desk in a well-tailored black suit. He was in his early forties, with curling black hair, heavy brows, and a closed, wary face.

"Ah," he said. "It seems I need to review my security arrangements."

Aeglica's shoulder lifted fractionally in something that might have been a shrug. "You place too much faith in firearms."

"They performed adequately in testing." Pryce frowned.

There was a heavy pause. "There has been an attack on the Prince of Cups."

"So I hear."

"Miss Kane wishes to ask some questions."

The Prince of Coins went back to his paperwork. "I do not wish to answer them."

I had a feeling Aeglica wasn't going to come back with "Okay, fine, we'll go then."

"This matter falls within my domain," he said instead. "You will answer."

"Your duty is to protect the Council as a whole, not to involve yourself in disagreements between its members. If I was responsible for the attack on Miss Saint-Germain, then it would be outside your jurisdiction. And if I was not, then you are simply wasting your time. You may see yourself out."

I'd half turned to go when Aeglica walked calmly forwards, caught Thomas Pryce by the throat, and threw him through the window. And here was me thinking I was going to be bad cop. Aeglica crunched through the glass to the gaping hole where the window used to be and stepped off the building.

Shit.

The whole place was in lockdown, so there was no hope of a lift, which meant I had to run down twenty-six flights of stairs, and past several security teams, who, fortunately for me, were still mostly unconscious. Four minutes later, and knackered, I staggered out into the plaza. Aeglica was waiting for me in the centre of a spider-web of cracked paving stones. The Prince of Coins was impaled on a bit of modern art. He did not look happy.

"That," said Pryce, "was uncalled for."

A spider slipped from under the collar of his shirt, crawled across his face, and lowered itself off the edge of the sculpture on a long strand of silk. Another ran out from beneath his cuff and did the same. And eventually his entire body, clothes and all, dissolved into a teaming mass of spiders that swarmed down the somewhat dented sculpture. They gathered in the centre of the plaza and reformed into the shape of the Prince of Coins. He still did not look happy.

Aeglica turned to me. "Ask your questions."

There was something to be said for the direct approach. "Was it you?" I asked.

Pryce sighed. "No."

"Was that really worth being thrown through a window for?"

"Is that one of the questions?"

I sighed. "But," I tried again, "you've attempted to buy Julian out before."

"Yes, I have."

"So, it would benefit you to devalue her properties?"

He folded his hands in front of him, his expression unchanging. I made a mental note never to play poker with this guy. "The acquisition of the Calix Group is no longer part of our development strategy."

"What changed your mind?"

"Miss Saint-Germain was disinclined to sell. With enough time and energy, I'm sure I could have persuaded her, but there was little profit in it. I am not in the habit of using my business to pursue personal vendettas. I consider it unprofessional."

"No offence, but why should I believe you?"

"Because you have no choice, Miss Kane. If I had been involved in this affair and wished to conceal the fact, I could. It would take you a lifetime to understand even a fraction of my operations. The sooner you conclude that I am not, in fact, a plausible suspect, the sooner we can both continue our lives unmolested."

He was probably right, and I'm a big fan of being unmolested, but I'd come all this way, and I was buggered if I was leaving with nothing to show for it. "I'll need more than that."

He sighed. I got the feeling it was something he did a lot. "I am willing to release to you the full records of my previous dealings with the Calix Group. Anyone with a modicum of financial experience will be able to see that the project has concluded."

I did not, in fact, have a modicum of financial experience. I didn't even have a Business Studies GSCE. But Archer's wife—by which I mean, of course, Archer's widow—was a forensic accountant. We hadn't worked together much since I got her husband killed. But business was business, right?

"That'll have to do," I said. "Thank you for your time, Mr. Pryce."

"Do not impose upon it so lightly again." He nodded to Aeglica and disappeared back into the building.

"Well." I looked up at the Prince of Swords. "Thanks?"

"That is unnecessary. The Council has been threatened. The Prince of Coins was standing in the way. He had to be reminded of his loyalties."

"A twenty-six-storey fall is a pretty harsh reminder."

"He is young."

Aeglica turned and walked away.

I called a taxi because I'd had it. I'd climbed a wall, walked from Holland Park to Lime Street, got up twenty-six flights of stairs in the middle of a gun fight, and then down the same twenty-six flights of stairs in pursuit of a falling vampire. I sat down heavily in the back of the cab, and then realised my leg was bleeding.

Well, fuck.

Three hours later, I was explaining to a man in blue pyjamas that I had no idea how I'd torn the stitches out my leg. I just found it like that. Honest. And five hours later I was at home, face down on my pillow.

The next day I woke up around noon again, feeling like I'd been run over. I limped to my computer, where I had several emails from lawyer types working for the Prince of Coins that wanted me to electronically sign a series of hard-core non-disclosure agreements. I negotiated an allowance to share the information with an expert third party on a need-to-know basis, and then I emailed Lucy Archer to tell her I had a job for her. Lucy was more than capable of taking it from here, and I wanted to avoid getting into a long conversation with her, so I left them all to it.

By the time this had all been sorted out, it was early evening, and I made an executive decision to spend the rest of the day lying on a sofa, drinking heavily, with my leg in the air.

CHAPTER TEN

FROCKS & FUNERALS

I woke up in a complete panic midway through Sunday afternoon, remembering I had a werewolf funeral that evening and nothing to wear. I didn't even know if I should be looking for a cocktail dress or strategically placed animal skins.

I'd thrown the entire contents of my wardrobe onto the bed and was digging through the pile for the third time, wondering if I could get away with jeans and a black tie when the buzzer rang. I picked up the handset.

"Delivery for Kane."

Great. On top of everything else, someone had sent the world's least original hitman after me. "No one by that name here."

"As you wish, Miss Kane," replied the incredibly posh hitman/delivery guy. "I have a parcel for you from Miss Vane-Tempest and, with your indulgence, I shall leave it on the doorstep."

I ran to the window just in time to see a middle-aged man in an immaculate dark suit step into a silver Bentley Spur and drive away.

Huh.

Figuring I'd better get the parcel before somebody nicked it or pissed on it, I hurried downstairs. It turned out to be one of those white oblong boxes that I've only seen in tacky romcoms. I took it back to the flat and put it on my kitchen table next to a roll of Plenty and a bottle of ketchup. There was a miniature envelope tucked into the ribbon, and inside was a single square of eggshell card that read: *Wear this, T.*

Oh, my fucking God. I was Pretty Woman.

I opened the box. Lying in a bed of crisp crackling tissue was a dress. I lifted it out and looked at it.

It was a really fucking nice dress.

I know nothing about fashion, but even I could see it was a really fucking nice dress. Versace. It was black silk with sheer lace sleeves and a cut-away shoulder. It was fitted at the top, clinging in the middle, and flowing at the bottom. It almost certainly cost more than my car.

I put it back in the box and went to make a cup of tea while I worked out how I felt about this. On the one hand it was kind of a dick move. On the other hand, it was a really fucking nice dress. I wasn't sure how Julian would feel about me partying on another girl's ticket, but people who live in glass houses full of naked chicks shouldn't throw stones. I liked Julian, and the sex was . . . well . . . not something I was going to forget in a while, but that didn't mean I was going to sit around waiting for my prince to come. Especially when my prince had the attention span of a cupcake.

I took out the dress again. What were the chances it was an innocent gesture from a new friend who was concerned I might not have a suitable gown for the occasion? The cool silk poured over my fingers like shadow.

No. This was a fuck-me dress.

I was kind of out of my league here. Usually all it takes is a pint and a packet of crisps.

It was hard not to feel flattered in a prostitute-y kind of way. But at the same time, I really hate being told what to do. I'd just about resolved to wear a suit on principle when I somehow accidentally tried the dress on. The last time I'd done the fairy princess thing, I'd been seventeen, deep in the closet, dating an arsehole, and a cabal of vampire alchemists had kidnapped me on the night of my sixth form leavers' ball. And that had kind of put me off.

But this time it was going to be different. I was going to wear a fabulous dress and have a fabulous time on my own terms. In my own way. For me.

At a funeral.

For a man whose murder I had, so far, failed to completely solve.

Well, bollocks.

But, since I was back on the case, this would be a great opportunity to double-check the weird shit at Safernoc. Vampire politics were looking like a dead end, which moved the werewolves, and their forest full of monsters, up the suspect list again. After Mr. Squidgy, I'd been pretty certain that Andrew had just been in the wrong place at the wrong time, but if there were two killers, they could easily have two motives and two targets. Tara had been pretty adamant that werewolves don't kill their own, but after lovers, family were the next most likely suspects. I'd been okay to backburner the wolf connection when I had other leads, but right now I had squat, so I couldn't afford to dismiss anything. Unless it really had been Maeve all along, and this was a huge waste of time. I suppose I could have gone and asked her, but I had no reason to think she'd tell me the truth, and besides, I'd already caused enough trouble for Nim, so I didn't think she'd be all like, "Hey Kate, of course you can come and interrogate my people again."

Since I had a funeral to doll up for, and I wasn't going to get anywhere with the case by sitting on my arse, I multitasked. I backtracked through my mental case notes while showering, tending to my many wounds, wriggling back into the dress, doing make up and shit, and fretting about shoes. I tend not to wear heels because they make me fucking enormous, and they're really rubbish when you have to run away or fight something. Finally I settled on some knee-high gladiator sandals, and I was just admiring the ensemble in the mirror that came with the wardrobe when I realised I had nowhere to put my knives. And to think I'd been worried about the shoes. Having actually been to Safernoc, there was no way I was going out there again without my iron dagger, and I eventually strapped it to the outside of my thigh without wrecking the line of the dress too much. It wasn't exactly subtle, but I wasn't planning on wandering past any cops and I *was* going to have travel through a faery-haunted forest.

Then I cranked up my car and drove to Oxfordshire. At least I didn't have to stop for directions this time. When I came to the massive wrought iron gates, I turned through them onto a gravelled driveway. It was all way easier when you were actually invited.

I'd kind of expected getting through the gates would mean I'd arrived, but it just took me deeper into the forest. It was still early evening, but the trees strangled the light. Strange shadows moved in the mist. Nice place for a funeral. Atmospheric.

At last, the house loomed at me out of nowhere, reaching jaggedly towards the sky. It was one of those old English castles that had been knocked down, rebuilt, and extended so many times it was like Frankenstein's monster with buttresses. The sort of place with a

New Wing that was older than the United States. I drove carefully round the long-dry fountain in the centre of the courtyard. Through the moss and the weeds, you could still make out the statues in the middle: a circle of six howling wolves. Subtle.

I eased my second-hand Corsa between a Veyron and a classic E-Type. I wasn't sure if I should feel inadequate or just surrounded by wankers. Slithering free, I made for the main door, where a couple of waiters were standing around with trays of canapés. I helped myself to a roll of something posh and a glass of something expensive, and wandered inside. I found myself in a vast, echoing entrance hall, all stained glass and dark wood. I ate the canapé like that had been the plan all along, and wondered what the fuck to do next. Basically, I had to blend in at a funeral and figure out if anyone in the family had a reason to off the dead guy—y'know, without being massively offensive and disrespectful. "Sorry for your loss. Did you kill him?" tends not to go down too well.

Then I spotted Tara. She was wearing a dark gold dress that had no visible means of support, and was greeting people as they filed past her. I tagged onto a cluster of toffs to wait my turn.

Her eyes swept possessively over my body. "I'm glad you came, Kate Kane."

I wasn't quite comfortable doing sexy banter at a funeral.

"Least I could do," I muttered. "Sorry for your loss."

"We'll talk later, yah." She put a hand on my hip and steered me after the other guests, down the corridor and into a spacious room with no obvious function, probably a drawing room or a morning room or some other sort of room that ordinary people don't need. There were more waiters with more canapés, lots of people I didn't know, and Andrew laid out on a bed of fresh oak leaves by the far wall. I downed my drink and went over to pay my respects, feeling a bit of a knob since I hadn't actually known the guy.

Sorry you got murdered, mate.

He looked depressingly young and depressingly dead. I suddenly remembered I still had his iPhone.

A voice came from behind me. "I do not believe we have been introduced." The tone suggested this was a serious failing on my part.

I turned round. Generally I find old ladies come in two flavours: ones that remind me of my nan and ones that scare the fuck out of me. This woman did not look like my nan. At all. It was like she'd been whittled down until she was nothing but skin and ferocity. Like a Quentin Blake illustration without the quirky charm. A wolf watched me through amber eyes.

"I'm Kate Kane."

"I know who you are, Miss Kane. I said we have not been introduced."

I had a feeling this was not going well.

"Tara invited me," I mumbled.

"See that you do not outstay your welcome. This is a family affair."

"I'm just paying my respects."

"I doubt you know the meaning of the word," she snapped.

I smiled awkwardly. I had no idea how I was supposed to handle this. If she hadn't been about eighty and we hadn't been at a funeral, I might have had more options. Like decking her. Was I just supposed to stand here and let her lay into me for shits and giggles?

I was looking for a window to jump out of when I noticed that someone was coming towards us. It was the guy from my last visit, a whole lot less naked this time. He had that effortless grace that posh people have when they're in formal clothes.

He took the old woman by the arm. "Grandmamma," he said, with a hint of mischief, "I don't think you've been formally introduced. This is Katharine Kane, a private investigator who's looking into Andrew's murder. Miss Kane, this is Henrietta Vane-Tempest, Dowager Marchioness of Safernoc."

"Stop trying to manage me, Hetty." The old woman tore her arm away. "If I wish to be introduced to somebody, I shall ask."

"This isn't your pack anymore, Grandmother. You will sit down and you will be polite to Tara's guests."

The Marchioness actually snarled at him. It was a savage, inhuman noise no little old lady should be able to make. Her grandson bared his teeth and growled back. And I thought my family was fucked up.

The Dowager finally retreated and sat down, glaring.

"Now, if you'll excuse me, I'm going to get Miss Kane a drink."

He offered me his arm, and I took it gratefully. "That's the best thing anyone has said to me all evening."

We skirted the crowd. Small talk, small talk, small talk, help. And we hadn't been formally introduced, which was apparently a big deal round these parts. I didn't think him throwing me off his land counted.

"I'm Henry, by the way. My friends call me Harry. Bunny calls me Hal."

"Dude, that's a lot of names."

"Well." He smiled. "At Roedean my nickname was Binky."

"You can call me Kate," I said firmly. "You know your granny's kind of evil, right?"

He laughed, not entirely happily. "She was an alpha werewolf, and a good one. That requires a certain strength." He paused. "But yes, she's a terrible human being."

Interesting. "Bummer."

"As you so astutely observe: bummer."

It was probably nothing, but a ruthless, psychotic old woman who was clearly hostile to outsiders was too good a lead to pass up. "How does she feel about vampires?" I asked, in what I hoped was a casual sort of way.

His eyebrows went up. "Are you interrogating me, Kate?"

"Maybe a little bit."

He thought about it for a moment. "She doesn't like vampires, and she didn't approve of Andrew dating one, but I don't think she had him murdered, if that's what you're getting at."

"I probably wouldn't have been quite that blunt about it, but I have to cover all the angles."

"It's all right. If I was investigating a murder, she'd be my prime suspect. She'll do anything to protect the family."

He plucked two glasses expertly from a passing waiter and handed one to me.

"Thanks." I knocked it back. "Sorry, I'm shit at parties. Who'd be next on your list?"

He smiled at me. "Oh, I see what you did there."

I gave him my best innocent look, which did not look very innocent.

"All right," he said, "I'll play. But only because I honestly don't think it was any of them. My number two suspect would probably be

Jumbo." He indicated a large, balding man dozing in one of the few available chairs. He didn't look like a killer. But who does? "He's our PR man and general fixer. Terribly clever chap. Fingers in a lot of pies."

I was about to make a joke, but I realised it was too obvious.

"Don't let him fool you," Henry went on. "He's nowhere near as harmless as he looks. He's got the contacts to do it, and the will if he wanted to, but no motive whatsoever."

We seemed to be doing what BBC costume dramas called "taking a turn about the room." Henry steered me expertly through the crowds and the canapés.

"But doesn't Jumbo work for the pack?" I asked. "What if someone ordered him to?"

"He doesn't really do orders."

"What about the rest of them?"

"Well. Bunny's in charge, but that's just not the way it works."

We got ourselves tucked into a corner out of the way of the other guests. "Sorry, who's Bunny again?"

He burst out laughing. "Tara. We called her Bunny at Roedean." There was a pause.

"Why would you do that?"

"It's just a nickname. Who knows where nicknames come from?"

"If people started start calling me Bunny, I'd want an explanation."

He patted my hand reassuringly. "Don't worry, you don't look like a Bunny. Anyway, if Tara had wanted Andrew dead, she'd have done it herself, and we'd all know about it."

"I bet that makes for awkward Christmases."

"Less than you might think."

"So there's no one else?" I pressed him.

He shook his head. "If this were a country house murder, I'd suspect Tara's mother, but only because she has no connection to the crime whatsoever." He gestured discreetly. "That's her over there. See the resemblance?"

I could definitely see the resemblance. Tara's mother was tall, blonde, and fabulous. And I wasn't going there. I have a one generation at a time policy. To go with my one supernatural creature at a time policy. And my not at a funeral policy. I needed another drink.

"She seems . . . nice. Unmurderous." I was really trying to avoid the word MILF.

"She is," agreed Henry. "Nice. And unmurderous."

"You do realise that now we've had this conversation, she probably did it."

Suddenly Henry's head snapped up like a meerkat, and he actually sniffed the air.

"What's wrong?"

"Who are they?"

Kauri and a few other performers I recognised from the Velvet were standing respectfully by the body. Kauri was wearing a dark suit over a white shirt and a black velvet corset. There was a dusting of gold across his eyes. He had that sad, quiet look you get when you don't want to piss on other people's grief.

"That's Andrew's boyfriend. And Cabaret Baudelaire."

Henry relaxed. "I should have guessed. It was kind of them to come."

"Come on," I said. "I'll introduce you."

Henry followed me across the room. "And you said you were shit at parties."

I did that thing and left them having a not-entirely stilted conversation about the dead guy. I didn't feel like making small talk with strangers, and I didn't think I could learn much more in here, so I grabbed another drink and slipped out into the corridor. I was leaning away from suspecting the werewolves. I obviously couldn't take Henry's word for it, but the way Andrew had died didn't seem their style. The Dowager looked as ruthless as they come, but if she wanted to stop a member of her family dating a vampire, surely she'd just kill the vampire? And werewolves didn't generally need to summon monsters to do their murdering for them—unless it was an exceptionally thorough cover-up. Which basically left me back where I'd been last Sunday: with the exsanguinated body of a guy nobody wanted to kill. I was fast running out of options that weren't "random act of monster."

Passing another one of those pointless function rooms, the sound of lowered voices made my PI senses tingle, and I couldn't help lurking by the doorway. If someone came by, I could always pretend to be lost or drunk, and I wouldn't even be lying.

"You will not tell me how to manage the affairs of this family." That was Tara's voice. She sounded narked. But then, that was how she usually sounded when I was around.

"This is an insult to the memory of our cousin. There are vampires here and, worse, mortals." I recognised that voice too. It had been horrible to me earlier.

"That is my decision, not yours."

"Your decisions will lead the pack to ruin," snarled the Dowager. "We should have strangled you at birth. That I should live to see my family ruled by the daughter of a whore and an exile."

Wow. Henry had said his grandmother was a terrible human being.

"Your counsel is noted." Tara sounded calmer than I would have. "Leave me."

I nipped out of the way as the Dowager swept out. I leaned against the wall and decided to finish my drink while I waited for the coast to clear. Then I could rejoin the party. Joy.

"You've got a lot to learn about spying on werewolves." Tara stepped round the corner. "You smell of cheap cigarettes and dirty sex. I'd recognise it anywhere."

"I bet you say that to all the girls."

"I bet you say that to all the girls as well."

Busted.

She put her hands flat to the wall on either side of my head and leaned over me. This woman had no concept of personal space. "You should be careful, Kate Kane. My indulgence has limits."

Being trapped in a corner by a hot lingerie model might be fun under the right circumstances, but right now I wasn't sure whether it was sexy-threatening or just threatening. I had a knife, but stabbing the host at a funeral would probably be considered rude. Besides, she was a werewolf, and it would just piss her off and ruin a perfectly good dress.

There was only one thing for it. Sex my way out. Oh, my life is so hard.

I raised my knee and slid it up the inside of her thigh. "You should be careful who you pin to walls, Tara Vane-Tempest."

She hooked her foot round my leg, holding me off balance, and pressed in further, a spill of golden hair brushing my cheek. I was even less in control of the situation than I thought I was. I could feel the heat of her body . . . quite a lot of her body, actually. Her eyes gleamed amber.

"Who killed Andrew?"

Well, fuck.

I'd just lost sex-chicken. I tried to lean back, but the wall was there. Damn you, wall.

"I don't know for certain," I babbled, trying to wriggle away from all the skin and warmth and eyes and hands. "I'm still sort of working on it."

She caught me under the chin, forcing me look up at her. "Tell me." Her breath rushed across my lips like a kiss.

"It's complicated. I need more time. There was a mage involved, but—"

"I thought so." Tara pushed away from me and swept off. I guess sweeping ran in the family. Well, fuck. Fuck. *You fucked up, Kate Kane.*

I had to warn Nim that I'd just dropped her in it. And I was stuck in a tight dress without a phone in a Gothic ruin full of werewolves. I grabbed one of the catering staff, who directed me to, I shit you not, a telephone room. A room. For a telephone. What the hell.

Sitting in state on a mahogany table was an actual black Bakelite. You know, one of the manual dial things. Nim changes her phone every couple of months, and I didn't have the new number, but one of her lieutenants—Rachel, the Guardian of the Watchtower of the East—did weird telecommunications magic from a call centre in Hackney. I dialled that number and got through to an automated voice, which told me my call was important. It started playing that tune you always get when you're on hold: *da da da da dada daa, da da da da dada daa, didi dum didi dum di dum dum dum.*

I spoke into the music. "I need to speak to the Guardian of the Watchtower of the East." The line faded into an eerie static. And then a voice with a broad Estuary accent said: "Hi, this is the Guardian of the Watchtower of the East. I'm not 'ere right now. Please leave a message after the beep." *Beep*, said Archer's voice in my head.

There was a beep, then silence.

"Fuck. Uh, this is a message for Nim. From Kate. Kate Kane. I forgot about the werewolves, and they know. They'll be coming for you. Be ready. I'm really fucking sorry. Fuck."

I fucking hate answering machines.

I put the phone down and went back to the party, hoping to find Tara and explain. But she was already tinging on a glass for silence.

"Brothers, sisters, friends," she said. "We come together to guard Cousin Andrew on his final journey. The woods are dark and our enemies myriad. But we are the wardens of the ways between worlds. From the beginning, we have stood and we have watched and we have fought. Tonight, we commend Andrew's body to his ancestors. The shadows will come for him, and we will hold them back."

Beside her, Henry began a low, mournful howl and, one by one, the others joined in until the room echoed with the grief of wolves. At last, Tara threw back her head, the strength of her voice uniting the others. I stood quietly and listened. It should have been weird as hell, but I guess pain is pain.

Tara put one hand to her shoulder and released whatever was holding her impossible dress in place. There was the briefest flash of skin and then an enormous golden wolf was shaking out its coat. The French windows had been thrown open and people were spilling onto the terrace, some of them sprouting claws and fangs and gleaming lupine eyes. There were about a dozen full werewolves, emerging from discarded gowns. One of them was silver-grey and lean. I would have recognised the Dowager anywhere. Henry had thrown off his jacket and torn off his shirt. A moment later, he padded outside in wolf form to join Tara.

I hung back, not sure what was expected of me. I had no intention of taking my dress off. Unless I got a very good offer. And, to be honest, I didn't fancy wandering round the forest of Safernoc again. On the other hand, I had to find Tara as soon as possible, and I guess, since Maeve was probably off the hook for Andrew, I should have been looking a bit more deeply into the monsters that seemed to be trying to kill his family.

It wasn't long before I was the only person left in the room. Not fun. Oh wait, not the only person left.

The man Henry had called Jumbo uncurled himself from an armchair and came reluctantly to his feet, stifling a yawn. He finished his drink, ate a canapé, and sauntered over to me.

"Playing the wallflower, Ms. Kane?"

"Is that a polite term for standing around like an idiot?"

"I rarely use polite terms for anything. But you do look a little lost. I take it nobody has explained the traditions to you?"

"I need to find Tara," I said. I didn't think it was worth mentioning that I needed to find Tara to try and talk her out of eating one of my ex-girlfriends.

Jumbo laughed, an unhurried, indulgent sort of laugh. I think it meant *I'll try to help, but you're fucked.* He stretched out a hand, his fingertips lengthening one by one into claws.

"Well, my dear," he drawled, "you'll have to catch her first. And that would be quite extraordinarily dangerous. I strongly recommend that you remain with the main hunting party and do not even consider taking one of the horses off the beaten path into the dark heart of the woods. Nor should you follow the ghost lights until you reach the withered grove and the realm of the pale stag."

It's possible the angry silver faery with the antlers I'd met last time I was here was something completely different, but I doubted it. "What's the deal with that thing?"

Jumbo wagged a chiding claw at me. "One shouldn't delve too deeply into family secrets. It's a powerful local spirit, and that's all you need to know."

"Look, I'm all for privacy and everything, but I'm investigating a murder here." This was getting serious, so I ditched my drink. "Faeries hold grudges. Trust me, I know. So, as far as I'm concerned, this stag thing is a suspect."

"You reason that such a creature, angered from years of conflict with our family, would choose to lash out at one of its most isolated and vulnerable members?"

"Basically . . . yes."

"I fear you're, if you'll forgive the expression, barking up the wrong tree." Jumbo twitched an infuriating eyebrow at me. "Without going too deeply into our family history, the stag and his servants hunger for lives and souls, not for blood. If you wish to see his workings for yourself, you need only join the hunting party."

"You wouldn't be trying to get me killed, would you?"

"You hardly need my help for that." The tips of Jumbo's ears were narrowing lazily to points. "Come, let us join the others."

He led me onto the terrace. Andrew's body was being gently lifted into a hearse drawn by two black horses. They even had those plume things on their heads like in BBC costume dramas.

"The wolves have already breached the woods," explained Jumbo. "They'll hold back the worst of the shadows while we protect poor old Andy."

The family were gathering round the hearse, some on foot, some of them on horseback armed with shotguns, and some piled onto the tallyho wagon. Kauri and the other vampires had fallen in with the hunters, keeping clear of the horses.

"This is pretty hard-core for a funeral procession," I said.

"You do realise that all that talk about holding back the shadows wasn't symbolic? As you astutely surmised, Ms. Kane, our family has many enemies, and we're never more vulnerable than when we're dead. Now, if you'll excuse me, I'm about to lose the power of speech." Jumbo's jaw lengthened into a canine wedge, his teeth growing into fangs. He dropped briefly to all fours and sprang forwards like a sprinter, running with surprising speed to join the rest of the pack.

CHAPTER ELEVEN
SILVER & STONES

I went to get myself a horse. Servants were giving them out like party favours. I'd never actually learned to ride, because I wasn't middle class enough, but horses just seem to do what I want. I think it's a faery princess perk. I was helped onto what was blatantly the beginner model, and I declined the complimentary shotgun. I had to go sidesaddle, which turned out to be bloody uncomfortable, but at least I wasn't flashing my arse at a funeral. I had no idea how normal people got this to work, but I thought very firmly about where I wanted to go, and the horse trotted over to join the rest of the party.

Somebody sounded a horn, a chorus of howls answered from the woods, and the procession moved slowly forwards. As we neared the treeline, ghostly figures like the ones that had watched me chase the pale stag began sliding from the shadows. Shots rang out. Here and there, the wraiths dissolved into mist. Then the first wave of shifters charged towards the undergrowth, shaking loose more of the pale spirits. Some took to the air and were brought down in a hail of shotgun pellets. The rest were set upon and torn to ribbons of smoke by claws and fangs.

I stuck a hand up my skirt and grabbed my knife. The spirits were coming thick and fast, filling the air with clinging vapours. The shotgun fire was almost continuous now, a staccato cracking like fireworks. Something rushed towards me, reaching out with slender, ash-pale fingers. I slashed into it, and it recoiled with an inhuman shriek, scattering papery flakes of leaves and bark. Another came at me, and Jumbo burst from the pack, in full Hammer Horror wolfman form, and dragged it down. We pressed forwards, spirits falling to knives, claws, and shotgun blasts, and eventually they stopped coming.

The woods grew dark and quiet.

From the deepest shadows came a sweet and melancholy music, silver voices singing softly. I'd heard that before. My fingers slackened on my knife. I thought I might want to go towards the music. And then I changed my mind. One thing I've learned in this business is that ghostly singing chicks are never good. For the first time that evening, I felt real fear from the pack. There was a shimmer of light between the trees, and suddenly we were surrounded.

Surrounded by ghostly women riding honest-to-God motherfucking unicorns, and singing at us. Each held a slender silver bow. One of them tilted her head curiously at me.

I heard a volley of gunshots, and small wounds, weeping pale blood, opened across her face and body. She didn't even flinch, she just carried on singing. Then she raised her bow, a gleam of moonlight catching on the arrowhead.

Here lies Kate Kane, shot by a ghost on a unicorn. Beloved daughter. Sorely missed.

The arrow whistled past me. And from behind, I heard a strangled howl. Even partial shifters were damn difficult to stop, so an arrow shouldn't have been a big deal unless it was . . .

Well, fuck.

Ghost chicks on unicorns with fucking silver arrows.

More arrows came raining down on us. It was chaos. The wolves scattered but had nowhere to go. Some of them charged directly at the spirits, others scrambled beneath the hearse and the tallyho wagon. I pressed myself to the neck of my horse. Sorry, mate, better you than me.

To my right, Kauri flew forwards in a rush of shadows. Arrows struck him in the chest, but, being a vampire, he didn't really give a fuck. He crashed into one of the unicorns, bringing it thrashing and screaming to the ground. The other vampires attacked as well, falling on the riders in a blur of flashy supernatural powers. World's deadliest boylesque troupe.

An arrow grazed my arm. Bleeding again. Sigh.

This dress was not going to make it, was it?

I'm not the heroic type, but between sitting here waiting to get shot and trying to do something, I decided to do something. I wheeled my horse to face one of the women. I could tell the poor animal was terrified, but it charged anyway. Another arrow whistled past me. The next thing I knew the unicorn's horn rammed through my horse's neck and damn near stabbed me in the ribs. I rolled clear as my faithful doomed steed toppled to the ground in a mess of blood and flailing hooves. I'd have felt sorry for the fucker if I hadn't been in serious risk of joining it.

While the unicorn was ripping its horn free from the horse carcass, I dragged myself to my feet and threw myself over its neck to face the rider. She wrapped cold, dry fingers round my throat and squeezed. Long experience has taught me that when someone is trying to strangle you, the trick is to stay calm and fuck them up as fast as possible.

I hooked a hand over her shoulder to brace myself and drove my knife up into her heart. Her flesh cracked like an eggshell, spilling silver fluid all over my now completely ruined dress. And this is why I can't have nice things.

The ghost's fingers were still tight on my throat, so I wrenched my knife out through her chest cavity and kept hacking until she was just fragments of dust and a puddle of goo.

Victory!

Except for the part where I was sitting backwards on an angry unicorn.

The beast reared underneath me, snorting and making horrible, high-pitched noises. I threw myself flat to its back, got my legs round its neck and hung on as tight as I could. I was really glad everybody else was too busy getting killed to see this. If there was ever a time for latent faery princess powers, this was it. I concentrated really fucking hard on wanting the thing to calm the fuck down.

It really didn't want to. It was nothing but hate and malice wrapped in a horse skin.

Well, I wasn't going to do anything with my face in its arse. I waited until it had all four feet on the ground and swung myself round.

"Right, you fucker," I growled in its ear.

It jerked its head back and tried to stab me in the face. Bastard. I caught its blood-slick horn in my left hand, and my mother's strength surged through me. For once I didn't mind. This fucker was going down. Digging my other hand into its mane, I twisted its head around. Either it was going to do what I wanted, or I was going to break its fucking neck.

It fought me for a bit, its panicky breath steaming in the air, and then went to its knees. Very carefully, I let it go, and it didn't freak out and try to kill me again, so I called that a win. I half-heartedly patted its neck, and it rose smoothly to its feet.

Holy shit. I'd got a unicorn. Where was I going to park it in central London?

The rest of the fight wasn't going so well. Several members of the pack had been injured. There weren't enough vampires to keep the archers busy, and my technique of getting your horse killed wasn't scalable. I was going to have to try to take out another ghost, and I had no experience of unicorn-based combat. If I was lucky, I'd be a quick learner.

I set my sights on another of the unicorns and readied my knife. Before I could charge, a flash of silver-grey broke from the woods. The Dowager Marchioness of Safernoc clamped her jaws round one of its legs and tore through bone and tendon. It went to the ground with a shriek, pinning its rider under its flank. The Dowager circled, belly low to the forest floor, then shot forwards again, ripping out the beast's throat with merciless efficiency. I didn't wait to see the rest.

I looked for a new target and saw Henry scything through the rest of the ghosts, forcing the unicorns to the ground with his weight, and tearing the riders apart. One of them turned to flee, but the Dowager cut it off and brought it down. The song finally ended.

The woods grew dark and quiet.

I trotted back to the main party on my unicorn, hoping no one would ask too many questions.

"Who's hurt?" asked Henry.

I realised both he and the Dowager had shifted back into human form and were stark bollock naked. I looked away quickly. I'm just not into casual wang. Or, for that matter, anyone who gets free travel on public transport.

Jumbo eased out from under the hearse, his face losing its wolfish features as he rattled off a list of names and injuries.

"Any fatalities?"

Jumbo shook his head. The wounded were being helped onto the tallyho wagon and the Dowager—back in wolf form, thank God—leapt on to guard them on their way back to the house. The rest of the pack pressed on into the forest with the hearse. I wasn't sure what I was supposed to be doing, but then I saw a glimmer through the trees.

I guessed this was one of the ghost lights I'd carefully avoided following last time, and shouldn't follow now if I had any sense.

I followed it.

As soon as I left the path, I lost sight of the funeral party, the woods closing round me like a claw. The undergrowth was dense and the trees tangled together, but the unicorn seemed to know what it was doing. It seemed suspiciously keen to carry me to towards certain death. Fucker.

The lights never seemed to get any closer, but they multiplied like stars coming out, leading me to the place where the forest was dying. At first, all I noticed were some withering leaves, but soon the moon shone down through skeletal branches onto a floor littered with dry bones and dust. At last, we came to a ring of dead trees, and my unicorn just wouldn't move.

I slithered to the ground.

"You'd better wait, you fucker. Or I'll hunt you down and turn you into magic glue."

It gave me a look with its dead black eyes that I decided to take as a yes.

Knife in hand, I stepped into the circle of trees. I felt a familiar chill, like stepping into cold water. I've walked between worlds before, but you never quite get used to it. I looked over my shoulder to see what I'd got myself into. Behind me was a blasted heath, dead trees scattered on an ashen plane. A vast pale moon hung low in a starless sky, washing the land in light the colour of bone. Well, Toto, I wasn't in Kansas anymore. I was in a fucking faery realm.

In the middle of the grove, a great golden wolf was locked in combat with the most fucked-up animal I'd ever seen. It was a gigantic, corpse-white stag, its flesh blistered and sloughing away to the bone. Its many-tined antlers were honed to points and hung with strips of rotting velvet. I guess when I'd seen it before it had its friendly face on. Faery lords were an extension of their worlds, or maybe the other way round, and everything here was, well, dead and desiccated. I guess Tara had been telling the truth all along. There was no way this thing, or anything that worked for it, had killed her cousin.

As I watched, Tara sprang for the stag's throat, but it batted her aside, its antlers opening a jagged cut across her flank. She hit the ground, rolled, and came to her feet snarling.

Well, thank God I was here with my very small knife.

Not wanting to get myself immediately killed, I waited for an opening.

The stag lowered its head and charged. Tara held her ground, twisting aside at the last second to strike at its haunches. She brought it down, and I lost track of them in a whirl of dust. The stag threw her off and rose to its feet, its form shifting into something vaguely human. If you count massive, horned dudes with hooves as human. He wore a crown of antlers and held a spear of bone, which he hurled at Tara. It pierced her flank, knocking her down just as she was getting up. The ex-stag reached out his upturned hand, spreading his fingers wide and then curling them inwards. Tara convulsed on the ground as tendrils of silver mist streamed from her wounds towards her attacker. They gathered round his fingers and pooled in the palms of his hands as he shuddered in what seemed to be pleasure.

Fuck. Kate. Do something now.

As usual, I had no fucking clue what was going on, but there was no way it could be good.

I ran forwards, jumped onto his back, and tried to drive the knife between his collarbone and neck. He made a pissed-off noise and flexed his shoulders, at which point his flesh gave way under my fingertips and his entire back peeled away, dumping me on the ground in a pile of flaking skin and ash. At least he wasn't gooey. He turned on me, twisted one massive finger into my hair, and hauled me to my feet. It really fucking hurt. He clamped his other hand over my mouth and nose. I tried not to panic, but I was out of fucking options. I'd dropped my knife, I couldn't reach his body. All I could do was claw pathetically at his wrists. And I was feeling weaker by the second, like something I seriously wanted to keep was being sucked out of me.

And then he was gone.

I hit the ground hard, gasping for breath and half-blind. When I felt capable of it, I looked up. Tara had the stag-dude-thing pinned to the ground and was mauling the fuck out of him. I let her get on with that. When she was finished, he was nothing but dust, fragments of bone, and a shattered crown. I crawled to my feet and followed her back to our world. As we approached the edge of the circle, a cold sensation crawled over my skin, and I could see the woods again. The unicorn had buggered off, though. Fucker.

Back under familiar stars, Tara shifted. It was just my luck. Alone in the woods with a naked, sweaty lingerie model, and I was too beaten up to properly appreciate it. She descended on me.

"What the hell did you think you were doing?"

"I needed to talk to you." It sounded a bit weak, even to me.

"You could have been killed."

"So could you."

"I had the situation under control." She loomed over me, getting a lot of mileage out of a couple of extra inches of height.

I tipped my head back so I could look her in the eye. "Yeah, getting stabbed like that was a winning strategy."

"I would have handled it. This is my life, and it is dangerous. I can't protect my pack with you in the way."

"I'm so sick of the 'stay out of my world' speech. You invited me here. Yes, you saved my life, but I saved yours. Can't you get over yourself for ten fucking seconds and admit that?" I turned away from her. I'd heard all this before.

Tara grabbed me by the shoulder and spun me round, catching me by the waist as I tried unsuccessfully to pull back. She reached out and twisted a lock of my hair around her finger. I looked down and saw it shone white in the moonlight. "You see," she said softly, "he could have sucked you dry in seconds. I don't want anyone hurt on my account."

In a moment of horrified vanity, I checked the rest of my hair, but it was okay. God, what if it had grabbed my boob or something? "I'm fine. But, listen, about the murder. I really don't think the mages had anything to do with it."

Tara's eyes flashed angrily. "There will be retaliation. Blood demands blood."

"Seriously, the mages had nothing to do with your cousin. One of them attacked Julian, and Nimue is handling it. And I really, really don't think it was a mage that killed Andrew."

"I cannot put my faith in the Witch Queen. Somebody conjured something that killed one of my people. If it was not one of her court, it was still one of her kind."

Oh, this was not going well. I'd just about managed to keep Julian from going all blood on the walls, and, although I was about sixty percent certain I could use the same technique on Tara, it would be the last nail in the coffin of my professionalism.

"It's not worth starting a war," I insisted.

"Yes. It is. And I will not discuss this further."

She let me go and turned to leave, so I caught her by the arm. "Well, I'm not finished talking about it."

She snapped back around and slammed me into a tree. Her body was burning hot. "When I say a conversation is over, it is over. Do not lay hands on me again. You are no longer amusing, Kate Kane."

My mother was probably having a field day. I marshalled her strength and shoved Tara away from me. She flew backwards, transforming in mid-air and landing on all fours. I didn't think wolves could look surprised.

"I'm not your fucking sex toy." I stomped into the woods with great dignity.

Tara overtook me in two bounds and shifted back into human form. "You have no idea where you're going."

"Away from you is good for now."

"We've subdued the spirits for the moment, but these woods are still dangerous. And you still have no idea where you're going."

I kept stomping, dragging the tatters of my dress through briars and fuck knows what else. Suddenly I felt a finger tracing a line across my bare shoulder.

"Is being my sex toy really such a bad thing?" asked Tara huskily.

My pride said yes, it was. Other parts of me had other ideas. I accidentally stopped stomping.

She slid one hand round my waist, pulling me back against her very naked body. Her heart pounded a hunter's rhythm along my spine. Her other hand cupped my chin, drawing my head around, as she leaned over my shoulder. Her hair spilled across my arm. Her breath warmed my skin.

Just say no, Kate. Just say no.

"There's a power in you, Kate Kane," whispered Tara against my lips. "You smell of dark woods and wild places."

Tara smelled of blood and sweat and excitement. *Ngh*. I needed a way out of this. One that didn't involve fucking a werewolf. Maybe.

"I thought it was cheap cigarettes and dirty sex," I said, preserving my modesty with witty repartee.

"I can help you, yah."

"With the dirty sex?"

"That too."

The hand round my waist dipped lower. Quite a bit lower.

Come on, Kate. You're at a funeral. And you have to be able to look at yourself in the mirror tomorrow.

I caught her by the wrist. "Buy a vibrator."

She kissed the corner of my mouth. "The chase has barely begun, Kate Kane. One day you'll beg me to fuck you."

It was the kind of line you could only get away with if you were an alpha werewolf.

I pulled out of her arms. "You've got a long way to go before that'll happen. Now come on, let's bury your cousin."

She didn't really have an answer to that, so she led me through the woods to the foot of a small hill covered in white stones. The rest of the funeral party—at least the ones that were still reasonably intact—were waiting with the hearse. Tara handed me over to Jumbo and climbed to the top of the hill, where she addressed us.

"Brothers, sisters, friends. In this place we have laid our dead to rest for ten centuries. Now we send Andrew to join our ancestors in whatever world awaits us next."

In subdued silence, they took Andrew's body from the hearse and carried it up the hill. They laid it beside Tara, who lifted a large white rock and placed it at his head. And then, one by one, the rest of the funeral party came and added their own stones to the cairn until Andrew's body disappeared into the hill.

CHAPTER TWELVE

RATS & NUNS

My sleeping patterns were fucked again. By the time I drove back to London, it was four in the morning. I did my now-customary face-plant and woke up at noon, with the weird realisation that there was nothing I was meant to be doing. Technically, I'd put myself back on the case, but progress had stalled. The Prince of Coins probably wasn't involved, but it would take a while for Lucy to confirm that. And I'd ruled out both the Vane-Tempest clan and their whacky supernatural neighbours. That left me with a grand total of zero suspects and zero leads. I could just about pin it on the Dowager or Kauri if I tried really hard, but while I was hardly a beacon of professional ethics, I drew the line at fitting people up. Maybe I would have to accept that I wasn't going to get this to make sense.

That was when I realised I had no reason to get out of bed. I tried to think of this as a win. I'd sort of closed a case, and nobody was dead who hadn't already been dead when I started. But then there was the war I'd accidentally started between the mages and the werewolves. I told myself there was nothing I could do about that.

I decided very firmly that I was going to get up and do things and, to my surprise, I did. I peeled off the ruins of my dress and had a shower (this was almost getting to be a regular thing). I tended to my not-very-sexy wounds. The old ones looked like they'd heal up fine, but the white streak in my hair was freaking me out. Tara's *my life is dangerous* bullshit was infuriatingly unattractive, but thinking about it, that thing had come *really* fucking close to actually killing me. I went to get dressed and noticed I hadn't done any laundry for weeks. It was officially dress-down Monday. I dug the pair of jeans I'd worn least recently out of the bottom of the basket and grabbed the very last T-shirt from the back of the drawer. It turned out to be one of Eve's. At least it was black, but it had a stick man on the front above the slogan "Stand back, I'm going to try science."

Well, it hadn't worked for us.

But today was my day for being a grown-up and doing laundry, not feeling sorry for myself.

This turned out to be more of a challenge than I expected, because I'd run out of those washing tablet things.

It was time for a list.

A couple of hours later, I'd bought cleaning supplies, put my laundry on, stuck all my old bottles in the recycling, changed the bin liner, Skyped my dad, picked up an email from Lucy confirming that it would, indeed, take a while to get anything from the documents I'd sent her but she thought it all looked kosher, cleaned a bunch of crap, and was ready to think about being a go-getting young professional.

I'd let a lot of things slide since Archer died. I needed to find someone to redo the website. Eve had designed it years ago when she was a nerd-for-hire, and I was pretty sure things have moved on since 2006. Wasn't I supposed to be tweeting? *I am on a stakeout #donttellanybody.* And then there was Archer's name on the door. This one I'd been deliberately putting off, which was stupid and sentimental but, you know what, fuck it. I was going to leave it up there. It was the least I could do for him. *Beep.*

Shit. My phone. I'd left it under the pile of clothes last night, and now it was whining that it was low on battery. I went to plug it in and I saw I had a missed call from an unknown number.

Huh.

I checked my messages. Julian's voice poured over me like hot fudge sauce on an ice-cream sundae. "Hello, sweeting, I'm just thinking about you. If you want to know what I'm thinking, call me back."

Perhaps I'd totally misread the situation. Perhaps I hadn't given Julian's attention span enough credit. But I'd kind of assumed it was a one-off, and now I was confused. Did this mean we were dating? She had taken me for pudding, but I'd thought that was about getting into my pants. It had, after all, worked. But then she *had* told me half her life story while my pants were clearly accessible, and that had been . . . sweet.

I had a don't date vampires policy for a reason.

On the other hand—now that I knew it was an option—I really wanted to see her again.

No, wait, this was crazy. She was an eight-hundred-year-old vampire. For all I knew, she had ex-girlfriends stacked under her floorboards like Lego bricks. Maybe it was her hobby: "Hi, there's this murder I want you to investigate, can I buy you pudding, look at my lesbian sexpile, let's shag, let's shag more, now I will kill you." And it's not like I had a great track record with relationships, either.

There was only one sensible option that an ordinary, rational, safety-conscious person could take. I had to do another background check. This time a "does she murder her girlfriends?" check, not a "would she kill a random guy outside her own club and then not pay you?" check.

I had a quick poke round the usual places—the National Archives, the Criminal Records Bureau, government agencies, that kind of thing—but found nothing I hadn't found last time. Vampires are very good at staying out of the public eye, and they tend to work through intermediaries. I spent some time looking into the Calix Group. Three of her venues had been brought up on public health violations within the last six months. Julian had mentioned someone calling the health inspectors, but I couldn't quite see how it fit into anything, and it wasn't really what I was after right now. I made a mental note to come back to it later and went on digging around for evidence that dating her would go horribly, horribly wrong.

Time for a different strategy. Start from the beginning.

I Googled the Order of St. Agrippina, not really expecting to find anything, but it turned out they had a website. They were a group of exorcist nuns based out of Rome. That shouldn't have been weird, since I've met and exorcised demons myself, but it totally was. There are plenty of groups that deal with supernatural shit, but they don't normally talk about it on their website. Well. They don't normally talk about it on their website and expect to be taken seriously.

I clicked past Today's Homily and the Welcome from Sister Ignatia to the history of the order. It wasn't particularly helpful. You can just about get away with mentioning evil spirits and possession and the power of Christ, but "In the year of our Lord 1206, Sister Julian did get turned into a vampire, lo" is probably pushing your luck. There was, however, contact information for their archivist, so I registered a fake email and pinged off a quick query, claiming that I was writing an academic paper on the history of demonic possession with a particular focus on the all-female Catholic orders of the twelfth century. I didn't push too hard for specifics, but I said that I'd heard about an incident involving a member of their order and an entity called Anacletus the Corruptor, and was wondering if they had any more information.

That was about all I could achieve without leaving the house. If I wanted hard information on Julian's past, I'd have to find someone with access to a thousand years' worth of obscure information, half-forgotten secrets, and forbidden knowledge dredged up from the darkest recesses of the city.

Thankfully, I knew someone like that.

His name was Jack.

He and someone I thought was probably his sister had a market stall near Camden Lock, where they sold shiny tat to teenage goths.

I got there just as he was packing up. He looked much like he always did, small and scrawny, with a floppy black emo fringe and too much eyeliner. He looked about eighteen, but he'd looked about eighteen for the last ten years.

"It's been ages," he said. "Buy me a waffle?"

"Sure."

I picked up his box of bling and tucked it under my arm. There was a waffle stand across the road, in front of a shop that seemed to sell exactly one type of boot. I bought him a waffle with everything on it, and a coffee for me, and we wandered into the covered part of the market until we found a wall to sit on.

Jack squashed up really close and shovelled too much waffle into his mouth with his fingers.

"You've got cream on your nose," I told him.

He wiped it off on the back of his hand, licked it up, and then smiled shyly at me. "Can I have some of your coffee?"

I handed it over.

He took a sip and made a face. "I don't like it without sugar."

"Well, I'm sorry I ordered my coffee the way I like it."

He giggled and then grew serious. "There's something nasty in the sewers."

When Jack wasn't running his stall or charming people into buying him waffles, he was basically a swarm of rats. It meant he'd lived in some pretty weird places.

"Sorry to hear that."

Jack shrugged. "We moved out of there months ago. Got a cellar now."

"That sounds nice."

He nodded vigorously.

I finished the last of my coffee. "So, look, I wanted to talk about something."

"Okay! The Veiled Lady walks again, the Library of Lost Books has closed its doors for the war with the Fifteen Hundred, the Prince of Wands is seeking the key to the Discarded Stair, and there are delays on the Circle line between Embankment and Barbican."

The rats are all part of this weird group mind thing called the Multitude, and Jack sometimes forgets I can't hear what he's thinking, which can make him pretty difficult to talk to.

"Errr," I said, when I could get a word in edgeways. "I wanted to talk about something specific."

"Oh."

"What can you tell me about Julian Saint-Germain?" I asked.

"That's not specific at all." Jack looked confused.

"Okay." I tried again. "Does she, for example, murder her girlfriends?"

Jack twitched his nose thoughtfully. "Only once."

As far as I was concerned, that was one time too many. "Uh, what happened with that?"

"She made her a vampire."

"Just to check: do you mean made her a vampire *and then* murdered her, or do you mean made her vampire *which constituted* murdering her?"

"Ummm . . ." Jack licked the remains of the waffle off the polystyrene tray. "The second one."

Well, that was a relief. That *was* a relief, right? I must have looked pleased or something, because Jack went chattering on eagerly.

"But then they went away. And then the Morrigan fell. And then she was at the Conclave. That was where all the vampires talked a lot. Julian Saint-Germain used to eat rats. She used to be called Julian of Colchester. She came here when she was alive. Then she went away. Then she was dead and she came back. That was when she ate the rats. Lots of rats." Jack made a pouty face.

Eve used to have one of those posters where it's all shots from *Star Wars* and then you step back and it's Darth Vader's head. Talking to Jack was kind of like that. And the best thing to do was to wait for the whole picture to come together.

"Then she stopped eating rats and started having lots and lots and lots and lots of sex. Then she was at the Wars of the Roses. That was where all the people fought a lot. Then she was at the theatre dressed as a boy. That was when she stabbed a man in the eye over a bill. She did a lot of stabbing when she was alive."

I was starting to get a headache.

"She used to stab vampires and demons. Once she stabbed a faery lord with an iron sword and threw him in a hole." Jack suddenly remembered what I'd actually asked. "She never stabbed her girlfriends, though. Unless she went away and stabbed them. And then we wouldn't know."

"What happened to the one she turned into a vampire?" I wasn't sure I really wanted the answer.

"She was in the theatre as well, but then they went away and then she was a punk rocker. And then there were a lot of fires. My sister likes punk rock. And fires."

At least she wasn't murdered. In my experience, most relationships end with a lot of fires, one way or the other. I tried to work out how I felt about Julian now and came down on the side of weirdly reassured. She'd been doing crazy, irresponsible shit for the best part of eight hundred years, but that was kind of what I'd signed up for. And if anyone would know about a secret pile of mouldering corpses, it would be the rats.

Overall chance of getting murdered: low.

Overall chance of miserable, soul-destroying break-up: moderate.

Overall chance of lots of red-hot monkey sex: high to extreme.

Overall chance of boredom: zero.

I was liking those odds.

"Come on," I said, "I'll take you to dinner."

Jack smiled and grabbed my hand. His fingers were slightly sticky with cream and maple syrup, and his nails were painted in chipped black varnish.

I'm not a cheapskate, but Jack really really likes KFC. There was a branch just round the corner on the High Street. I bought us a bumper bucket of undifferentiated chicken fragments, with coleslaw and beans, added a box of hot wings for three quid, and threw in a bottle of Pepsi Max. Once I'd bought enough chicken to feed a swarm of voracious rodents, we scrambled over the railing and sat on the edge of the lock, with the bucket between us.

We didn't talk much. It was one of those low-key English sunsets, pretty in a grey way.

I was actually doing okay.

Jack hoovered up the chicken, stripping the bones and flinging them into the lock. I ate a couple of hot wings to keep him company. And then my phone rang. Unknown number. Again.

I picked up. "Kane."

"There's been another one." Ashriel's voice drifted over the line like digitally transmitted aural sex. "It's fucking nasty, get down here now."

He hung up.

Wrong as it felt to get excited about the death of an innocent person, at least this proved I hadn't been going crazy the last few days. I was back in the game.

I said good-bye to Jack, and left him sitting on the lock, staring into the sunset and eating beans. Then I grabbed a cab to Brewer Street.

Twenty minutes later, I was in the unisex bog at the Velvet, ankle-deep in blood and sewage.

Being a PI is such a sexy, exciting job.

Ashriel was leaning by the door, his usual incubus smoulder dampened by the ming.

"So . . . what happened, exactly?" I asked.

"You're the detective. We think it's probably the plumber."

There really wasn't much to go on: a shattered toilet, a wash of dirty water covering the floor, scraps of shredded clothing, and a scattering of stripped bones.

I really wished I hadn't had that KFC.

I pulled a pair of latex gloves out of my inside pocket and put them on. Then I crouched in the filth and fished out a long bone, probably one of the arm ones. Not for the first time, I kicked myself for having spent A-level biology staring at Patrick. The bone had been thoroughly gnawed. Hundreds of tiny teeth marks pitted the surface. I put it in the sink and checked another. Same story. Whoever this was, they'd been killed and eaten. Hopefully in that order.

I plunged my hands back into the sewage and made a slow, methodical search of the bathroom floor. Ashriel came and squatted down next to me. He smelled considerably better than the rest of the room.

"Can I help with that?" he offered.

"You want to stick your hands in poo and look for clues?"

He shrugged. "I've not got a fetish or anything. I just thought it'd go faster with two of us."

"Dude, you are more than welcome. I just thought you'd be squicked out."

He laughed. "I used to live *in Hell*. I'm basically unsquickable."

"Well, I'll do this bit, you take here to the door, and we'll meet in the middle."

I found a wrench and a plunger, a mobile phone that had seen better days even before it'd been chewed and drowned, and a big chunky ring of keys, practically a life story in themselves. I was just sorting through them when Ashriel yelped and jerked back so quickly he nearly fell over.

"Unsquickable, huh?" I reached over to steady him.

Ashriel was shaking his hand in an *ow fuck* way. "There's sanctified steel down there."

I felt around where he indicated, and eventually my fingers closed on something hard and round. I cleaned it up in the sink, shook it dry, and put it on the palm of my hand. It was a tarnished metal ball, about the size of a Mint Imperial, with a hole through the middle.

Huh.

I put it down carefully and continued the search from where I was. Scattered across the floor I found five more balls and a worn cross made of the same metal. I laid the bone and the pieces of metal out next to the sink. There was a loop on the top of the cross about the same size as the holes in the beads.

We had a dead plumber. With a rosary. With pieces of a rosary. With pieces of a rosary that looked really old. That made no sense.

"Can you think of any reason your plumber might be carrying this?"

Ashriel peered over my shoulder. "Actually, that's some serious hardware. It takes more than a few Our Fathers to make steel burn like that."

"And you're sure your plumber wasn't a demon hunter in disguise?"

"I'm pretty sure she was just a plumber. We investigate that sort of thing pretty thoroughly. Although . . ." He trailed away, staring at the crucifix.

There was an obvious conclusion here, but I wasn't jumping yet. "Seen it before?"

"One a lot like it," he said cautiously.

"It's hers, isn't it?"

His eyes shuttered suddenly. "I don't know what you mean."

"Julian. She used to be a demon-hunting ninja nun. Also there was something about pudding."

His eyebrows went up. "She told you?"

"Doesn't she say that to all the girls?"

"No. Really not."

I wasn't sure whether to be flattered or freaked out. I decided I'd worry about it after I'd dealt with the dead plumber.

There was just too much here that made no fucking sense at all. I really needed a cigarette.

"Going for a smoke. By the way, what was her name?"

"Whose?"

I gestured to the floor. "The plumber."

"I didn't ask."

"Find out for me."

I went into the alley where poor old Andrew had bought it and lit up. There was a white van parked at the end, which had "J. Brown, Son & Daughter, Plumbers, est. 1976" painted on the side. Well shit. Make that "J. Brown & Son." I heaved out a smoky sigh.

There'd been three attacks now. Two on the Velvet, one on Julian. That alone didn't add up. These things escalated. This thing wavered. You don't follow up an assassination attempt with an exploding toilet. What was with that, anyway? There was no pattern here. Mages who summon bloodsucking star demons don't fill rooms with sewage. And what about the rosary? That had to be a message. Which also meant it had to be an old enemy, not a new one.

Unless it was an incredibly elaborate bluff by someone who'd found out that Julian used to be a demon-hunting nun, sourced an original thirteenth-century, mystically sanctified rosary, and planted it in a toilet, along with a swarm of killer whatevers. I'd seen some byzantine shit in my time, but if we were up against someone who would go to that much trouble for a red herring, I was going home.

It also confirmed that Maeve was off the hook. For some of it, anyway.

Oh fuck. Maeve.

I flicked my cigarette down the sewer grate and ran back into the Velvet, shouting for Ashriel.

"Did you tell Julian about this?"

"She's in charge. I went to her first."

I pulled out my phone and dialled her number. It rang for a while and then went to the default voice mail service. I didn't leave a message. She wouldn't have picked it up anyway. I turned back to Ashriel.

"Where the fuck is Julian?"

"Do you really think she tells me where she goes?"

I don't even know why I was asking him. I suppose I was hoping for "she's having a quiet night in with some Horlicks."

I knew exactly where she was.

I had to get to Tottenham. Now.

CHAPTER THIRTEEN

FIRE & MIST

 had just enough presence of mind to grab the rosary bits before jumping in a cab. It should have taken half an hour, maybe only twenty minutes, at this time of night, but after an hour we were still driving, and the meter was climbing.

"Uh, what the hell are you doing?" I asked the driver.

"Nearly there, just a bit further." He spoke in a weird, faraway voice.

"I think I'll just get out here."

Something was messing with this guy's head, and he clearly shouldn't be in charge of a cab.

I got out somewhere by the reservoir, moonlight gleaming on the flat, wide water. It was strangely silent. And then I realised there wasn't any traffic. I crossed the bridge and turned down Forest Road to Tottenham Hale. As I walked, a mist thickened around me, and, even though the road was straight, I kept feeling as though I'd taken a wrong turn.

This had Nimue written all over it, and if I wasn't careful, I'd end up wandering Tottenham 'til dawn.

I closed my eyes and tried to feel the shape of the enchantment. It was woven with the currents of the city like a stone shifting the ripples of a stream. I didn't know much about magic, but I was pretty sure this was some serious shit. If I concentrated, I could feel the mist pulling me in two directions, as though it couldn't decide whether I was an innocent, to be gently led aside, or an enemy to be drawn deeper.

I knew how it felt. I was pretty sure I was here to save someone's arse, but I wasn't sure whose. One of these days, I'd get a girlfriend nobody wanted dead.

But it wasn't like I had a choice: spell or not, I was going in.

I let the mist draw me down Ferry Street. I didn't see a single fucking soul.

I passed a random pub (traditional Sunday roasts: £6.95). It had just gone chucking-out time, but no one was being chucked out. It was all closed up and silent, no cars in the car park.

I kept walking, past quiet apartment blocks, a deserted car wash, and bus stops with no buses and no one to wait for them. At a barren junction, I saw a glare of light through the mist. An empty KFC, lights still on.

It was official. I was in a zombie movie, except there were no zombies and everybody was tucked up safely at home. Nim had got sixty thousand people off the streets.

More houses, more shut-up shops, another pub as quiet as the first. I finally passed a late-opening Tesco that wasn't as late opening as it should have been and turned onto West Green Road.

Julian was stalking down the street, somewhere ahead of me, the tails of a military coat billowing behind her and her boot heels striking the pavement steady as a metronome. I'll say this for Julian. Even on a psychotic vengeance crusade, she had one hell of a sense of style.

"Come out, come out, wherever you are," she called in an eerie sing-song.

She passed a lamppost. There was a blur of motion, and a second later it crashed through the window of a Celebrations party shop, scattering shards of glass, streamers, and feather boas into the street. A solitary helium balloon drifted out into the mist.

"I can do this all night." She dusted her hands off theatrically.

I yelled out her name, but my voice was lost in a roar of engines as Michelle's gang swept in from all sides, the decals on their bikes actually burning, and tracks of fire streaming in their wake. I ran for the shelter of the shattered shop front.

Michelle swerved to a halt in front of Julian, the bike skidding away on its side as she leapt clear.

Julian put her hands on her hips. "So this is the Witch Queen's cavalry."

Wings of flame erupted from Michelle's shoulders and a burning sword appeared in her hand. I was sensing a theme here. "I don't do banter," she said, and swung her sword straight at Julian.

Of course, Julian wasn't there. "And what exactly do you do?" She was standing on the top of the railway bridge half a street away.

Once again, I'd brought a knife to a super-power fight. I was seriously outclassed, and I couldn't see what the fuck was going on. Also, somebody might set me on fire. I scrambled out of the wreckage of the store and up the broken security grill. By the time I'd got onto the roof ledge, Michelle was flying, the tips of her wings cutting golden arcs through the mist.

The rest of the bikers were fanning out into what was clearly a well-rehearsed deployment pattern. The ones on the quickest, lightest bikes criss-crossed the street, layering trails of fire into a barricade, and suddenly the sky lit up like Guy Fawkes's night as the mages launched their attack.

They threw fire. A lot of fire. Some breathed it from their mouths, some shot it from their fingertips, some lobbed great balls of the stuff. One conjured a flock of fiery birds that soared towards the bridge.

Julian vaulted backwards out of sight, and I heard the explosions from a second barrage on the other side of the road. A moment later she dropped to the ground again, driven back by a crossfire of, well, fire. Michelle swooped out of the sky and rammed her sword through Julian's back.

The next few seconds seemed to go on forever. My proto-girlfriend had just been pretty thoroughly stabbed, and I had no idea how to feel about it because she was blatantly the bad guy.

But I really did kind of like her. Yes, I was a faery-blooded, thirty-something PI with trust issues and a drinking problem, and she was a psychotic undead nun with a pudding fixation, but I really thought we were in with a chance.

A weird sort of hush had fallen over the mages like they couldn't believe it had worked.

Julian turned round slowly and caught Michelle by the throat, wrenching the sword out of her grip. She forced her back, holding her at arm's length. With her free hand, Julian took hold of the burning blade and began to shove it backwards through her own chest. Michelle grabbed onto Julian's wrist and wrapped her other hand round Julian's neck, flames pouring from her fingers.

I started to scrabble over the rooftops towards the bridge. Fuck knew what I thought I was going to do when I got there.

The sword came free and clattered to the ground. Julian tore Michelle's hand from her neck, yanked her forwards, and bit her. The fire went out.

The mages went ballistic. Literally. A torrent of flames filled the road from both directions, creating a vast inferno beneath the railway bridge. I had to shade my eyes from the heat and the glare, and when I looked back Julian was walking out of the fire, dragging Michelle's limp body with her. Julian's clothes were charred and tattered, her skin streaked with ash. She did not look happy.

She threw Michelle at the feet of her followers. Michelle tried to stand but then collapsed. I'd thought she was dead, but it looked like she was just damn close to it.

Julian gave a flourishing bow. "Next."

A couple of the older mages exchanged brief looks and stepped forwards. Each stretched one hand towards Julian and the other towards their comrade, and chains of fire bound the three of them. Julian fell to her knees, screaming, and the scent of burning flesh seared the air.

The bikers ran forwards, wielding chains and tire irons, for a game of splat the vampire.

Fuck fuck fuck.

I had to do something. But what? If I did nothing and Julian died, I'd feel like shit. And if I got in the way and Julian killed someone, I'd feel like shit.

Julian lashed out wildly as the mages closed in on her, flinging them aside and dashing the weapons out of their hands. This was getting really fucking nasty. Mages were falling, but they kept coming. And as the fire under the bridge died away, they were joined by more from the other side. I didn't know how long Julian was going to last.

Then one of the mages holding the chains gave a terrible shriek and fell to the ground, flames erupting from beneath his skin. Fire magic is fucking dangerous, and this was why. The other one staggered back, blisters bursting across her arms and face. The chains vanished.

Unbound, Julian ripped through the remaining bikers. The ones that could run, ran, leaving Julian alone on a bloody, burned-out street, surrounded by crumpled bodies and discarded motorcycles. She walked over to one of the fallen and lifted him to his feet.

"Tell your mistress I am still waiting."

She dropped him and he fled.

One of the other mages was crawling towards his bike. I caught a familiar flash of orange hair.

"Do you have a death wish, little wizard?" asked Julian, as Ector pulled his bike up and got on it.

"Fuck you, you dead bitch!" he yelled. He revved his engine and raised his right hand, a plume of flame solidifying into a burning lance.

Then he charged, fire blazing in his wake.

Julian dodged aside, grabbed the bike in one hand and Ector in the other. The bike spun through the window of a Western Union. Ector dangled.

"Foolish." Julian snapped his neck.

She dropped the body and walked away.

My rosary was starting to feel just a little bit trivial. Ector had been pretty annoying, but now he was dead. I guess this should have changed how I felt about Julian, but it didn't. I'd always known what she was.

I climbed down from my ledge and hurried after her.

Nimue stepped out from a side street. She was wearing faded jeans and a grey hoodie. She'd grown out her hair so it fell past her shoulders in loose, dark coils.

"You wanted to see me?"

Julian flicked ash from her ruined epaulettes. "You attacked me, I let it go. You attacked me again, for that you die."

Before she could develop that thought, a sleek black limo eased its way down the street and pulled to a halt amidst the wreckage. The doors opened, and Tara flowed gracefully out like she was at a movie premiere, followed by Henry and some other pack members I vaguely remembered from the funeral.

"Miss Vane-Tempest, fancy meeting you here," said Julian, with a slightly ironic look.

Tara tossed her hair haughtily. "This is a family matter, Saint-Germain."

"Oh yes, they got one of your pups, didn't they?"

"On your territory."

"Ah, do you wish to lodge a complaint with the management?" Julian bared her fangs in something that could have been a smile.

"I have come for vengeance."

Julian's teeth glinted. "Get in line, dear heart."

"There are five of us and ours is the greater claim."

"Amazingly, I don't care."

"That is enough." Nimue didn't raise her voice, but it carried on the wind. "There are no claims here. No vengeance will be taken."

Claws scythed from the tips of Tara's fingers, and she strode forwards. "I will not tolerate your impudence, witch."

Nimue raised her hand, and Tara went slowly to her knees before her. "You stand in my place of sovereignty. You will offer me no harm, but hear my judgement."

Julian came flying forwards, fangs bared. And the next moment she was kneeling too, snarling up at Nimue.

Although she looked serene, I'd known Nim for years, and I could see the tension running down the line of her neck. I couldn't imagine how much this was taking out of her. I ran across the street towards them.

"One of our courtiers was responsible for the attempt on your life, but not for the attack on your property," Nimue told Julian. "She has been punished for her crimes, and you will take no further action against her or us." She turned to Tara. "Neither we, nor any of our court, had any part in the death of your cousin. We swear this by the earth, the sky, and our true name. You will no longer seek our blood, nor the blood of our people. You will both leave this place and return to your places of power. And for what has happened here tonight, neither we nor our court shall pursue you. This is our judgement. Your wealth, your title, and your strength are forfeit should you defy us."

Nimue stepped past them and went to tend the wounded.

Julian and Tara both got slowly to their feet. I guessed this was my cue. I stepped forwards.

They glared at me.

"What are you doing here?" demanded Julian.

"I came to tell you it wasn't the mages."

Tara gazed haughtily down at me. "You're a little late, Kate Kane. I think we've already established that."

"You didn't believe the witch, did you?" Julian sounded pretty scornful for someone who had been kneeling on the ground a few moments ago. "Witches lie."

"She swore on the land and on her name," said Tara. "If she is lying, then she has sacrificed everything for that lie, and we have no need to punish her further."

Julian sneered. "That's all very kumbayaya, but somebody's fucking with me, and somebody's going to pay."

"Well, that's your problem, Saint-Germain." Tara swept her hair over her shoulders and caught my hand. It was so unexpected, I didn't have time to pull away. She raised it to her lips and kissed it with a bit too much linger. "Always a pleasure, Kate Kane." And having casually fucked my relationship, the whole family got back into the limo and left.

Julian's eyes narrowed. "I've been stabbed, set on fire, and given orders by a witch. That better not be what I think it is, sweeting, because I'm having a very bad night."

"She was just being a dick. Julian, can we please focus on the murders?"

"You don't have a good track record in that area."

It was a cheap shot, but I let it slide, given the circumstances. "I tried to tell you. That's why us mortals have a legal system. Sometimes you're going to finger the wrong person."

"Don't I know it, sweeting. So, who are you fingering now?"

I pulled the pieces of the rosary out my pocket. "I found these at the scene."

Julian stared.

"Are you okay?" I awkwardly patted her shoulder. I'm not very good at comforting people at the best of the times. This was a long way from the best of times. But, to my surprise, she put a blackened and blood-stained hand on top of mine like she really appreciated it.

"This is probably quite bad," she said in a small voice.

"Bad how?"

"There's only one person I can think of who would still have this."

"Anacletus?" I suggested.

She nodded.

"What are you going to do?"

She seemed to give it some serious thought. "I'm going to take you home and fuck you senseless."

"I'm not objecting, but how will that help?"

"It'll take my mind off it."

"Fair enough. Where to?"

"Can we go to your place?"

"Sure, I'll call us a cab."

She grinned, an impish look spreading across her face. "No need for that, sweeting."

I'd assumed she meant "I will summon us a sex-mobile with my vast wealth," but then she swept me into her arms.

"Now, wait a minute," I protested.

And the next thing I knew we were on the roof of the news 'n' booze, the motion so swift and sudden, I barely felt it. I considered making a fuss, but then realised that struggling would look even more undignified than being carried across London by someone a clear foot shorter than me.

At first I was gritting my teeth—I don't much like being in the passenger seat of a car if I can help it—but slowly I relaxed. It wasn't something I'd have volunteered for, but, truth be told, it was kind of nice. A new perspective. The world went by in ribbons of glittering light. The night air beating against my face made me feel free, and Julian's arms were strong. God, I was getting sentimental in my old age.

CHAPTER FOURTEEN
STORIES & TRUTHS

As soon as I'd let us into the flat, Julian was on me, shoving me hard against the door. The acrid scent of ashes rose up from her tattered clothing, but her mouth was soft and sweet, the familiar taste of wine and roseleaves sweeping over my tongue and making me dizzy. I put my hands flat to the walls on either side to steady myself, the peeling paintwork catching under my fingertips. Julian's teeth grazed my neck. I heard a harsh gasp and realised it was me.

Julian pressed an answering murmur into my skin. "Kate. Kate, the prettiest Kate in Christendom."

Wow. I never thought I'd shag someone who used the word "Christendom."

I caught the gleam of her smile through the gloom of my dingy hallway. If I'd known I was going to get laid here, I would have fixed the lights. Her hands curled into my hips, her body moving against mine as she stretched up to kiss me again, and I stopped thinking. She was relentless, our kisses fierce and tangled, pleasure consuming me like fire. I felt her hand at my belt, undoing the buckle, and then she was slipping under the waistband of my very functional boyshorts. I really wished I'd worn better underwear. Her fingers danced over my skin like she was mapping me. I shuddered. And then she pressed between my legs. My sudden cry broke the kiss, and I scrabbled at the walls, trying to regain a bit of control.

Julian undid the buttons of my shirt and slipped her free hand beneath the fabric, cupping my breast and curling her tongue under the top of my bra. "It's all right," she whispered. "I'll take care of you."

I was trying to think of a witty comeback when she slid a couple of fingers into me, the heel of her hand grazing my clitoris, and then I had no chance. I moaned and wrecked the wall a bit more.

Look. I sometimes have trouble letting go. What if I need that stuff? Everyone holds themselves back. It's what you do if you want to stay sane. But when I was with Julian, sane didn't come into it. She made me want everything.

And I wanted this. This mad swirl of desire. Kisses of blood and roses. Pleasure that could undo me. I closed my eyes and let her have me. And, in moments, I came apart on her fingers with a desperate prayer to a God I didn't believe in. I half collapsed on the bliss of it, hands catching at Julian to stop me sinking onto the floor. She steadied me round the waist as I gasped my way through a pretty awesome orgasm. And just when I was coming down, and breathing and seeing and functioning seemed to be options again, she bit me. And a second one hit me like a train.

"Wow." Julian wiped her mouth on the back of her hand. "You look really hot when you come."

"Guh," I said.

She navigated me through my own flat to the bedroom.

"Oh, look," she observed, as we passed through my living room, "you've cleaned all the things."

"Guh," I said.

She peeled me out of my coat and jacket, and I crumpled onto the bed. Julian left her clothes in a pile on the floor and pounced on top of me.

I made my mouth work. "God. Anyone would think you were some kind of ancient immortal sex monster."

"You know what they say. She who would shag ancient immortal sex monsters must take care lest she become an ancient immortal sex monster."

"Who the fuck says that?"

"Germans."

I caught her behind the neck and dragged her down into a kiss. "I'm still wearing way too many clothes," I said, when I came up for air.

Julian resolved the issue and then crawled back up my body, her skin gliding over mine. I skimmed my hands down her back, making her purr.

"This is weird." I kissed the side of her neck. "We haven't been interrupted by monsters, yet."

"Well, if it'll get you in the mood, there's a very real chance that a two-thousand-year-old vampire who really likes to watch could creep up on us at any moment."

In hindsight, monsters hadn't been a great subject for sexy banter. I was supposed to be taking her mind off Anacletus, not dragging him into bed with us.

"I'm not really into that."

She licked the dried blood off my neck, the tip of her tongue teasing at the wound. It was a strange sensation, a kind of stinging pleasure. Propping herself on her elbows, she looked down at me, my blood glistening on her lips. "What *are* you into, sweeting?"

I slid out from under her and pressed her down onto her front, kissing the nape of her neck, a few strands of her hair curling feather soft against my face.

"Oh, you know, this 'n' that."

I dragged my tongue along the curve of her shoulder blade, heat dancing under the skin where I touched it.

"Well," she murmured, "let me know if you find anything you like."

I ran a fingernail down her spine, and she gave a full-body shiver. "That's quite fun."

She made small, contented noises as I strung kisses across her back. Her skin had that oddly untouched quality that vampires have, unscarred, unblemished, and unaging. She was as pristine as a sheet of paper. Only a dusting of freckles over the tops of her shoulders and a beauty mark at the top of her hip reminded me she was real. Well, that and the way she sighed and wriggled underneath me.

I took my time, savouring her. Like a pudding. My every touch won a gasp as Julian gave herself easily over to pleasure. She was languid and shuddery when I rolled her onto her back again, but her eyes gleamed with a sharp and feral focus.

You had to admire Julian's commitment to getting off.

She was beautiful like this, beautiful and mine.

I fell into her kisses, wine and roseleaves and a little drop of poison. She dug her hands into my hair and pulled me hard against her mouth, her hips arching restlessly under mine. Struggling free, I pushed my knee between her thighs, and she wrapped her legs around me, the heat of her body enveloping me in a second embrace. Madness and desire swept through me like partners in a riotous, never-ending waltz. I smothered a cry in Julian's skin, my hands sliding frantically down the outside of her legs. I grazed my teeth across her nipple and she twisted into my mouth with a moan. My kisses tumbled downwards, wild and chaotic, the taste of Julian sweet against my lips.

I hooked one of her legs over my shoulder and traced my tongue up her thigh, leaving behind an invisible signature of lust. Julian had gone as still as a snake ready to strike, her body taut as a bow string. I licked the tender crease at the top of her leg and she gave a stuttering gasp. Her head fell back against the pillow.

"Oh, you fucking tease."

I looked up with a grin. "Ask me nicely."

"Please, Kate. Pretty please. With fucking sugar on top, you fucking tease."

I stroked my tongue lightly over the folds of her cunt, and she made a throaty sound of pleasure. "You have a dirty mouth for a nun."

She writhed about, chasing my touch. "And I'm starting to think yours is all talk."

I put it to use, slowly exploring her with my lips and tongue, and sliding a finger into her. She felt like raw silk, and she tasted purely of Julian. And when she came, she clutched at my shoulders so hard it drew blood, and cried out my name like it was the only word she could remember. When we untangled, she drew me lazily into a kiss. Wine, roseleaves, and Julian, my Julian.

I nestled myself against her shoulder, my hair spilling over the pillow and across her chest, her fingers moving idly through the strands. She carefully teased out the white streak. "What's this?" she asked, sounding a bit surprised.

"Oh, it's nothing. A zombie faery stag tried to suck my life out."

"That's not nothing, Kate. What were you doing?"

I did my best to shrug while lying in a postcoital pile. "It doesn't matter."

"It matters to me."

"I said it was nothing."

Julian wriggled free and pulled the duvet round herself. "Is this how it's going to be?"

"This?"

"You run off and do madly dangerous things and then won't talk to me."

"What I do with my life is none of your business." I claimed an edge of the duvet for myself. "You don't get to tell me what to do."

"I'm not trying to tell what you do. I just care about you."

"You only met me a week ago."

Julian sighed. "I said 'I care about you,' not 'you are my reason for existing.'" She turned back and took my hand. "You're hot, you're funny, I like fucking you, I like talking to you, and I don't want you to die. And if you die, I want to know what killed you, so I know who to be cross with."

Huh.

"Uh, sorry," I said at last. "I might have issues."

"Don't we all, sweeting?"

I struggled into a sitting position and kissed Julian lightly on the shoulder. She made a happy noise. "It happened at the werewolf funeral," I explained. "I needed to talk to Tara, and I followed her through a gate into the realm of the pale stag. The pale stag kicked my arse."

"You know I'm going to be very cross if you keeping running through the woods with other women."

I gave her a look. "Are you really getting jealous over my near-death experience?"

"I have a very simple rule: no one's allowed to get my girlfriend killed but me."

"Aww, I'm touched."

"Are you okay now?" She nuzzled into me.

"I think so. I'm not keen on the . . ." I pointed at my white hair.

Julian brushed it back from my face. "I don't know what you're complaining about. It's totally sexy and mysterious."

"You say that about everything."

She pushed me back onto the bed. "That's because it's true." She leaned down and licked my nose.

"Ew."

She laughed. "So you're okay with me sucking your blood, but nose-licking is outside your comfort zone?"

"I'm a complicated woman." I rolled her off me. "I'm going to need more of that duvet. And you'd better not watch me while I sleep."

Julian pouted. "I bet you look adorable. Like a snuggly little ferret."

"I hate you." I pulled the covers round me in a manner not remotely adorable, snuggly, or ferret-like.

Julian crawled in beside me and curled up behind me, her skin cooling slowly. "I'll keep you company 'til you drop off."

"So," I asked, settling in sleepily beside her, "do you still have the nun costume?"

"No, sweeting, I lost that years ago."

"I bet you could get one, though. On the internet or something."

She slid an arm over me, her fingers caressing the underside of my breast. "Why, do you feel in need of spiritual succour?"

"I'm always up for a bit of succour."

And on that optimistic note, I fell asleep.

I woke up a few hours later to find the bed empty. I wasn't entirely surprised by that, but when I rolled over, I saw Julian was standing by the window. She was wearing my fluffy white bathrobe and staring at the pieces of the rosary resting in her hand.

I pulled myself into a sitting position. "Are you okay?"

"Go back to sleep, sweeting."

"I can't, you're brooding too loudly."

"I'm not brooding, I'm just thinking." She came and sat next to me on the bed. "I don't know why Anacletus would come for me now."

"It might not be him." I wrapped my arms round her. She leaned back against me, tucking her head under my chin.

"Well, I can't think who else it could be. Who else would send me this?" She held up the crucifix, the moonlight slithering over its tarnished surface.

"And you really have no idea where he is?"

"I tracked him for a while, but he vanished somewhere in Transylvania in the fifteenth century."

"Transylvania?" I smothered a snigger.

Julian sighed. "Are we going to have the Dracula discussion? Fine. A powerful vampire from Wallachia did indeed show up in London in the 1880s and try to take over. I'm certain he was of Anacletus's bloodline. He drew people to him and broke them."

"And you lot let someone write a book about this why?"

"That was one of Sebastian's schemes," said Julian, with a look I couldn't read.

"One of Sebastian's schemes?"

"The Prince of Wands is the oldest and most duplicitous of the four princes."

I kissed the top of her head. "So you just let him do random shit?"

"Sebastian plays a deep game. I learned long ago to pick my battles against him."

I had a sudden thought. "Oh, oh, what about that other one? With Brad Pitt and Tom Cruise?"

"Fictions, my friend." Julian smirked. "The vulgar fictions of a demented American."

That perked her up for a bit, and she seemed happy to be held, so I held her.

"Well, look," I said eventually, "worst-case scenario. Let's say Anacletus does rock up. Can you take him?"

"I honestly don't know. I sometimes think he's already won."

I wasn't sure I liked where this was going. "Huh?"

"Am I not what he made me?" She'd gone all serious and brooding again.

"What, a lesbian? I think you were ahead of the game on that one."

"No, a vampire, a hedonist, a debaucher, a corruptor." She pulled out of my arms and brooded broodily across the room.

"It's not the same." I scrambled up and went after her. "I've never seen you debauching anyone who wasn't well up for being debauched."

"Neither did Anacletus. All his victims wanted what he gave them. Eventually."

"But you didn't."

"Oh, I did." She pulled my dressing gown tightly around herself. "It's just the fear that held me back was stronger than the desire that drew me on."

"But you're still not like that. You don't break people. You just get them off."

She sighed and wedged her hands into the pockets. "It's the same thing, Kate. It comes from the same place."

"So what if it does?" I stepped forwards, kissed her. "I'm not broken."

Julian drew back a little. "You've only known me a week."

I kissed her again. "I'm not broken."

"It's not that simple."

"Yes, it is," I said. "I've had people telling me they were bad for me my whole life. But I have rights too. I can make my own decisions, and I know what I want. That's you, by the way." She met my gaze, her eyes a little wide. "And I'm going to get pretty pissed off," I continued, "if you start getting all 'you do not understand my vampire torment' on me. I've been there before, and it gets really old really quickly."

She gave a little smile. "Well, I'd hate to be boring."

I held out my hand and, after a moment's hesitation, she took it and let me lead her back to bed.

I drew her down next to me and carefully unwrapped her fingers from around the crucifix. "You know, I do sort of know what it's like."

"You mean because you've got a splash of faery blood?" She raised an eyebrow. "It's really not the same thing."

I put the crucifix on the bedside table. It was, after all, still evidence.

"It's more than a splash, it's a whole fucking bucket. My mother's the Queen of the Wild Hunt, so you can stop trying to play 'my darkness is darker than your darkness.'"

She looked contrite. "Sorry. Please tell me more about your darkness."

I thwapped her lightly with a pillow. "I just meant that I know what it's like to have power that comes from something that's fucking ancient and fucking evil and gets a deeper hold on you every time you use it."

"Okay, maybe that is a little bit similar. My experience of faeries is strictly limited to killing them."

"Oooh." I bounced up and down. "Is it time for another adventure from Sister Julian, Pudding Nun?"

"Oh, all right, get back into bed. But you're going to sleep straight after. And no asking silly questions."

I unwrapped her from my dressing gown, and lay down, pulling her with me so I could fold myself around her.

"Once upon a time," began Julian, in a determined voice, "there was a nun called Sister Julian."

"Pudding nun!"

"I said you weren't allowed to interrupt."

"No, you said I wasn't allowed to ask silly questions."

Julian gave an aggrieved sigh. "Once upon a time, there was a nun called Sister Julian, Pudding Nun, who belonged to a sect of holy warriors called the Order of St. Agrippina. One spring morning, the Mother Superior received word from a priory in what is now Clerkenwell that some bad shit was going down in England."

"And," I added helpfully, "she sent a crack team of ninja nuns to investigate."

Julian poked me.

"That was a statement, not a question."

"It was a statement of interrogative intent."

I kissed her shoulder and she forgave me.

"And, lo," she went on, "the Mother Superior did decree that a crack team of ninja nuns should be dispatched forthwith to the island of Britain. Arriving in Clerkenwell, the holy sisters heard tell of knights errant, their armour decorated with hearts and flowers."

"Hearts and flowers. Hard-core." I slid my hand up to her breast and circled a nipple lightly with my thumb until Julian shuddered.

"More than you might think," she said, a little breathlessly. "The heart didn't have quite the same connotations that it does today. These knights roamed the lands performing mighty deeds of arms in the name of love."

"Oh, I hate guys like that."

"By which I mean, of course, killing things, burning stuff, and raping people."

My hand stilled. "That's a bit of a mood killer."

"These knights," she continued, "swore fealty to a being they called the King of the Court of Love and recognised no authority but his. Richard, *Cœur de Lion*, had gone abroad to kill people in the Holy Land, taking most of England's knights with him, so the country was vulnerable to otherworldly invasion."

"This sounds like a job for Sister Julian, Pudding Nun."

"And so it was. The court itself was easy to find, for it was a shining white castle on an emerald hill, but it was well guarded, so the holy sisters were called upon to subdue a number of the King's knights and avail themselves of their armour."

"Do you still have the knight costume?" I asked.

"We said no questions, sweeting. Besides, chainmail is just not sexy."

"It's sexy in my head."

"You have fun with that."

I stoked my hand over Julian's hip and down the slender line of her thigh. "I am."

"I'm trying to weave a story here," she complained, wriggling. "You're distracting me. But don't stop. The knights did not roam the land in bands, so each of the holy sisters was forced to enter the court alone. They had planned to meet inside the walls, but it was a faery place and its rose-hung bowers and golden archways twisted and misled, and they could not find one another. Sister Julian—" she sighed "—Pudding Nun, searched for her sisters for hours or days in the shifting marble cloisters and endless, petal-strewn gardens of the Court of Love. Two she found dead, and two were simply lost and never seen again."

I gave her a squeeze and nuzzled her ear.

"The six that remained came together in the labyrinth and fought their way to the great bower, where the King of the Court of Love sat upon a throne of gold-veined marble decked with lilies. He was a vision of immortal beauty, with sweeping gossamer wings and hair the colour of fire. He was clad in diaphanous robes and, as they approached, he drew two slender blades."

"Where was he keeping them?" I asked, sleepily.

"I said no silly questions."

"That isn't a silly question. He's basically naked."

"They were beside his throne, okay? The sisters had come prepared and riddled his pristine flesh with iron crossbow bolts. Even so, he was strong and swift, and he cut down three of the sisters before the others could react. The battle that followed was short and bloody. He was greatly wounded, but still he slew two more of the sisters before he finally fell. Sister Julian ran him though the heart with an iron sword, and then, taking the blade from one of her lost sisters, she hacked the body into pieces. She gathered the parts in a cloak of iron rings and warded the body with a holy token. Then she fled the crumbling palace that had once been the Court of Love. She disposed of the remains of the faery lord in a well at the priory and returned alone to Rome."

"Wow, you really know how to pick a bedtime story."

"Oh, because the last one was full of kittens and sunshine." She caught up my hand and kissed my fingertips.

"How am I supposed to sleep after a story like that?"

She flipped over, her grin gleaming in the dark. "Maybe you're not."

CHAPTER FIFTEEN

SAUCEPANS & DONUTS

What with one thing and another, I didn't get much sleep, but when I woke up, Julian was still lying next to me. She bounced chirpily out of bed and said something about trying to make coffee. When I heard the first crash, I thought I'd better get up.

Julian was wearing one of my shirts and standing in the middle of my tiny, messy kitchen. All my pans were on the floor.

"Who keeps saucepans in an overhead cupboard?" she asked. "I could have been hurt."

"You're immortal."

"Yes, but that doesn't mean I want pans falling on my head. Where do you keep your coffee?"

"In the freezer."

She yanked it open and started rummaging. "That is actually the last place I would have looked."

I leaned in the doorway while Julian made coffee. There was a pyramid of mugs balanced precariously in my drying rack, and she plucked one from the top. It had been Archer's. It said *Now panic and freak out* on the side. She poured me a generous measure of coffee and handed it over, inhaling deeply with a blissed-out look on her face.

"Oh, not coffee as well," I sighed.

"I hear it tastes terrible, but it smells divine."

We went into what the floor plans optimistically called my reception area.

"So, I've been thinking about the case," I said.

Julian gave me a look. "I'm a bit insulted by that."

"I meant between."

"My, my, aren't we the multitasker?"

"That's why they pay me the big bucks." I paused. "Not in a prostitute way."

She sat on my dining table and put her feet on one of the chairs. "What've you been thinking?"

"I think we've been getting distracted—"

"You can say that again, sweeting."

"No, I think we've been distracted because we've been focusing on *who* is trying to get you, instead of *how* they're trying to get you. You had health inspectors into three of your places a couple of months ago?"

"Yeah." She shrugged. "But it wasn't a big deal. There was an electrical fault they put down to mice, poorly timed flies in the kitchens of one of our restaurants, and something grim happened to the pipes in a hotel."

I really wished I had Archer's whiteboard. I bet there's an app for that. iMurder or something. And I'd thrown away my empty bottles.

"Okay, if we put those three events on the timeline, as well as the attacks, then we get a very different picture. At first it looked like someone was going for you personally, but that makes no sense if you take the plumber into account. If the killer knows where you sleep, there's no point killing randoms at your club. Besides, we know that doesn't count, because it was Maeve."

"Can we assemble all the suspects in the room?" asked Julian excitedly.

"That's just the point. We don't have any suspects—unless you count the two-thousand-year-old vampire who could paste us over the walls—but, the thing is, we don't need any. If we ignore Maeve and include the health violations, then all these attacks have two things in common."

"Is one of those things ick?"

"Yes."

"Wow, I was joking."

"No, you're dead right. And it's not just ick, it's backed-up pipes, vermin infestations, and people being torn apart by rats. I'm afraid we're looking at a sewer monster."

"So what's the good news?" Julian quirked a brow.

"Well, the other thing they've got in common is that they're attacks on your power, not on you. What that says to me is that this is someone who doesn't have very much personal knowledge of you."

"You're forgetting the rosary," said Julian. "That's pretty personal."

"But it's from eight hundred years ago. Whoever it is, even if they knew you used to be a secret ninja pudding nun, they clearly don't know where you live or how you get to work, or they'd just job you in the street. When Maeve went after you, she had enough of a connection to send a tentacle space monster to your home. Where I was trying to shag you."

"Hmm, maybe I will hire you again. You're pretty good at this." Julian grinned at me.

"You did notice it's my job, right?"

"Yes, but there aren't that many supernatural detectives in London. So where does this leave us?"

"With an icky random. It's not a lot, but it gives me a direction. I'm going back to the Velvet to see if I can get more on where this is coming from."

Julian nodded. "While you're doing that, I'm going to have to talk to the Council. I need to keep them informed, or they'll get pissy and start barging in on me all the time when I'm trying to have fun." She looked down at herself. "Can I keep this shirt? Mine's wrecked."

"Are you sure you can bring yourself to wear something without ruffles?"

"I'll cope."

Ten minutes later, after dressing and kissing me good-bye, she was gone. I texted Ashriel to let him know I was coming, and took the Tube to Piccadilly Circus. I had a pretty strong sense where all this ick was leading, but I wanted to make sure I was absolutely correct before I followed it down the sewers.

The crime scene had been cleaned up, which I suppose is what happens if you run out in the middle of an investigation to try and stop your vampire girlfriend from freaking out and tearing down Tottenham.

"We have to stop meeting like this." Ashriel reeked of lies and seduction, sweetness and ruin. As usual.

"What, you mean at murder scenes?"

"Oh, by the way," he said suddenly. "Alice."

"Huh?"

"The plumber. Her name was Alice. Alice Brown."

"Thanks."

I went downstairs and poked about in the broken toilet. The really sad thing was that this was not a personal low. The inside of the S-bend was covered in tiny claw marks and scratches, but other than that—and the usual things you find down toilets—there wasn't much to go on. I'd never been a Girl Guide, and I didn't know much about animal tracks, but it looked like a metric arseload of rats had burst through the bog and eaten someone.

Rats just don't do that.

And even if they did, you'd expect some of them to get killed in the crush. There should have been little furry corpses all over the place.

I had another look at Alice's bones, which Ashriel had put in a box for the coroner. Guess it was going to be a closed casket funeral. I took a few photos.

Finally, I checked the alley where Andrew had been found. And there it was: the sewer grate. I'd been pretty sure I remembered seeing—and smelling—one nearby.

Well, fuck.

Words could not express how little I wanted to hunt a killer sewer monster in its home territory. I'd been there before. It's just messy. And there was no way I was casually popping into a sewer on spec—they're a huge underground labyrinth, prone to flooding, and full of really nasty diseases.

Here lies Kate Kane. Died of leptospirosis after swimming in a river of poo. Beloved daughter. Sorely missed.

So, before I went any further down shit creek, I was going to need some proper safety gear and a clue where I was going. I had gear back at the office. As for the clue . . . it meant paying a visit to one of the somethings that lived under the city. There were a lot of somethings to choose from. There were rumours that Mercy used the sewers to move around, but I was sick of asking for favours from vampires. A few years ago I'd had to deal with this crazy spider goddess who lived under the Northern Line, but I really didn't want to talk to her again. Then I remembered that Jack had mentioned something nasty down there. Of course there's always something nasty in the sewers, but a lead was a lead.

So it was back on the Tube and back to Camden. I armed myself with a box of Krispy Kremes and found Jack and his sister Nancy at their stall. She was slouched sullenly against a wall, playing with her lip piercing, and he was selling a spiky tongue stud to a cybergoth. His eyes lit up when he saw me, but that was probably the donuts.

"Hi Kate." He waved cheerfully. "Are those for me?"

"I can wait."

Nancy huffed out a long-suffering sigh and stomped over to the customer.

"So like," she said in a tone of deep boredom, "you should totally buy it because it's like shiny or whatever and we want to have donuts."

I passed the box to Jack, who tore it open and dived in.

"The other day," I began, "you said there was something nasty in the sewers."

"Mmmrmff." Jack had just stuffed two different donuts into his mouth.

"Finish chewing first."

He swallowed and thought for a moment. "Yes. I did say that." He grabbed for another donut.

"Any idea what? Or where?"

Jack shook his head, which made his fringe fall into his eyes. "Mmmrmff."

"Do you know anyone who would?"

He nodded, and then, when his mouth was empty, said, "Come on, I'll show you."

Leaving the stall with his sister, he took my hand and dragged me off into Camden. Jack didn't say a lot, which suited me fine. He had, however, consumed a lot of sugar. This led to twitching and pogoing, like he badly needed to go to the loo. We ended up on the Tube to Aldgate.

Jack spent the journey twirling on the poles, swinging on the handrails, and stealing people's food until I asked him to sit down. Then he went sulkily into a corner and ate a copy of the *Metro*. He'd cheered up again by the time we got off and was casually telling me how many plague victims had been buried in the area as he led me round the corner to one of London's stranded churches. It was an eighteenth-century stone tower with obelisk, next to a 1970s concrete office block, with the Gherkin glittering in the background like a giant glass dildo.

Jack scurried up to the door, and I followed him inside, a bit dubiously. It was one of those trendy High Church Anglican places: big gold organs, shining stained glass, statues. But pleasantly light and airy with it, like they were saying "God is Great, but he's also really nice when you get to know him." I picked up a leaflet about how Jesus was a swell guy who hung out with "excluded members of society" and took a moment to wonder if that included swarms of rats in human form.

The church was empty except for an unassuming man in his late fifties sitting in one of the pews. As a general rule, I'm suspicious of unassuming men in their late fifties because they're usually terrifying supernatural monsters.

He smiled like my granddad. "Hello." He was wearing a clerical collar and a tweed jacket.

"Hey!" Jack's body dissolved into a writhing pile of rodents that scampered across the church.

The vicar stood up and stepped into the nave. The floor around his feet seethed with rats.

You see. Always terrifying supernatural monsters.

The rats that had been Jack disappeared into the sea of furry bodies.

"I'm going to go out on a limb here and guess you're not a real vicar."

"Actually," he said mildly, "I'm a curate. I go by Edmund Carew. But you're not here to speak to me. You are here to speak to the Multitude."

As he spoke, his voice began to change. It was soft at first, but suddenly I realised I was not hearing one voice, but many, until it became a vast and endless chorus of echoes.

This was officially outside my comfort zone.

"Uh, I suppose so."

"And what will you give us if we answer your questions?" asked the Multitude.

He probably wasn't going to be satisfied with a box of donuts. "What do you want?"

I braced for *your immortal soul* or *your left eye and your tongue*.

"We want you to help someone." His sleeve rippled and a stream of rats cascaded down his hand and onto the floor.

"Anybody in particular?"

"A woman from this parish. She needs employment and a place to stay."

"Uh, I got my last partner killed, and my spare bedroom is tiny."

"Those are our terms."

"Okay." I was just glad the deal didn't include the words *inhabit your x* or *devour your y*. And I guess I could use a receptionist. I've always wanted a Miss Moneypenny.

"We will send her to you this evening. As for what you seek, the creature makes its lair beyond the River Fleet."

"And this is the thing that's attacking the Prince of Cups?"

"That we do not know. It is ancient, but it is not what once it was. It has been a danger in the world below for decades, but only now has found the strength to threaten the surface."

I was going to be really pissed off if I went down a sewer and killed the thing, and it turned out to have nothing whatsoever to do with the case.

"Any chance of a guide?" I asked.

He returned to the pew and sat down, rats swarming up and into his body, disappearing and reappearing in a way I didn't like to think about too much. To give him his due, they seemed to be pretty happy with the arrangement. He brought his hands together and rats gathered on his palms. "We will not risk any part of ourselves, and we will not risk those under our protection. Even without the creature, the Fleet is dangerous. It, too, is ancient and not what once it was. Its waters are fickle and rise swiftly."

"Uh, thanks. And just to check, you didn't eat a plumber yesterday?"

"No."

"Cool. Had to ask. You know how it is."

I got the fuck out of there.

Leaving the rats and the Gherkin behind, I got back on the Tube again, and headed to my office. Once I was there, I dug out my sewer kit. Overalls, waist-high waders with tungsten-studded soles that grip but don't spark, heavy-duty gloves, a hard hat with a miner's light, gas mask, gas meter, and a bandolier for my knives—the sort of thing they'd lock you up for even thinking about wearing in the street. I was slightly depressed I lived the kind of life where you needed a sewer kit, but the only thing more depressing than having a sewer kit is needing a sewer kit and not having one.

I stuffed everything into a bag for later and then fired up my computer to see what the press was saying about Tottenham. I checked the BBC news website, navigating down to local. Rioting on West Green Road. Well, there's a reason it's a classic. It was that or gas main explosion. I opened up my email, and there was a message from the Archivist of the Order of St. Agrippina.

Dear Dr. Smith,

Thank you for your email. Our order has a long history of helping those afflicted by evil spirits, and our records are extensive. Our archives are, of course, based in Rome, and our documents are too fragile to transport or subject to modern digitisation techniques. I have found no references to an Anacletus the Corruptor in our records. However, if you have any further requests please do not hesitate to contact me. I would be more than happy to look into them on your behalf. It is my pleasure and my duty to share the history of our order with all those who seek to learn of it. If you should find yourself in Rome at any point in the future, do not hesitate to make an appointment.

Respectfully yours,
Sister Benedict

Huh.

With hindsight, it had probably been overly optimistic to expect, "Why yes, one of our nuns was transformed into a killer sex vampire in 1194." I chalked this one up to experience. Worst-case scenario: I'd made an order of demon hunters think I was an inept vampire spy. But they were in Rome and probably had better things to do than worry about me.

I spent the rest of the afternoon digging up blueprints of the sewer system while I waited for whoever the Multitude was sending over. Knowing my luck, it would be some kind of adorable scrappy orphan.

At about half past five, there was a rap on the door, and I looked through the frosted glass to see a silhouette that belonged in a Humphrey Bogart movie.

"It's open."

A femme fatale walked into my office. Even the slightly shabby trench coat couldn't hide the fact that this woman was gorgeous. Like a Greek goddess stepped down from a plinth. Waist-length wavy, black hair, eyes only one shade lighter, packing lashes that ought to have been illegal, full lips, high cheekbones, and bronze Mediterranean skin.

"Miss Kane, I presume," she said in a smoky Marlene Dietrich voice.

"Uh . . . yeah." Maybe I'd fallen asleep at my desk again.

"The Multitude sent me. I am Elise."

"And you're here for a job?"

"Yes. I require employment."

"Have you considered, for example, modelling?"

"I find it tiresome to be looked at."

I hastily averted my eyes. "Oh, right. Sorry."

"Are you homosexual, Miss Kane?" she asked.

I blinked. "Wow, you make it sound so clinical."

"I apologise. I was simply requesting clarification."

"Am I making it that obvious?"

"Yes, Miss Kane."

"Is that going to be a problem?"

"No, Miss Kane."

"You can call me Kate, you know," I said.

"Thank you, Miss Kane."

I've known some loopy dames in my time, but this one took the biscuit. And I was supposed to be employing her. God knew what I was going to do with her. Maybe I could use her as an umbrella stand.

"So," I tried, "what was your last job?"

"I reflected the desires of my creator."

O-kaaaaay.

"And, er, how long were you doing that?"

"Approximately six months."

There was a pause that could only be called awkward.

"Why the change of career?" I asked carefully.

"My creator attempted to have me destroyed."

"Destroyed?" I asked, even more carefully.

"Yes, Miss Kane. He put me in the boot of a car and sent it to a wrecking yard."

Bummer. That meant at least one them was a raging psychopath. For her sake, I hoped it was her. For my sake, I hoped it was him.

"Uh . . ." I tried to think of something comforting to say and came up completely blank. "Why did he do that?"

"He did not find me satisfactory."

"I find that hard to believe."

"My creator fashioned me to be his ideal companion. I embodied his desires and his secret passions and, consequently, I saw him as he saw himself. This, he could not abide."

"So he tried to kill you? Wasn't that a bit of an overreaction?"

"I cannot be certain, but my limited observations suggest that people believe they have the right to destroy that which they have created."

I tried to think of something comforting to say. Again. And came up completely blank. Again. "Who was this fucker?"

"His name was Russell."

"First or last?"

"I do not know, Miss Kane."

"That's it?"

"Yes, Miss Kane. He told me little about himself, and I was not permitted to leave his house until he attempted to destroy me."

"Okay, but if you ever see him again, tell me so I can kick his head in."

"As you wish."

I didn't know what else to say, and, in the absence of an immediate head-kicking opportunity, I changed the subject with subtlety and grace. "So, do you have any transferable skills?"

"I appear to be impervious to physical harm. I have no need to eat, sleep, or breathe, and I can bring a man to orgasm within thirty seconds."

There was another pause. Also awkward.

"Can you type?" I asked, finally.

"I suspect that I could learn, Miss Kane."

I gave up. "You're hired."

"There is also the matter of lodging."

She was still standing by my desk, hands folded neatly in front of her. I realised she literally hadn't moved since she'd come in. Her head was at the same angle, her fingers in the same position. Once I'd noticed, it started to creep me out a little bit.

"You can crash in my spare room until you get your own place," I told her. "I warn you, I drink, smoke, and wander around in my underwear. You should feel free to do the same. Uh, I mean, not the underwear thing. Not unless you really want to. Look. Just make yourself at home, okay?"

"What will my responsibilities be?"

"Answer phones, make coffee, do the stuff I don't want to do like reports, record-keeping, filing, and tax returns. Oh, and I need you to drive me to Farringdon in the middle of the night so I can go down a sewer."

"Thank you, Miss Kane."

"Guess we're done here. Grab your stuff, and I'll show the flat."

"I do not have any 'stuff,' Miss Kane."

"Can you stop calling me Miss Kane all the time?" I asked. "It's kind of weird."

"I apologise."

I took my quirky new sidekick home with me. She wasn't kidding about not having any stuff. I even had to pay for her Oyster card. From what I'd heard about her creator, I was mildly surprised she wasn't naked. She insisted on standing all the way home. She didn't even sway with the motion of the Tube. I guess, at the very least, he'd given her a good sense of balance.

I let us into my flat, making a mental note to get the hall light fixed, and gave her the grand tour. Thirty seconds later we were standing awkwardly in the living room.

"So . . . this is the place," I said. "If you need blankets or a pillow or whatever, there's an airing cupboard in the hall."

"Thank you. That will not be necessary. As I said, I have no need to sleep."

"Yes, but you might want to sit down."

"Thank you, but I prefer to stand."

I blinked. "What, always?"

"Yes."

"Well." I gave a sweeping gesture. "Stand wherever you feel most comfortable. Do you want me to make you up a corner or a cupboard or something?"

"No. Thank you."

We awkwarded for another long moment.

"So," I tried, "where were you before?"

"In a cube of metal in a wrecking yard. This is quite spacious by comparison. After the Multitude rescued me, I stood in a corner of a church, portraying the Virgin Mary."

I had no response to that whatsoever. "How about a cup of tea?"

To my surprise, she perked up. "That would be lovely."

"How do you like it?"

"Black and very hot."

She followed me into the kitchen and watched with a rapt expression as I made the tea.

"Will I be permitted to use these devices?"

"*Mi* kettle *es su* kettle."

"Is that a yes?"

"Yes, Miss Elise," I said.

"I feel you are mocking me, Miss Kane."

"*Moi?*"

"I notice," she observed, after studying the layout of the kitchen, "that you have heavy objects stored in an overhead compartment. That seems illogical."

Everyone has an opinion. They're my heavy objects, dammit.

"That's where they live."

"I apologise. I did not consider their feelings."

"I'm sure they'll forgive you." Then I realised she was serious.

I grabbed two mugs from the pyramid. One of them was mine—which you could tell because it was scavenged from a promotional stand and advertised a recruitment company—and the other was Eve's—which you could tell because it was black and had a weird message on it about being the only one here with the antidote. I'd never understood that mug. It was nice to know Eve could still make me feel slightly stupid a year after we'd broken up. I poured out two mugs of Tetley and passed one to Elise.

She wrapped her hands around it with a look of genuine pleasure. "You really like tea, huh?"

"I like the heat."

"I could have just boiled you some water if you wanted."

"Ah. That had not occurred to me." She dipped a finger into the steaming liquid and then took a sip.

"Look," I said. "I don't mean to be rude, but are you some kind of robot or something?"

"I am a statue, Miss Kane, carved from stone and animated with stolen fire."

Eat your heart out, Dr. Frankenstein. "And you don't need to devour human flesh or anything?"

"No, Miss Kane."

"Right." I'd had my fill of weird conversations for one day. "I need to grab a couple of hours' sleep. I'll be up at ten. Here, have some cash in case you want to do anything or go anywhere. Consider it an advance. There's a spare key behind the door and a spare mobile in one of the drawers somewhere."

"Goodnight, Miss Kane."

With that, I went to bed at half past seven in the evening. My sleep patterns were so fucked.

CHAPTER SIXTEEN
SEWERS & GOTHS

I woke to the beeping of my phone and the smell of fresh coffee. Fifty percent win. I zombied out of bed and pulled on some clothes. It was a good thing I remembered I had a guest. I could imagine the conversation now: *You appear to be naked, Miss Kane. Is that your customary habit at this hour?*

I went into the kitchen where Elise was just pressing the plunger on my *cafetière*.

"I successfully operated the devices, Miss Kane."

"Go you." I sat down in front of a pile of bananas. Elise passed me a cup of coffee, and I nursed it lovingly. "What's with the bananas?"

"I took the liberty of examining your refrigerator and found it empty except for a jar of pickled cucumbers, half a packet of bacon, and several bottles of Newcastle Brown Ale. Reasoning that you would require something to sustain you on your nighttime journey in the city sewers, I took it upon myself to procure some suitable nourishment."

"So you bought bananas?"

"Bananas are exceedingly practical, Miss Kane, for they are both portable and high in energy. They are, as they say, good for you."

I finished my coffee and gamely ate a banana. I do not like bananas. They're basically mush held together with stringy bits. And Eve once told me they were technically nuts, which blew my mind. Then she told me that peanuts weren't nuts. And then I dumped her. Though not, admittedly, for a couple of years.

I checked my sewer kit and stuck my knives into the bandolier. Since there was no danger of running into the rozzers where I was going, I took the lot. I tossed Elise the keys, and we went down to the car, where I hopped into the passenger seat.

"Wait a minute," I said, as Elise got in next to me, "do you actually know how to drive?"

"I am not certain, but it cannot be that difficult."

"Okay, switching sides now."

Elise didn't budge, but sat there running slender fingers over the dashboard and the steering column.

"Come on, get out." I might have sounded a little bit anxious.

Here lies Kate Kane. Driven into a wall by a statue without a licence. Beloved daughter. Sorely missed.

"A moment, Miss Kane." She turned the key and my death trap on wheels sprang perkily to life.

I put my head in my hands as she turned on the windscreen wipers and the hazard lights. Then she turned them off, adjusted the mirror, and pulled out.

Huh.

"And you've never done this before?"

"I had never operated the coffee-making device before, either."

"They're not really the same thing."

"Not in detail, perhaps, but in essence."

"Remind me to get you to look at the washing machine."

"I look forward to it. I like washing machines."

Okay, that was two things I knew she liked. Hot water and washing machines. It was like we'd known each other our whole lives.

"You like washing machines?" I asked.

"I like the vibrations."

I took the high road and concentrated on giving Elise directions.

Twenty minutes later, we left the car in an underground lot near Farringdon Station. I bundled my kit and my bandolier under my arm and went off looking for a manhole. Normally when I do this kind of thing, I just try to act like I'm supposed to be there. Generally people don't question you if you're wearing a hard hat. This time, however, I had a supermodel following me around. We looked like a small lesbian Village People tribute act.

I found an easy-lift manhole cover just off Farringdon Road. Despite the name, it was not, in fact, easy to lift. I guess the Council wanted to discourage casual sewer tourism. I was about to channel my mother's power when Elise gracefully bent down and pulled it open.

"If I'm not back by four," I said, "I've probably drowned in poo, and there's fuck-all you can do about it, so keep the car and have a nice life. And if a crazy vampire chick shows up looking for me, tell her it was fun."

"As you wish, Miss Kane."

I climbed down the rusty metal ladder into the darkness. At the bottom, I slung on my bandolier and checked my gear for the last time. From here, there was no turning back. Metaphorically. Not literally. I had every intention of coming right back here, ideally in about an hour's time, having beaten the bad guy and got the girl.

I was in a narrow entrance gallery, dripping brick walls dimly illuminated by my miner's light. I always expect the sewers to smell way worse than they do. It wasn't really bad. Just quite bad. And it would get better when I joined the main tunnel. It's basically all about shit-to-water ratio.

I made my way down the feeder tunnel, which narrowed gradually until I had to crouch. Balancing myself against slimy walls, I followed the gradient over a series of what, for the sake of my sanity, I decided to call small waterfalls. Finally, I splashed into the sewer proper. This was the real deal: a fifteen-foot oval of hard-fired, nineteenth-century brickwork supported by heavily layered arches sometimes nearly six bricks deep. The Victorians might have been a bunch of mass-murdering, misogynistic fuckheads, but they sure knew how to build a shit pipe.

It was at about that this point that I realised "beyond the River Fleet" wasn't very helpful. Downstream would take me to an outfall pipe and the Thames, so I headed upstream instead, wading knee-deep through grey, fast-flowing water. I had to stay right in the middle of the river because, even with my special sewer-diving boots, I couldn't keep a grip on the sloping, slime-covered floor. And even then, I had to pick my way around dodgy-looking clumps of stuff that I knew from experience would belch a load of sewer gas at you if you kicked them.

It was just ducky.

As I went deeper, I began to notice a strange, heavy mist in the air, which told me I was probably going the right way. Or the wrong way, depending on how you looked at it. I passed interceptor sewers, each disgorging yet more sewage into the river.

And then something hit me.

It came from behind and above, nearly sending me face-first into the Fleet. I dropped to one hand and one knee, murky water rising to my chest and spilling down my waders. I'd have been grossed out if I didn't have bigger problems. The bad guy wrapped a slimy, splay-fingered hand round my throat and I felt tiny mouths burrowing at my skin. Another hand clamped round my elbow and started trying to pull me off balance.

I yanked the steel knife out of my bandolier and slashed back and down as hard as I could. I heard a wet, tearing sound, but the creature just tightened its grip.

This was not the time to worry about the personal and metaphysical consequences of invoking otherworldly magic.

I mustered all my mother's strength and stood up, throwing the thing backwards. Power and adrenaline surged through me, the world snapping into focus around me.

In the Deepwild, my mother stood laughing, knee-deep in a river red with blood.

I turned. My attacker was back on its feet. It was person-shaped, clad in tattered rags and rusted chainmail. Its skin was pallid and glistening, and its long blond hair was matted with filth and lank with sewer water. Its mouth was a distended circle of hooked teeth surrounding a sharp, probing tongue. Dozens of similar mouths twitched open and closed on the palms and fingers of its outstretched hands. But its grey eyes were shockingly human. And it didn't look as though it liked me much.

I lunged forwards with my knife a split second before the creature came for me. It reached for my throat again and I severed its hand at the wrist, slamming my free hand into its chest.

It reeled away from me.

I'd say I felt like I was dancing, but I hate dancing, and this was effortless.

It lifted the stump of its arm, gristle and mucus oozing out of the wound and rapidly coagulating into a new hand. Mouths burst open across the surface.

Well, fuck.

We circled each other, looking for weaknesses and openings. Worst-case scenario: I'd stab it with each of my knives in turn until

I found one that hurt it. I looked again at its armour. You don't often meet squidgy, sewer-dwelling, lamprey-mouthed, blood-sucky things wearing chainmail. I could just about make out the remains of a tabard, embroidered with a faint pattern of flowers and a single bleeding heart.

Huh.

I sheathed my steel knife and reached for cold iron.

The creature rushed forwards, grabbing for my knife hand. It latched onto my wrist but I pushed forwards. As I came in, its other hand clamped over my face, rasping tongues scraping at my lips and eyes as teeth hooked into my skin. I forced my way through and drove my dagger into its chest. It recoiled, shrieking and hissing, and tried to flee.

Without even thinking, I caught it by the hair, twisted its head back, spun the knife in my hand and plunged the blade through its pulsating mouth and into whatever was left of its brain.

It slipped twitching into the sewer, and shrivelled away to nothing, leaving me with only a handful of hair, which I dropped and let the Fleet carry away.

Slowly my senses returned to normal, and I almost regretted it. I was breathing heavily, my waders were full of shit, and my face hurt. Great. I put my dagger away and tried to gather my thoughts.

I was pretty sure I'd just found what killed Andrew, and I was pretty sure I knew what I was dealing with. Given where I'd started and how far I'd come, I was probably under Clerkenwell. The smart thing to do was get out of here, talk to Julian, and come back in force.

Uncharacteristically, I did the smart thing.

About a quarter of an hour later, I was pulling myself awkwardly back up the ladder with boots full of water. I rapped on the underside of the manhole, and Elise lifted it up. It felt unbelievably good to see a dreary London night waiting for me on the other side. Sewers really do give you a sense of perspective.

"How was your trip, Miss Kane?"

"There were no fresh towels, and the service was terrible."

"I sense you are mocking me again."

I crawled out onto the road and schlooped out of the waders, emptying their contents back into the sewer. The shit-to-water ratio up here was not good. I reeked, and I needed to see Julian quickly, but I needed a shower more.

We went back to the car, threw a rubber sheet over the seats, and rolled down all the windows. In some ways, this was worse than the sewer. Given the choice between wading through shit and sitting in it, I'd pick wading every time. I tried to ring Julian, but, of course, it went straight to voice mail. I was starting to suspect that she saw telephones purely as a means for her to contact other people. Besides, it's not like she'd be able to a fit a mobile in those trousers.

"You appear to be injured, Miss Kane," said Elise.

"Bloodsucking poo monster. It's no biggie."

We got home. This was the bit I hated most. The aim of the game was to get as much sewage as possible off yourself without getting any of it onto your stuff, and to do it quickly to make sure your house didn't smell of poo for the next ten months. I took off my socks and overalls and bundled them into the waders, wrapping the whole lot in the plastic sheet I'd just been sitting on. Underneath I was still wet and smelly, but nowhere near as wet and smelly as I had been. Then I squelched inside, put everything in the bath and hosed it down. I moved all that to the sink and got into the shower myself, stripping off layer by layer once the water ran clear.

It took a while, but eventually it turned into the best feeling ever. Not being covered in crap was awesome. I towelled myself off with my nicest, fluffiest towel, eying Julian's crucifix, which was still lying on the bedside table. Figuring I should give it back to her, I stuck it in my pocket as I dressed. I said good-bye to Elise, who seemed to be taking this completely in her stride, jumped back in my still-very-smelly car, and sped to the Velvet.

Tuesday night was subVersion, their goth, kink, and kinky goth night. Outside, there was a long, excitable queue of people dressed almost entirely in black. Ashriel was standing in the door, shirtless. Gosh, the dude had definition. No wonder all the ladies went for him. Well, that and the sex-death hellpower. He was wearing thick leather bands on each wrist and a dog collar with a dangling lead. I couldn't help myself. I pulled on it, grinning.

"Are you really yanking the chain of an incubus?"

"Are you really managing a line of horny goths with your shirt off?"

"*Touché*. Julian's inside. Usual place."

They were playing Combichrist's mid-noughties masterpiece "This Shit Will Fuck You Up," and the dance floor was heaving with writhing, angry bodies. The air was once again full of sex and sweat and leather, to which I brought the faintest suggestion of raw sewage. I liked to think it was an improvement.

I eased myself through the crowds, tripping over riding crops and trying not to snag my shirt on anyone's nipple clamps, past the velvet rope, and up the spiral stairs to Julian's lesbian bonk pit. She'd redecorated. The hangings were still red velvet and the *chaise longue* was where we'd left it, but there were handy chains dangling from the ceiling, many of them in use. Julian was lounging about as usual, her booted feet resting on the bowed back of a woman who showed every sign of getting off on the arrangement. Julian was sipping languidly from the wrist of another, who also showed every sign of getting off.

"Having fun?" I flopped down beside her.

"Always, sweeting."

"Is this your thing, then?" I asked.

"You're my thing."

"Because I have to tell you, it's not my thing. I find three-ways stressful, so I don't think I'll ever be ready for a—" I started counting. "—six . . . seven . . . eight-some."

"Don't worry, sweeting." She gave me ravishing smile. "This isn't about me, it's about them."

"Well, that's really community-spirited of you."

"Not at all, their pleasure is my power. I haven't slept with anyone since I met you, and I don't intend to."

"For someone wearing another woman's blood, you say the sweetest things."

She wiped her lips and kissed me.

"Anyway, I've cracked the case," I told her, some time later.

She sat up. "Time to go, kittens."

I waited until the women had unchained each other and departed.

Julian reached up and brushed my face with light fingertips. "Who've you been playing with?" she asked.

"The King of the Court of Love."

"What do you mean?"

"It's not Anacletus," I said. "It's the King of the Court of Love. I got these bites fighting one of his minions, probably the same one that killed Andrew."

Julian raised a sceptical eyebrow. "That makes no sense. I chopped him into pieces centuries ago."

"He's put himself back together. He's under Clerkenwell right now."

"Can they do that?"

"You don't know a lot about faeries, do you?"

"Who does?" She shrugged.

Basically nobody, unless you happen to be killed by one, captured by one, or descended from one.

"Let me put it this way. You know how you sometimes get that feeling like you're the only real person in the world?"

"All the time, sweeting."

"For faeries," I went on, "that's really true. They sort of make their own worlds on the edges of ours. It's like they're the world and the world is them. You chopped the King of the Court of Love into pieces and threw him down a well. And then the people of London poured shit on him for eight hundred years. That kind of thing's got to change your world view a bit."

"I'd almost feel guilty if he wasn't trying to kill me."

"You shouldn't. They don't feel the way people feel."

"Well, he's doing a pretty good impression of it."

"But that's all it is: an impression." Shit, this was hard to explain. I knew some stuff about faeries, but sometimes I didn't know how I knew it. I'd probably inherited it, and that was fucking scary, because it meant some part of me thought that way too. "It's like when my mum took my dad. She didn't love him. She didn't even fancy him."

Julian blinked. "Then why would she take him?"

"It's like," I tried, "he was a character in a story she was telling herself."

"Can we make this more about me, sweeting?"

I leaned in and kissed her. "Bad news, you've run into one of the few creatures in the universe more narcissistic than you are. It's never going to be about you. It's about him, the King of the Court of Love, and everything else is just, like, scenery in his world. He doesn't hate you, he's not angry at you, but having an enemy is part of who he is now."

Julian nodded thoughtfully. "In which case, how do we kill him, and properly this time?"

"I have no idea," I said. "I've never fought a faery lord. The ten killer nuns choppy choppy strategy seemed to go quite well."

"Quite well? You've got a pretty funny definition of quite well. Nine of them died and he's after the tenth."

"Yeah, but it took eight hundred years."

"Pardon me for considering the long game." Suddenly she leapt to her feet, her head turning towards a noise I couldn't hear. "Something's wrong."

She tore down the curtains over the gallery and, at that moment, the King of the Court of Love himself swept into the Velvet. He was about my height, maybe a little taller, slender and angular, with grey-brown wings folded at his shoulders, and ankle length hair flowing behind him. It was the colour of withered things, worms and insects weaving through the strands. He was wearing a twisted circlet of barbed wire and a robe made of some kind of glistening membranous material that I thankfully couldn't identify. But beneath it I could see that his body was criss-crossed with scars, which seeped with yellow pus and maggots. He had another coil of wire curling round his arm like ivy and, on the other wrist, like a lover's token, a string of tarnished steel beads. His face was eerily pristine.

He was followed by four of his knights, all of them still wearing ruined armour and tattered heraldry. They looked human, more or less: one of them had flies swarming from his eyes and mouth, the skin of another blossomed with rot and mildew, the third was a patchwork of squirming rats pressing outwards from his flesh, and the last, who was covered in strange lumps and pustules, had Ashriel impaled on a steel lance. As they came in, he thrust the lance into the wall, leaving Ashriel pinned and helpless.

The music cut out, replaced by screaming.

The King of the Court of Love drew twin swords from beneath his wings and started cutting people down with unhurried grace.

With a snarl, Julian vaulted over the railing. And, like that, she was on him. I lost them in a whirlwind of teeth and steel.

The rest of the club was carnage. Anyone who wasn't falling to the knights was stampeding. I saw the Rat Knight throw someone to the ground, the rats embedded in his flesh tearing free and reducing his victim to nothing but chewed bones. Well, I guess that explained Alice.

For an unhelpful moment, I was frozen. I really wanted to swoop in and help Julian. But people were dying. It wasn't sexy or glamorous, but the most important thing right now was to get the fucking fire doors open. I climbed up the railing and took a flying leap onto the bar. I landed in a crash of broken glass, pulled myself to my feet, and ran the length of the bar until I reached the fire doors, where poor old Andrew had waited pointlessly for his lover on the night he died. I kicked them open and started screaming for people to get the hell out. A tide of drunk, terrified goths poured into the alley, carrying me with them.

I forced my way back inside, through the last of the fleeing crowd, just in time to meet Mr. Lumpy coming the other way. He ripped a gilt railing from the bar and swung it at me hard. I ducked, and it shattered one of the mirrors on the other wall. I went for the iron dagger strapped to my arm, and he brought the bludgeon straight down towards my head, forcing me to roll past him through a scatter of broken glass.

Well, this was fun.

He spun around as I was coming to my feet and swung at me again. I dodged and dived forwards, ramming my dagger into his gut. His waxy white skin burst open, splurging congealed fat and matted black hair all over my hands and the floor. He shoved me backwards, my feet slipped on the crap that had just spilled out of him, and I landed flat on my back. Never a good place to be. Not in a fight, anyway.

He took the railing in both hands and thrust it down towards me. I rolled aside and the metal end gouged a chunk out of the space where my chest had been. I rolled back and grabbed the pole with my free hand. Mr. Lumpy brought all his weight to bear on it, forcing it down onto my throat. His wound was still dribbling lumps of fat and grease onto me, and the distorted, oozing face looming over mine was absolutely not the last thing I wanted to see before I died. I spun my knife, wriggled my arm free, and stabbed the blade into the vulnerable flesh beneath his chin.

His mouth opened, and he vomited his insides all over my face, before falling forwards on top of me. I heaved the body aside, wiped the gunk out my eyes, and sat up.

The Velvet was empty except for Ashriel's body pinned to the wall. *Well, fuck* didn't cover it.

CHAPTER SEVENTEEN
CHESS & BRIMSTONE

I scrambled to my feet and ran across the room to Ashriel. Normally, a little thing like a spear through the chest wouldn't bother a demon, but Ashriel was a celibate incubus and nowhere near full power.

As I approached, he cranked open his eyes. "Fuck."

"This is going to hurt," I said. "How do you want it, slow and careful or quick like a plaster?"

He winced. "Why don't you just leave it? It's not so bad."

"Quick it is then."

"Wait—"

I braced my hand against Ashriel's shoulder and yanked. He fell to the ground, groaning.

"Are you going to be okay?" I tossed the spear aside and knelt down next to him.

He was on his hands and knees, struggling to breathe, oily, black blood pooling onto the floor beneath him and forming a network of shadowy cracks like the beginning of an earthquake.

He was not okay. Demons don't really belong in our world, and it takes a lot of effort for them to keep a physical body. Beat them up badly enough, and the whole thing falls apart, and they get dragged back to Hell.

The ground broke open, fire and darkness pouring upwards through the widening fissures. A clawed hand reached out, seized Ashriel by the throat, talons hooking into his flesh and dragging him downwards. He gave a terrible scream.

I've had quite a lot of experience of this kind of thing, but I've never wanted to stop it happening before.

A couple more hands forced their way out and snatched at his wrists. Ashriel pulled his hand away, shredding his skin against the claw that held him, more blood spattering onto the floor and opening new portals full of scrabbling claws and fingers trying to push through.

I pulled out my sanctified steel knife and swiped at the nearest hand that wasn't Ashriel's. It let him go, but another rushed up to take its place. I stabbed a few more but this was clearly a holding pattern, and not a very good one. I was bad at whack-a-mole even when I wasn't kneeling on the edge of a portal to Hell. I hooked him under the arms and tried to pull him towards me. But even with my mother's power, I wasn't stronger than an army of demons.

This was looking pretty bad.

Hell was literally opening under Soho, and it wouldn't go away again until it got what it wanted. Closing that fucker would take proper angel magic, and I didn't have any.

Oh, wait. Yes, I did.

I pulled Julian's crucifix out of my pocket and flung it into the portal.

There was a high-pitched shriek and a flash like magnesium, and the ground snapped closed, leaving nothing but the faintest scent of sulphur and Ashriel sprawled face down on the ground, still bleeding but not in a drag-me-to-Hell kind of way.

I got the first-aid kit from behind the bar. It didn't really have anything for impaling or hell-sucking, but there were bandages and plenty of gauze. I helped Ashriel into a sitting position and started patching him up as best I could.

"I think you're kind of fucked here."

He gave me a sickly smile. "It could have been a lot worse. Thanks."

I kept bandaging. Thick black blood was seeping through the layers. This stuff was probably worth a bomb on the occult black market. "It doesn't seem to be healing very well."

"Celibacy and being run through don't really go together. It'll take a while." He waggled an eyebrow. "Unless you want to take one for the team?"

"I'm on none of your teams. And I'm most definitely not on the 'get your soul sucked out through your vagina' team."

"I was kidding. The last time I fell off the wagon was a hundred and ninety-seven years, five months, and three days ago."

"Nearly got your two-centuries token, huh?"

"But in this state," he went on anxiously, "I'll take months to heal. And I can't help Julian with a hole through the middle of me."

This could get awkward. "Just so you know," I told him, "if you start taking people, I'll fucking put you down."

"I am what I am, Kate."

"I thought you'd made a choice to be different."

"And I make it every day, but now I need to help my friend."

"What happened? I kind of had a grease monster in my face."

"That faery took her. I don't know where."

"I do. And I'm going to get her back."

He stared at me. It takes a lot to startle an incubus, but I'd managed it. Go me. "That's insane. That thing took Julian out. You're a mortal."

"Mostly mortal. And you want to go after it, and you're a complete mess."

He ran a hand through his hair, pulled himself to his feet, limped over to one of the less trashed booths, and flopped down. "I have to do something."

"No, you don't." I sat down opposite. It was like we were on the worst date ever. "*I* have to do something. You have to stay here, get better, and not shag anybody to death."

"At least tell me you've got a plan."

"I've got a plan."

"Really?"

"No, of course not. But I'll figure something out."

He put his head in his hands. "We're fucked. Worse, Julian's fucked."

"We're not fucked," I said. "We know what it is and where it is. It's just a question of taking it out. But first we need a clean-up crew. Because this is a fucking disaster area."

I pulled out my phone and was halfway through dialling Patrick's number when I realised how weird it was that I could still do that so easily after more than a decade.

He answered on the first ring. "Katharine."

"We've got a situation at the Velvet. Get here now."

"I'll always be there for you, Katharine."

"Just do your job, Patrick." I hung up. "All right," I went on. "Operation Rescue Julian. Go."

We sat there in silence for a couple of minutes.

"Well, I'm in," offered Ashriel.

"Great. So we have a mighty army of you and me. And we have to assault the impregnable otherworld fortress of an indestructible faery lord to rescue an eight-hundred-year-old vampire who's more powerful than either of us."

"You make it sound so simple."

"We're going to need backup, aren't we?"

"Backup? We're going to need front-up. And maybe side-up as well."

"Okay," I said. "Who's the most powerful person you know?"

He thought about it for a moment. "The Metatron. But we haven't spoken for a really long time, and I don't think he approves of my lifestyle choices."

"Okay," I tried again, "who's the second most powerful you know?"

"Lucifer."

"One more time. Who's the most powerful person you know who wasn't actively involved in the War in Heaven? Apart from Julian."

"Anacletus."

"Okay. Really one last time. Who's the most powerful person you know who wasn't actively involved in the War in Heaven, isn't the person we're trying to rescue, and might actually help us."

"Tricky. I know plenty of minor demons, but they don't approve of my lifestyle choices either. Since they took out the Morrigan, the major powers in this city are the vampire princes."

"Aeglica should help us," I said. "This is kind of his bag."

"This is the plan then, is it?" Ashriel spread his hands despairingly. "We assemble an unlikely team of misfits, descend into the sewers, and learn important lessons about friendship while getting murdered by faeries."

"Pretty much. Unless you have a better idea?"

"Unbelievably, I don't. So, who's the most powerful person you know?"

I didn't even have to think about it. "Nimue."

"Do you think she'd help?"

"Julian just tried to murder her, but, I don't know, it's complicated."

"Isn't everything?"

"Katharine." That was Patrick, creeping up on me as usual.

Speaking of complicated. "Hey." I didn't look round.

"Katharine, are you all right?" He leaned over me and took my hand. I pulled it back. "You're hurt." He glared at me. And then his voice trembled. "You're bleeding."

He had a point. There'd been a lot of broken glass, and I'd spent a lot of time rolling in it. I could feel cuts stinging on my arms, but my coat had protected me from the worst of it.

Patrick turned away dramatically. "Stay back. I am not certain I can control my hunger."

"Patrick, stop being a dick. We've got a bunch of bodies to deal with, and a bunch of people who saw something really fucking weird and could be anywhere by now."

He still had his back to me. "You should have sealed the area."

"Then everybody would be dead."

"Some sacrifices are necessary. Nobody knows that more than I."

I sighed. "Well, it's too late now. Handle it."

"What happened here?" he demanded.

"Faery lord. Massacre. He took Julian."

"Details, Katharine."

I gave Patrick a play by play, while he made calls. Finally he put the phone down.

"See, Katharine," he said, "see where your involvement with Julian Saint-Germain has led you."

I sighed. "I'm not the one who got kidnapped. I'm fine."

"Nevertheless, she put you in danger."

"Shut up, Patrick. I've got a rescue to plan."

"What about Kauri?" suggested Ashriel. "He's young, but he's still a vampire."

"Katharine," interrupted Patrick. "You can't. It's too dangerous."

I face-palmed. "Patrick," I said wearily, "I'm busy. I'm putting a team together to go down the sewers and rescue my girlfriend. Now get out of my face."

"I will not permit it, Katharine."

"Not up to you. I'm going."

"Then I'm coming with you."

I slumped onto the table. "You know, fine. If you want to come, you can come. Because, honestly Patrick, I don't care what you do. Just don't fuck this up."

"I will protect you."

"Fine. Whatever. We'll meet at the old Sessions House in Clerkenwell at half eleven tomorrow night."

"Is tomorrow soon enough?" asked Ashriel.

"It'll have to be. We have to go at night so the vampires are at full power, and we have to wait for the waters to go down."

"She could be dead by then."

"She's in a faery realm. They don't have time like we do."

"So, then, we can take as long as we like? We could get the whole Council in, even the Arcana?"

"They don't have time, but they don't like it when you take the piss. Faery realms take everything personally."

He nodded and eased himself painfully out of the booth. "I'll see you tomorrow then."

"As will I, Katharine." I didn't even look at Patrick.

Great, so it was me, my dickhead ex, and a celibate incubus. Not so much the Magnificent Seven as the Barely Adequate Three.

I pulled out my phone and called Kauri.

"Hello?" He answered just when I was about to hang up.

"Hi, how would you like to come rescue Julian and/or avenge your dead boyfriend?"

There was a long silence.

"Sorry, who is this?"

"It's Kate," I said. "Kate Kane."

"Okay, that's a lot less spooky. But didn't they already catch the killer?"

Fuck, this poor guy was way out the loop. I took a deep breath.

"Long story short: So Andrew was killed by a bloodsucking faery creature, which I thought had been summoned by some kind of sorcerer, and then when I told the mages about it, one of them—who was also Julian's ex-girlfriend—tried to kill Julian in self-defence by summoning a different bloodsucking monster. But then yet another monster killed somebody else after that mage had already been dealt with, so then it turned out that when Julian was alive, she chopped up a faery lord and threw him down a well, and he's the one who's been sending the things that have been killing the people." Okay, that wasn't particularly short.

There was another long silence.

"Was I meant to understand any of that?"

"Big bad faery shit lord killed your boyfriend and captured your vampire granny. A bunch of us are getting together to fuck it up. Do you want in?"

"Flats or heels?"

"Waders," I said. "He's down a sewer."

"You're joking."

"Afraid not. We're meeting at the Sessions House in Clerkenwell at eleven thirty tomorrow night . . . er. . . . I mean tonight, technically."

"I'll be there."

So that made it me, my dickhead ex, a celibate incubus, and the most fabulous man in fangs.

I called a cab and headed for Holland Park. Aeglica's place looked way spookier at half three in the morning. I hauled myself over the wall and landed slightly painfully in the rose garden. Shoving my way through the overgrown briars, I found Aeglica and Mercy sitting at a stone table, playing chess in the uncertain moonlight. Mercy had put back her veil, and tendrils of weed-green hair were spilling over her shoulders. Her chin rested on one black-taloned hand as she contemplated the board with what I thought was a faint smile. She moved a piece.

"Check. And you seem to have a guest."

"What is it this time, Miss Kane?" Aeglica asked.

Mercy turned towards me. She looked like the Phantom of the Opera without his good side. But there was something familiar about her eyes.

"Julian's been kidnapped."

"What happened?" He slowly rose to his feet.

I gave him the short version.

He nodded, turned, and walked away.

"Um," I said, "we were heading out tonight."

He paused. "I must go."

"Just so you know," I told him, "if you go now, you'll be swimming through a river of shit."

"That does not matter."

I'd kind of been hoping to get the bulletproof Geat to come with us, but it looked like there was no Aeglica in team.

"It will soon be dawn." I really hadn't expected Mercy to bail me out.

Aeglica turned his head back towards us. "The Council has been attacked. I must retaliate."

Mercy glided across the grass and took his arm with surprising gentleness for a scary monster. Aeglica looked down at her. "It is unwise to strike," she murmured, "when you are weak and your enemy is not. Besides, we have yet to finish our game." She slipped her clawed hand into his and led him back to the table.

"We're meeting at eleven thirty in Clerkenwell." And with that, I left them to it.

Me, my dickhead ex, a celibate incubus, the most fabulous man in fangs, and an indestructible Geat. Things were looking better than they had an hour ago, but I was now officially out of ideas. It felt pretty callous to just go home and go to bed, but I would have felt even worse if I got my girlfriend killed because I'd pulled an all-nighter.

CHAPTER EIGHTEEN

POLO & MARBLE

I got home at five, feeling shitty. I ate a banana, which didn't help. Elise was sitting in the middle of the floor with the bits of my washing machine spread around her. I couldn't tell if the whole scene looked like something out of the Tate Modern or something off a really specific fetish site.

"This device has not been well cared for," she said. "It is sad."

"I'm not sure washing machines get sad."

"I know. That is the problem."

I had too much shit going on to worry about the emotional well-being of my washing machine. I went to bed.

I woke up about three hours later to the smell of fresh coffee and the realisation that my girlfriend had been captured by an amoral, immortal monster. It had not been a good day so far, and it had the potential to get a lot worse. I lay there moping for a while and, finally, Elise came in with a cup of coffee.

"Are you quite well, Miss Kane?"

"I'm sad, Elise, like a washing machine."

"The washing machine is feeling better now. What are you sad about?"

I told her what had happened. To my surprise, she bent over and hugged me. I was prepared to be totally freaked out, but it was kind of nice. Like a teddy bear, only more attractive.

"Uh, thanks."

"Do you wish me to come with you to rescue Miss Julian?"

"Wouldn't you . . . maybe . . . sink?"

"Most probably. But since I have no need to breathe, it would prove only a minor inconvenience."

"It's really not nice down there. I promised the Multitude I'd look after you, and who's going to care for the devices if I get killed? I'd appreciate a ride though."

"As you wish, Miss Kane. I enjoy the car."

I had a shower, which woke me up largely because it really hurt. I was, once again, covered in sexy wounds. There were tiny stinging glass cuts running up my arms, and sucker marks all over my face. And that on top of the white streak in my hair and the stitches in my thigh. I was wrecked.

Operation Rescue Julian wasn't looking that great either. Somehow the eight-hundred-year-old sex vampire didn't have many friends. That just left rivals and enemies. More specifically, it meant Tara and Nim. I was pretty sure Tara didn't actually hate Julian, and I had no idea how she felt about me, or at least about the parts of me above the waist, but technically cleaning up psycho faeries was her goddamn job. As for Nim, I'd had a pretty eventful love life, but I'd never had my girlfriend literally try to kill my ex over a misunderstanding about a murder. So that could really go either way. I'd known Nim for a long time, and I really hoped I hadn't fucked everything up too badly.

Of the two, Tara seemed like the safer bet, so, as soon as I'd towelled off, I checked her Twitter feed. *Tallyho darlings. Opening match of the Autumn Nations. Cheer us on #awooo.*

I had no idea what any of that meant, so I asked Google. It turned out the Autumn Nations was a polo tournament held somewhere in Surrey. That did not bode well. Yes, my plans for the evening included infiltrating the kingdom of a deranged faery lord, but I didn't have a clue how to get into a polo match. Either way, I wasn't going to make any progress sitting on my arse.

I took my press pass and a banana, cranked up my car, and drove to Surrey. On the way, I flipped through my CDs, looking for something to take my mind off the fact that I was going to a polo match while my girlfriend was chained up in a sewer. If she wasn't already dead. But all I had was *Songs of Love and Hate*, *The Bends*, *Scott 4*, and *Bone Machine*. Wow, I'd be awesome on a road trip. In the end, I stuck on "Famous Blue Raincoat" and consoled myself with the thought that, no matter how bad things got, at least I wasn't Leonard Cohen.

After a while, streets gave way to woodland and I came to one of those car parks that's basically a field. A field they were trying to charge me twenty quid to park in. So I found my own field and stuck my car in it for free. As far as I could make out, a polo club was basically one big posh building and a lot of grass. The clubhouse had a serious *not for the likes of you* vibe, so I hopped a fence. There was a match going on. At least, I assumed it was a match. There were a lot of horses running around and people waving sticks. There was a fairly thin crowd, mainly bright young things with nothing better to do, drinking champagne and having picnics.

I snuck onto the fringes. The most effective way to look like you belong somewhere is to just do what everybody else is doing, which in this case meant watching polo. I had no idea what was going on. They call it the sport of kings. Probably because at your average comprehensive school you don't get "horse" as part of your PE kit.

It was fairly easy to pick Tara out. She was charging up and down the field with her golden hair streaming behind her. I hated to admit it, but some people are born to wear tight white trousers and knee-high boots. *Ngh.*

The game went on for about two hours. People hit balls to places. Occasionally they would go other places, and people would cheer. This is my experience of all sport ever. Afterwards, Tara's team looked happy, so I guessed they won. Awooo. I followed them round the perimeter, hopping a few more fences, to the horsey bit where they kept the horses. There were a couple of guys hanging around here, some kind of specially designated Horse Guardians or something, who didn't look like they'd be happy to let me go waltzing in.

I ran through my options. Let me through, I'm a faery princess? Stand aside, there's a slim chance that woman over there wants to fuck me? Surprise horse inspection? I went with my old fallback.

I waved my press pass. "*Horse & Hound.*"

They looked at me like I was mad.

At that moment, Tara walked by with a bucket of water. I waved hopefully.

"How do you keep tracking me down, Kate Kane?" she purred.

"Because you keep tweeting where you are."

She looked thoughtful. "Oh, yah. Silly of me."

"I need to talk to you."

"Well, come through, I need to take care of Trumper."

She was either talking about her horse or a member of her immediate family.

They let me through into the horsey bit where they kept the horses. There were horses here, many of them smelly. But I'd spent last night in a sewer, so I wasn't complaining.

"Have you met Tuffie and Smudge?" She gestured to a couple of girls I vaguely recognised from the funeral. I nodded a *hi* in their direction. "And you know Hal, yah?"

Henry was rubbing down his mount.

"Uh, well played, by the way." I gave a thumbs up and then immediately regretted it. "I thought the um . . . well played."

He looked round with a grin. "You don't know anything about polo, do you?"

I shrugged. "Horses and balls?"

"That's pretty much it, actually."

"The things you people do for fun."

Tara passed her horse to a groom, put one foot up on a hay bale, and rested a hand on her knee. "So what can I do for you, Kate Kane?"

"There's a faery loose under Clerkenwell. One of his minions killed your cousin."

"How do you know?"

"Because I met it and killed it back. And I have a souvenir." I pointed at my face. "Same marks."

"What makes you think it had a master?"

I took a deep breath, hoping Tara wasn't going to be a dick about this. "Because I was there when he took Julian."

Tara was a dick about it. "So this is about her."

"No, it's about your sacred duty to defend this world."

Her eyes bled to amber. "Do not speak of things you know nothing about. It is not my duty to rescue your girlfriend when she can't look after herself."

I wanted to tell her to stop being so fucking petty, but talking to her like that in front of her pack would have been kind of douchey. And I would have lost any chance of getting her onside.

"Look," I tried instead, "I'm asking for your help."

She tucked the streak of white hair behind my ear. "I can't help you, Kate Kane."

Well, fuck.

"I will not risk my people to rescue a vampire," she continued. "That's a matter for the Council. If this creature strays onto the surface, we will hunt it, but I will not take my pack into its realm."

"There's a bunch of us going down there tonight. We just need support."

To my surprise, Henry came out from behind his horse and spoke to Tara. "I'll go. With your leave. It would be a gesture of goodwill towards the Council. And a chance to avenge our cousin."

"If that's what you want." Her voice softened. "But remember, you're not expendable."

He smiled. "I'll be careful."

"When are you ever careful?"

"Then I'll hope to be lucky."

I felt a bit shitty busting up the family bonding. "We're meeting at eleven thirty at the Sessions House."

Henry nodded. "See you there."

Me, my dickhead ex, a celibate incubus, the most fabulous man in fangs, an indestructible Geat, and a shape-shifting toff. The King of the Court of Love wouldn't know what hit him.

That just left Nimue. Assuming she'd see me at all.

I got back to London in early evening because I stopped on my way home for a burger. Kate cannot live by banana alone. I took the Tube to Waterloo and did the ritual again. It led me in circles for a while before bringing me back to the Millennium Bridge just as the sun was setting. I climbed the steps and started walking until I came to Nimue. She was standing in the middle of the bridge, with the crowds parting round her like waves round an island. She was wearing a shimmering silver dress that faded into coils of mist as it touched the ground. Her hair was gathered beneath a net of shining thread and tiny pearls.

"You've got some nerve."

I'm crap at apologising, even when I mean it. Especially when I mean it. "I fucked up."

"Yes, you did."

"Is everybody okay?"

Her eyes met mine, as cold and dark as the river. "Do you mean how many of my people were killed by your vampire lover?"

"Um, yeah."

"Too many."

I tried again. "I fucked up."

"You've already said that."

I ran my hands anxiously through my hair. This wasn't going well. "I don't know what else to say."

"Neither do I."

There was a long silence.

"It was a faery lord."

Nimue folded her arms. "What's that to me? What do you want, Kate?"

"It's taken Julian."

The sky went suddenly dark and a wind came rushing up the Thames, beating the grey water into waves. Thunder rolled in the distance. "Tell me you're not here for her."

"I'm here for *me*. I want her back. And I'm going to get her back, whatever it takes."

The wind stirred the mist at her feet into fantastical patterns that shifted and swirled like the water below. "What it takes might be more than you can pay."

"Then that's how it'll have to be."

"Is she really worth it, Kate?"

I thought about it a moment. "Is anybody?"

"Yes," said Nimue.

I needed Nim's help, but there was no way she'd trust me while I was still an outsider. I took a deep breath. The spray from the river was cold against my face. "So how does this work?"

She reached out a hand, palm down. "Kneel."

"For serious?"

"Are you?"

"Can't we skip that bit?" I asked.

"Kneel." She didn't raise her voice, but when she spoke it cut through the wind and the noise of the crowd.

I dropped to one knee in the middle of the Millennium Bridge, as the first few drops of rain landed on the backs of my hands.

"Say the words."

I opened my mouth to say that I didn't know what the words were, but, at that moment, they came to me. Like magic. Which, of course, it was.

"I, Katharine Kane, do swear that I will well and truly serve my Sovereign Lady Nimue . . ."

In the Deepwild, my mother screamed, the trees splintering with her fury. Her presence filled my mind like knives, and then her voice tore out of my throat. "This one is mine, you cannot hold her."

"You have no power here, huntress." Nimue turned her hand sharply, and I felt my mother's presence recoil. I could speak again. In the Deepwild, my mother raged.

"And from this day forth," I went on, "I shall commit to her my faith, my blood, and my life."

As soon as I finished speaking, I felt sick. I couldn't breathe. The rain was suddenly warm against my skin. I closed my eyes against the panic, and then I was okay.

Or sort of okay. Something had changed, but I couldn't work out what it was. It was like remembering things you'd forgotten you'd forgotten. And even though I couldn't see her, I knew Nimue was there, watching me, the raindrops sparkling on her hair and the tips of her lashes.

"Rise."

And I did it without thinking.

"What the fuck was that?"

"A bond," she explained. "I share a part of your strength, and you share a part of mine. And you will not betray me again."

"I didn't mean to betray you the first time."

"I know."

"So what now?" I asked.

"Come."

I followed her across the bridge to Bankside and down a set of water-worn stone stairs that were usually sealed off. There was a thin strip of mud and shingle left by the tide. The choppy water was brown, with a sheen of orange light from the city sloshing over the surface. Rain was gathering on the brim of my hat and seeping through the felt, but Nimue wore the rain like a shawl, droplets dusting her arms and shoulders like diamonds.

"Wait here," she said, and stepped into the Thames.

As she walked, the water rose up to embrace her, silver spilling over the river as she vanished into the waves.

Normally, I'd have been pretty freaked out. As a general rule, you don't wander into the Thames. But somehow I knew that if Nim was in trouble I would feel it. I wasn't sure how comfortable I was with that. Well. It was too late now. I hoped I hadn't made a horrible mistake. I'm not a big fan of commitment at the best of the times, and here I was mystically bound to the service of the Witch Queen of London. But right now I needed her power. And I just had to hope that she didn't go to war with anyone I liked until I'd worked off my debt.

After a while, Nimue walked out of the river, the water cascading away from her, leaving her a good deal drier than I was. Across her folded arms lay an actual motherfucking sword. It had a scabbard and everything.

"If you're going to kill a faery lord, you'll need a weapon."

"Isn't that going to be a bit conspicuous?"

"Not in the battles you'll be fighting."

I didn't know whether that was reassuring or not. I was leaning towards not.

Nim drew the sword partway out of the scabbard. Although the hilt and the pommel were plain, the blade itself gleamed with shifting patterns.

"Whoa." I stared at it blankly. Honestly, I had no idea what a well-made sword would even look like. "Shiny."

"The blade is layered with the seven celestial metals and bound with powerful enchantments. There is nothing it cannot kill."

"I don't want to throw a spanner in the works," I said, "but I'm not sure I can use a sword."

She smiled. "The pointy end goes into the other man."

"I kind of assumed there was more to it."

"The blade will teach you. It wants to be used."

Great. Now I was going to have a sword telling me what to do as well.

"And this was lying at the bottom of the Thames, why?"

"You'd be amazed at the things people throw into water."

"Why haven't you given this to anyone else?"

"Michelle's essence would rebel against it, and none of my other followers would be suitable. Besides," she added gently, "I was saving it for you."

"You could have saved it a long time."

"Yet here we are. Although I hoped you would come to me for me."

My heart gave a painful little squeeze. "I didn't know you were waiting."

"I know you didn't." She looked down at the sword. "There's something else you should know. The blade was not made to slay mortals. It will shatter if it ever draws human blood."

"I'm not made to slay mortals either. To be honest, I'm not massively into the whole slaying gig. I'm a PI."

"I suspect you have many talents you have not fully explored."

"There are plenty of things I can do that I choose not to."

She looked away. "Perhaps you'll come to choose differently in time."

I took the sword and rolled it up in my coat. Which did not look in any way suspicious. "Well, thanks. And sorry for . . . everything."

"One last thing."

She'd already made me swear fealty and given me a sword. I didn't know what else was left. Nimue gestured, as if she was drawing something from the air, and a swirl of mist rose up from the Thames to envelop us. It felt like I'd stepped into cold water, and when I could see again, we were standing underneath Marble Arch, traffic roaring all around us, head lamps streaming white and gold in the deepening darkness.

"Well, that sure beats the Tube. Any particular reason we're here?"

"Maeve."

"Huh?"

"I'm commuting her sentence," said Nimue.

She put a hand on the white stone wall and whispered something I couldn't hear. The wall stretched like rubber, and a second set of fingertips pressed painfully through the marble, followed by palms, hands, wrists. And then, gradually, a stone impression of a face and body.

I looked round to see if anybody else had noticed this, but even the tourists didn't seem to be interested.

"Do you normally keep people in Marble Arch?" I asked.

"Among other places."

"How many people are in here?"

Nim shrugged. "More than ten, less than a hundred."

"There's a big difference between eleven and ninety nine," I pointed out.

"Not all my predecessors kept records."

"So it's like a prison for naughty wizards?"

"Basically."

About ten minutes later, Maeve was kneeling on the floor in front of us, drawing in great gulps of air. I felt really fucking sorry for her. I know she'd tried to kill me twice, but being trapped in stone looked like a world of not fun.

"Julian Saint-Germain has been kidnapped," Nim explained. "Help with the rescue attempt, and I will free you from the Arch. Refuse and you return to serve out your sentence. I'm sorry."

"I'm in." Maeve climbed to her feet.

"She's been taken by a faery lord," I added. "He's living in the sewers under Clerkenwell. It's probably going to be really fucking dangerous."

Maeve crossed her arms over her body and shivered. "I'm in. Really, I'm in. Whatever. I don't care. I'm not going back in there."

"Then I'll see you at half eleven tonight."

That made it me, my dickhead ex, a celibate incubus, the most fabulous man in fangs, an indestructible Geat, a shape-shifting toff, and someone who'd already tried to kill both me and the person we were trying to rescue. We'd got to seven after all. Still a bit light on magnificence, though.

CHAPTER NINETEEN

CHAINS & ROSES

I just had time to get home and discover my sewer kit was still fucked before we had to leave for Clerkenwell. It looked like I was going down there in my civvies, but considering I was probably going to get killed by a faery lord, I was slightly less worried about getting poo on my socks.

I tore through my kitchen, looking for something big enough to stash a sword in. If I had ever been to a gym ever I could have put it one of those long zippy bag things.

"It is time to leave, Miss Kane," said Elise.

"I need somewhere to stick a sword."

"Received wisdom suggests that the pointy end should go in the other man."

"Before that."

Elise's eyes flicked back and forth around my kitchen. "You have disordered the room. It is unhelpful."

"I'm having a crisis. I have to rescue my girlfriend from a killer shit faery, and I've got no way to carry my magic sword."

"May I suggest you use two of the refuse sacks? I believe if you were to secure them with the roll of parcel tape you keep in the second drawer near the sink, you could achieve the desired effect." I shoved the sword in a couple of bin liners and taped it round the middle. To be fair, a passing policeman probably wouldn't think it was a sword. They might just think it was, say, a shotgun. But it was better than nothing. We headed down to the car, running only a little late, and Elise drove me to the same all night multistorey we used the last time I had to jump into a sewer at short notice.

I scrambled out the car, and then stuck my head through the open window. "You've already heard my 'if I die' speech. So, yeah, not back by four, dead, blah blah, tell my parents, have my stuff, take care of the devices. I'll ring as soon as I get out because we'll need a pickup. We could be anywhere, and some of us could be injured. You did find that mobile, right?"

"I did, Miss Kane. Furthermore, I understand in such circumstances it is customary to pause dramatically and then say 'be careful.'"

"Don't do that."

"As you wish, Miss Kane."

I headed for the exit.

The car park was pretty near empty, just the occasionally dubiously parked van and oddly shaped shadows from the concrete pillars supporting the roof. Sometimes I think they design these places specifically to make you think you're about to get murdered.

I grabbed the hilt of my sword through the bin liner. Of course, if what Nim had said was true, it'd be useless against ordinary muggers. But maybe it would give me a psychological advantage. Because they'd think I was fucking insane. I walked quickly for the exit, trying to keep in range of the flickering strip lights.

Then I started to get that thing where you feel like there's footsteps echoing your footsteps.

I glanced over my shoulder, but there was nothing there.

And when I turned back Patrick was in front of me.

"Oh, you dick," I said. "You scared the crap out of me."

"It's not me you should fear."

"I'm not scared of you, I'm scared of creepy shit in abandoned car parks." I pushed past him. "Come on, we're going to be late."

Then the fucker bit me, and I blacked out.

Vampires are basically parasites, and when they bite you stuff happens so that you'll let them carry on biting you. Julian's orgasmabite was top of my list for fun ways to be incapacitated, but I've met vampires that make you hallucinate or forget, or just plain paralyse you. A bite from Patrick knocks you out like a horse tranquiliser. And then you wake up with a pounding headache while he's weeping in a corner about how hard he fights to control his terrible desires.

I woke up with a pounding headache, chained to the ceiling in Julian's BDSM bonk pit, while Patrick was sitting on the edge of the *chaise longue*, brooding at me.

"What the fuck?" I struggled in my bonds. "Seriously, what the fuck, Patrick? I honestly thought I'd seen all of the patronising bullshit you had to offer, but clearly I was wrong. Let me down right now, you impotent angst puppy."

Patrick looked at me sorrowfully. "It's for your own good, Katharine."

I rattled the chains again. Damn Julian for her sturdily constructed bondage playground.

"When I get out of here," I said, "I might actually kill you."

"That would be a small price to pay for your safety."

I made an undignified noise. It kind of went "Gyaaaargh!" When I'd finished with that, I tried to reason with him, even though long experience told me it would probably be useless. "Look, I don't have time for this."

"It is already too late. The others have followed the Prince of Swords and gone without you. Soon it will be over, one way or the other."

"Oh, you fuckguzzling shitweasel."

"I understand that you are angry, Katharine."

"I'm not angry!" I yelled. "I'm incan-fucking-descent. And you'd better not have lost my hat."

"No, I brought your hat. And this." He reached behind the *chaise longue* and set my sword over his lap. "What were you proposing to do with this, Katharine?"

"Pointy end in the other guy."

"This is magecraft. I warned you about the witch. She is not to be trusted."

"You fucking bit me. From behind. And chained me to the ceiling. You are the last person to be lecturing anybody about trust."

"But I love you," he said with infuriating, terrifying sincerity.

"You've got a fucking funny way of showing it. Now let me down. Or I'm getting down myself, and then I'm finding something long and spiky and ramming it up your arse."

"Be patient, Katharine."

Right. That was it. I called up my mother's strength . . .

And nothing came.

Well, fuck.

I reviewed the situation. My hands were cuffed to a rigid metal bar, which hung from a chain, which hung from a ring, which hung from another chain, which hung from an eyelet. They were designed to be set up and taken down quickly, but not by people whose hands were held three feet apart.

Well, fuck. Fuck.

Patrick had completely screwed me, and that was never a pleasant experience.

"Look," I tried. "What's the plan here? Seriously. What's the plan?"

He smouldered at me. "You will remain until morning. When I am certain you will be safe, I will release you."

"What about Julian?"

"You are my priority, not her."

"She's *my* priority, dammit."

"I'm just trying to protect you. From yourself, if necessary."

"Patrick, you are a wank-covered dick sandwich of a man."

I closed my eyes and searched for the hero inside myself. Okay, not so much hero as psychotic, bloodthirsty faery queen, but we work with what we're given.

In the Deepwild, my mother licked blood from her fingers and smiled mockingly.

Hi, Mum. Guess you're still pissed off.

The power was there, but trying to take it was like reaching through glass.

And then my mother turned and disappeared into the mists of Faerie, taking her power with her. And I was stuck chained to the ceiling at the mercy of my dickhead ex-boyfriend.

Well, fuck. "Fuck."

"Miss Kane." I twisted my head around and peered over the balcony. Elise was standing in the doorway of the Velvet, wrapped in the same big grey trench coat she'd been wearing when she came to my office. "Are you in need of assistance?"

"Who is that?" demanded Patrick.

"I'm up here, Elise," I shouted.

Patrick glowered at me. "If you care for this woman, send her away. I have no wish to harm anybody, but I will protect you whatever the cost."

"Shut up, Patrick."

Elise's steps rattled on the rickety stairway, and then she arrived in the gallery. Patrick vamp-bamfed in front of her, hissing.

"Excuse me, please," said Elise. "I need to unchain my employer."

"That will not be possible."

She regarded him steadily. "On the contrary, I believe it will be a simple operation."

Patrick's hand shot out and closed around her throat. He seemed to be trying to throw her off the balcony. He was not succeeding. I couldn't see the look on his face, but I had a good time imagining it. "What sorcery is this?" he snarled.

She placed a hand on Patrick's chest and shoved him away. He skidded across the floor like a hockey puck, and crashed heavily into the far wall.

"It is recorded throughout Europe as far back as first-century Athens," explained Elise.

Patrick sprang at her and struck her across the face. It made a sound like somebody dropping the Sunday roast on the kitchen floor, and he recoiled, clutching his hand. I could hear his bones snapping back into place.

"But many scholars believe it to originate from the time of King Solomon." Elise reached up and unhooked the bar from its chain. "Of course," she continued, "sorcerous techniques are often discovered in parallel in many parts of the world." She snapped my hands free. I felt a tiny bit guilty for ruining a perfectly good piece of bondage kit.

Patrick charged at us, all claws, fangs, and looks of personal betrayal. I brought up the bar and let him impale himself with his own momentum. It wouldn't kill him, just wreck his evening. I could have cut his head off as well, but that would have felt uncomfortably like murder. I know I'd threatened to kill him, but it turned out I'd been bluffing.

"So, in a way," concluded Elise, "attempting to categorise magic of any sort is a futile endeavour."

We stared down at Patrick. I'd got him square through the heart. I'm not exactly a demon-hunting ninja nun, but I've been dealing with vampires for more than a decade, and I know how to hit them where it hurts. He wouldn't be coming after me anytime soon. He was ash-pale and barely moving. Honestly, it was an improvement.

"Elise," I said, "this is Patrick Knight, my dickhead ex-boyfriend. Patrick, this is Elise."

"A pleasure to meet you, Mr. Knight."

"Trust me, it isn't. And, uh, thanks for the rescue."

"Not at all, Miss Kane. I enjoy being useful. When I saw him incapacitate you, I thought it prudent to follow in the car. I have left it outside."

I grabbed my hat and my sword. "I need to get back to Clerkenwell. Fast."

"I believe this is quite exciting, Miss Kane." Elise followed me outside.

It was getting close to half one when we got there, which was perilously close to drowning o'clock. We parked on double yellows, and I ran down Clerkenwell Road looking for a manhole, with Elise trailing behind me.

Even though it was after midnight, London's a busy place, and there I was sprinting along a fairly crowded street with a sword in a bin liner trying to find a hole to jump down.

It was probably the least subtle thing I'd ever done.

Oh no, wait. Asking my animated statue assistant/sidekick to rip open a sewer grating with her superhuman strength. *That* was the least subtle thing I'd ever done.

"It's all right," I told the startled passersby, "We're broadband engineers." I peered into the darkness, trying to make sure I wasn't going to jump into a pit of spikes or onto a hungry sewer crocodile.

"What network are you with?" asked someone in the slowly gathering crowd.

They seemed to like the idea of a company that sent emergency technicians down sewers at half one in the morning.

"I'm with Virgin," offered someone else. "The service is terrible."

I didn't really have time to invent a fictional telecommunications company. "My colleague will tell you all about it." I jumped.

There was that cold water feeling again and I landed on cracked, lichen-covered flagstones. I looked up and the light of the city was nothing but a distant glow. I was standing beneath an archway of congealed fat, threaded with brittle vines, and rotting grey-green roses. The whole place was lit by an eerie light that seemed to come from nowhere. Which was convenient since, with all the kidnapping, I'd forgotten my torch. Ahead of me I could see more archways and tunnels branching off in all directions.

Navigating a faery realm comes down to a mix of intuition, willpower, and luck. Not even the most basic rules apply. If you expect what's behind you to be what was just in front of you, then you're going to get lost in a straight corridor.

I pulled the bin liners off my sword and started walking.

I soon lost all track of time and space. I wandered through mazes built of bare twigs, moss, bits of barbed wire, and clods of disintegrated toilet paper. Sometimes I thought I was going round in circles, and sometimes I wished I was. Occasionally I was back in the sewer system, or at least something that looked a lot like it. Once, I came upon a moss-smothered sundial standing in a small courtyard. It seemed a bit pointless. There's no time in Faerie, and there was nothing to cast a shadow. I scraped the face clean. It was divided into eight sections, and instead of numbers there were words: attraction, worship, passion, rejection, fealty, death, valour, consummation. I suppose that was about as weird as you'd expect from a crazy faery lord.

I pressed on and finally found myself in a stone cloister that was half-swallowed by Victorian brickwork. The floor was slick with sewer water trickling from rusty pipes. The cloister overlooked a quadrangle of dead grass and filthy gravel. In the middle was a sunken fountain full of stagnant sewage, shattered pipework, and broken bits of statue.

I jumped down into the courtyard, but as I approached the fountain, a mass of heaving, rat-covered flesh burst out of the ruined pipes in a shower of shattered stone and sewer water.

The shock of the explosion knocked me off my feet, jerking the sword from my hand and sending it spinning across the floor.

Well, fuck.

It was a fountain, not a toilet, but I was pretty sure this was how Alice the plumber had died. I'm not a big fan of dying in general, but I really didn't fancy getting eaten alive.

The Rat Knight squeezed himself into a vaguely human shape and scrambled towards me on all fours, hundreds of squeaking, gnashing mouths thrusting out from his twisting flesh. If this thing got hold of me, I'd be a pile of chewed bones in seconds. I pushed myself away from him, hands and feet slipping on the slimy flagstones as I tried to get up. But his fingers closed round my ankle and started dragging me back. I could see broken rat bodies struggling under his skin, forcing their way to the surface to feed. On me.

I lifted my free leg and brought my boot heel down as hard as I could on his hand. There was a crunch of tiny bones and a pathetic squealing, and I yanked myself free and rolled to my feet. My sword was on the wrong side of the thing that was trying to eat me, but I managed to grab a piece of ancient lead piping. At least it was a weapon I knew how to use.

The Rat Knight rose to face me, a membranous fusion of rat bits peeling back to reveal something like human features. Rows of beady little eyes burst across his cheeks before being sucked back in. I think he was trying to smile at me.

I usually have a pretty high squick threshold, but this guy really pushed my *kill it with fire* buttons.

He seemed to be trying to say something, but instead of a tongue, a live rodent thrashed about inside his mouth, and all he could do was make an incoherent groaning sound.

I raised my pipe and made the *bring it* gesture. He came at me, frenzied rat mouths bulging out of his outstretched hands, and I smacked him upside the head with all my sadly mortal strength. It basically felt—and sounded—like smacking a hammer into a bag of rats. His head split open to reveal a soupy mess of mangled rat bodies that were immediately and messily devoured by a new set of mouths that squirmed up from inside the creature's skull. If I didn't have my imminent death to worry about, I'd have been seriously grossed out.

While the knight was busy eating himself, I managed to circle halfway round towards my sword. But then he was after me again. I tried to beat him back with my pipe, but this time he caught the blow on his forearm. The arm was mashed to a pulp, but the Rat Knight kept coming, pushing through my guard and trying to overwhelm me with sheer momentum. I threw myself aside at the last second, but he piled on top of me, biting and scratching. I brought my feet together, kicked up, and tried to shove him away from me.

If I'd had my mother's strength, I'd have flung him across the room. Instead, he went about five feet, and then came straight back at me. I flailed desperately, and my fingers closed round the hilt of the sword. With no time to think or plan anything clever, I stabbed wildly as the Rat Knight rushed over me, hundreds of tiny mouths and claws shredding my clothes and ripping at my skin in a frenzy. He'd run straight onto the blade, but it still took the longest few seconds of my life for the fucker to notice I'd killed him. He slumped on top of me, glassy eyes and rat corpses patchworking his flesh. If anything, I'd made him even squickier. I made sure he was definitely dead, rolled the body aside, and stood up, pulling my blade free.

Knackered but uneaten, I sat down on the wreckage of the fountain to catch my breath and clean rat gunge off the sword.

Okay, note to self: beware of exploding fountains, and don't drop your only weapon.

Part of me wondered what had happened to everyone else, but there was no point speculating. This was a faery realm, and I'd find them when I found them. If I found them.

I left the cloisters, and I was back in the maze. Eventually I came to a delicate arched bridge over a sluggish stream, where a willow trailed its decaying branches in the water. The handrails turned out not to be an option, as they were wound around with barbed wire and briars. I edged onto the bridge, and it shifted slightly under my weight, shaking flakes of rust loose into the water.

I wasn't that keen on trapping myself on a narrow strip of rickety metal, but I was even less keen on sloshing through the water, and there's never any point in going back on yourself in a faery realm. I was about halfway across when a fly landed on the back of my hand.

Perhaps I was being paranoid.

I quickened my pace, and the bridge creaked ominously.

A few steps further, and the air grew thick with flies, which crawled over my skin and tangled in my hair. They gathered together in front of me and poured themselves into the shape of a man. He was tall and slender, pale faced and dark haired, with sharp cheekbones and a pointy chin. He was wearing ragged chainmail and carrying a spear. And his eyes were black hollows swarming with flies that gathered in the air around him and trailed down his cheeks like tears.

I guess I wasn't being paranoid.

I took a few steps backwards because I really didn't want to fight a nutter with a spear on a narrow bridge. But then, glancing over my shoulder, I saw that the last knight had appeared behind me and blocked my retreat. Rot and mildew covered his body, and bones poked through his skin at the joints. He'd brought a rusty shield and a barbed wire flail to the Let's Kill Kate party.

This had just got interesting.

By which I meant fuck.

No seriously. Fuck. I was out of my league. I could take one unarmed man full of rats, but without my mother's power, I had no chance against two guys with weapons they knew how to use.

I tightened my grip on my sword, a weapon *I* didn't know how to use. A few coils of silver mist rose from the murky surface of the river, and for a moment, I thought I felt a hand on my shoulder. Then, without thinking, I stepped towards the Fly Knight, bearing aside his point with my blade and putting myself inside his guard. I seized the haft of his spear with my free hand and took another step forwards, driving my pommel into his face. He burst into a cloud of flies and I whirled round, bringing my sword up in a hanging guard just in time to catch the Rot Knight's flail in mid-flight. Its tails narrowly missed my face, wrapping round my sword instead. I snapped my arm back to free my blade, and the Rot Knight came forwards and smashed his shield into me.

I staggered back, winded, and found the floor wasn't where I expected it to be. Tumbling down the stairs, I landed in a heap at the foot of the bridge. The Fly Knight reappeared, spear in hand, and was about to shish kebab me when a rush of smoke and shadows came out of nowhere and threw him off. Kauri materialised and offered an exquisitely manicured hand to help me up.

"Honey, you look like you've been dragged through a sewer."

"No shit."

"I wish."

The Rot Knight was slowly coming down the bridge towards us while the Fly Knight had recovered and was readying his spear again. Things were looking way better than they had a minute ago. Sure, I was still in an underground faery realm being attacked by medieval dickheads, but at least I had company.

Kauri put his back to mine. "Okay, I'll take Pretty Fly For a White Guy and you take Tall, Dark, and Deliquescing."

He bamfed forwards, tendrils of darkness unfurling from his hands, and I turned to face the Rot Knight, falling easily into a guard. Nim had said the sword wanted to be used, but I hadn't expected to go all I Know Kung Fu. Right now I wasn't complaining, but I knew how this went. One minute, you're using skills you don't remember learning, and the next you're getting arrested for crimes you don't remember committing.

The Rot Knight advanced, swinging the flail in wide, slashing arcs. Parrying hadn't gone so well the last time, and I didn't really have an opening to attack him, so I fell back, waiting for an opportunity. The trouble was, he could come forwards faster than I could go backwards, and I was running out of options that didn't involve getting my face ripped off with barbed wire.

He brought his arm back for another attack, and I realised I had a very very narrow window when the flail was going the other way and his elbow was sticking out. But by the time I'd noticed, it was too late to take advantage, and I was forced to dodge awkwardly out of the way. He readied a fresh attack and, trying not to think about what would happen if I fucked this up, I went for it. I lunged forwards, bringing my sword down on his exposed forearm.

It was a bit like cutting into a mouldy orange. The skin split open and a rotting, pulpy mush oozed out. I pegged it backwards because the flail was still moving, but as the knight came round for yet another attack, the skin peeled away from his arm like stringy cheese, taking the weapon and most of his hand with it. Win. Before I could catch my breath, he came rushing at me, slicing his shield horizontally at my head. I leaned out of the way and the edge of the shield whistled past, too close for comfort. The force of the blow pulled the knight off balance, leaving him open, and I hacked into his exposed, mould-mottled ribs. The side of his chest crumpled inwards, and he crumbled slowly to his knees.

Monster Fighting Rule Number Twelve: Never Assume It's Dead.

I brought my sword round and smacked the knight over the head with it. His skull splodged into a mess of mould and goo.

Monster Fighting Rule Number Thirteen: No, Really, Never Assume It's Dead.

I stomped him into dust and kicked what was left into the river.

Kauri was still struggling with the Fly Knight. He had strength and speed, but the other guy could, well, turn into flies.

"Hold still, you buzzing shit," Kauri yelled, swiping ineffectively at the swarm of insects. "New plan, please."

"Take my hand." I coughed as flies pressed into my nose and mouth.

I pulled him after me up the riverbank and into the maze. A billowing cloud of flies streamed after us.

"This isn't really a plan, is it?" complained Kauri, as we ran helter-skelter through a series of twisty little passages.

"Got a better one?"

"Only if you know where to find a really big spider."

"Not at this time of night."

We kept going.

"Not being funny," said Kauri, "but why are we holding hands?"

"Faery realm. It'll separate us if we let it."

"So that's what happened to the others. I thought they'd just fucked off and left me."

We burst out of a tunnel into some kind of statue garden. Four great arches like the one I'd first seen, all lined by corridors of dead trees, surrounding a central plaza of dead grass and dead roses. Ashriel was slumped against one of the statues, breathing heavily, his shirt soaked with blood.

"Incoming," I yelled, as we ran towards him.

The air grew heavy with flies, and suddenly the Fly Knight was in front of me with his spear raised. I damn near ran straight into it.

Here likes Kate Kane. Should have looked where she was fucking going. Beloved daughter. Sorely missed.

I brought my sword across just in time to knock the point of his spear away. I aimed a swipe at him, but he dissolved into flies. Again. Fucker.

"Get down!" shouted Ashriel.

I threw myself to the ground as a gout of sickly green fire roared overhead. Charred fly corpses rained down on me like confetti from a wedding in Hell. I got up just in time to see Ashriel falling over.

Kauri stepped out of a swirl of shadows and caught him. "Honey, you are so fucked."

Ashriel gestured weakly. "Next time I'll let you get eaten."

"Are you going to be okay?" I asked.

"Probably pushed my luck with the hellfire."

"Well, take a moment."

"Is that safe?" Kauri glanced round nervously.

I shrugged. "I think we're a long way past safe."

We propped Ashriel up against one of the plinths, and I did my best to put his bandages back in place.

He lifted his brows. "You shouldn't put me on a pedestal, Kate."

"Oh, shut up."

Kauri tilted his head to look at the sculptures. "Is that the guy we're here to kill?"

We were on the edge of a circle of eight marble statues, still surprisingly clean and intact. They did, indeed, show the King of the Court of Love in his better days, complete with ankle-length hair, sweeping wings, and sculpted man-titty. He seemed to be making a sequence of dramatic gestures to a random woman that the artist hadn't bothered to carve in any detail. In one, he was kneeling at her feet, in another he was lying on a bed of roses bleeding from the heart. In yet another, he turned away from her weeping. In the last, he had her pinned underneath him, and there was no doubt what was going on there. I added that to the long list of reasons why Faerie was fucked up.

"Yep."

"What sort of person decorates his home with statues of himself?"

"Faeries. Ultimate narcissists."

Suddenly a crossbow bolt whistled past my ear and embedded itself in Kauri's heart.

"Fu—" he said, and keeled over.

I whirled round to see dark figures stepping out from the archways.

Ashriel rolled off the plinth and landed in a heap on the floor. "Great," he sighed. "Just what we need. Killer zombie nuns."

CHAPTER TWENTY

HEARTS & FLOWERS

I ducked down behind the pedestal as another crossbow bolt zinged past me. Oh, this wasn't good. I peeped round the edge. They had us surrounded. A pallid woman in a tattered habit stood in each of the four archways. They were packing some serious medieval firepower and they had us in a kill zone. I had to pick my next move very carefully, because I had this funny attachment to my lungs. Why hadn't Nim given me an enchanted shotgun?

"Bugger," observed Ashriel.

Across the garden, the two nuns who'd already fired were reloading. And I was, as usual, low on options.

"Cover me." I crept round the statue, trying to keep it between me and as many nuns as possible. "I'm going in."

He hauled himself up and lobbed a weak burst of hellfire at the nearest nun. It distracted her just long enough for me to charge and I barrelled into her, swiping frantically with my sword. I didn't want to think about how close I came to getting a crossbow bolt in the chest, and there was still another nun behind me who hadn't fired. I circled round and under the arch, and turned to face Sister Zombie. As long as I could keep her between me and the others, I'd probably be okay.

She dropped the crossbow, and, liking those odds, I attacked. I slashed at her head, but she darted forwards and caught my wrist with her forearm. She was pretty quick for a dead woman. I glanced down just in time to see a blade shoot out of her sleeve. I had to get me one of those, but first I had to stop it going through my liver. I brought my other hand round and pushed her back. She spun away from me.

We faced off. Mine was bigger, but I was pretty sure she could use hers better. I aimed a quick cut at her wrist, but she danced away, trying to draw me back into the courtyard where her undead mates could shoot me full of holes. They'd converged in the middle of the room, crossbows reloaded and ready.

Well, this was it. I was trapped. I couldn't go forwards without getting shot, and I couldn't run away without leaving Kauri and Ashriel to get killed by ninja zombie nuns. And, for that matter, if I killed the nun in front of me, I'd just make it really easy for the three others to take me out.

"Can we talk about this?"

I took the silence that followed as a pretty definite no.

Here lies—

There was a snarl, and a blur of sandy-coloured fur. Henry came racing in from one of the corridors and piled into the three nuns, pinning one to the ground, and catching another between his jaws and flinging her against a statue.

I rushed Sister Zombie, driving her back with a furious series of cuts, until I pinned her against a plinth. I went for her arm, and she dodged sideways, so I turned my hand and struck the other way, catching her across the side of the face. She fell, and Henry brought down the last of the others before padding over towards me. He shifted fluidly into his human form. "I was worried something had happened to you."

I maintained scrupulous eye contact. "It did," I said, "but I staked it."

"Should I ask?"

"Best not."

And speaking of staking, I ran over to Kauri. I yanked the bolt out of the poor bugger's chest, and he snapped upright like Uma Thurman in *Pulp Fiction*.

"Well, that was annoying. Stupid bloody professional vampire hunters."

"Tell me about it." Ashriel was slumped on the floor, looking even worse than he had two minutes ago.

"You did run right into them," said Henry chidingly. "What were you thinking?"

I glared. "It wasn't like we had a choice."

"What do you mean? Everyone's been behaving like complete berks since we got down here. I've spent the last however long chasing my tail, trying to get everyone back together."

I stared at him. "You can navigate Faerie?"

"You can't?" He blinked. "Oh yah, silly of me, must be a wolf thing. If I'd known you'd all be running around like headless chickens, I wouldn't have come alone."

After Safernoc, I should have realised that Henry was way better qualified to handle creepy faery shit than the rest of us. "Henry, I'm not sure whether I want to hug you or smack you. Does this mean you know where you are?"

"I don't know where I am, but I know where I'm going. This place reeks of its lord."

"Right," I said. "New plan. Stick with Henry, and all hold hands."

Kauri cracked up.

"What's wrong with you?"

"You've got to admit, this is pretty funny. We're in a sewer, going to fight an evil faery lord, holding hands like a bunch of school kids, and one of us is naked."

I sighed. "I've spent this entire case sifting through poo. I'm long past worrying about my dignity. Now, if everyone's ready, let's go."

"Um, Kate." Ashriel sounded like he'd had it. "I . . . I'm really not ready. I'm kind of fucked over here. You'll just have to leave me."

I looked up. "Oh no you don't, you're not doing the 'leave me, save yourselves' bit. You're coming with us, or we're getting you out."

Kauri cracked up again.

"Will you stop it?" I really wanted to throw something at him, but I had nothing except a dead nun and a sword. "This is a serious rescue operation."

He wagged his finger at Ashriel. "You should have gone before you left. If I have to stop this mission one more time, we're all turning round and going home."

Ashriel flumped onto his side and started laughing too. "Oh, we're fucking dead," he cackled. "We're so fucking dead."

Henry was kneeling by the nun I'd skewered. "Uh, sorry to interrupt your frankly bizarre behaviour, chaps, but these things seem to be getting better."

"Well, of course they are, puppy," said Ashriel, calming down a fraction. "They're stuck here, much like we are."

I peered at the body of Sister Zombie. Nim had said this sword could basically kill anything. Then again, I guess these women were already dead and tied to the faery realm we were currently inside. "Wow, bummer for them. Can we unstick them? I don't fancy being hunted by indestructible killer nuns."

"Not really my forte." Henry shrugged. "I just bite things."

"We have to do something," I insisted. "Otherwise they'll just keep coming."

Ashriel winced. "I don't suppose any of you have a priest in your pocket?"

"No," Kauri giggled. "I'm just pleased to see you."

Ashriel collapsed again.

"Less banter," I growled, "more options."

There was a thoughtful pause.

"Well," offered Ashriel, "I suppose I could suck their souls out. It'll stop them coming after you."

Henry glared. "I don't think so."

I thought about it a moment. "I guess that'd be better for us, but not for them."

"I'd let them go again," said Ashriel. "If I get out of here."

Henry stood up and leaned against one of the statues, keeping a careful distance between himself and the sex demon. "So you're saying you'd suck their souls out, but you wouldn't inhale?"

"Can you do that?" I asked.

"Of course. We trade in souls all the time."

"You would give them back again, right?"

"Yes, I'd give them back again. Though they'd be worth a fucking fortune."

Henry did not look impressed. "We're really going to trust the word of a demon?"

Ashriel put his hands up. "Look, worst-case scenario I take them to Hell, which isn't that much worse than where they are now. And at least it gets them out of your hair."

"Nuns or no nuns," I said, "I'm not leaving you here."

"And I'm not trusting him on his own with four innocent souls," snapped Henry.

Kauri was laughing again. "All we need now is a fox, a chicken, and a bag of grain."

"Not helping." I ran my hands through my hair and took a deep breath. "Okay, new new plan. Henry, get Ashriel out of here. You can find your way out, right?"

Henry shook his head stubbornly. "I'm not going. You need me."

"It's not your fight. And I'm not leaving anyone trapped here. Not even four zombie nuns, if I can help it. If we're all killed, you can get the pack and finish what we started. Also, we don't really have time to argue about this."

"All right. But I'm doing it for the nuns, not the incubus. And if he double-crosses us, I'll tear him to pieces."

Ashriel scowled. "Put your dick away, Fido. I'm not in a position to be double-crossing anyone."

"Still not helping," I said. "Now do what you have to do, Ashriel, and get out of here before you get killed."

Ashriel staggered over to the nun I'd cut down and knelt beside her. Her hand shot up and closed around his throat, but she was still too weak to be any threat. He leaned over her, put his lips close to hers and slowly inhaled, drawing out a ribbon of multicoloured light. The body went limp. Ashriel clambered painfully back to his feet and exhaled, blowing iridescent spirals into the palm of his hand, where they formed a tiny, shining sphere. He did the same thing to the other nuns, until he was holding four balls of light in one tenderly cupped hand.

I peered at them curiously. Each one was a constantly shifting pattern of colours, and each one was different. "You take care of those."

He nodded. "I will."

"Can you walk?" Henry asked.

"Just about."

Henry huffed out an exasperated sigh. "Come on, I'll carry you. But no funny business."

"Don't flatter yourself."

Henry shifted back into his wolf form and Kauri helped Ashriel onto his back. And then Henry padded off through one of the arches, and they disappeared into the darkness.

I took Kauri's hand, and we pressed on into the maze. I felt like we should have been hurrying, but I knew it wouldn't make a difference. We'd arrive when we arrived, and it was probably best if I wasn't knackered when we got there. We kept wandering through tunnels and corridors and bowers until we came to another open space. In the centre was a heart-shaped archway made of the same congealed fat and grease. A swing hung from it on ropes of glistening grey-green roses.

Maeve was sitting on the swing with her eyes closed, murmuring softly under her breath. She opened her eyes. "I was beginning to think this was a really elaborate trap."

"Please, I'm not that subtle."

"She really isn't," agreed Kauri.

"I suppose," said Maeve, "you want me to lead you to the King?"

"You can do that?"

"Yes. I'm a Priestess of the Quiet Gods. It's what I do."

"Then how come you all got separated?"

She shrugged. "They wouldn't trust me."

Kauri's eyes flicked over her. "No offence, honey, but you're not exactly trustworthy."

Maeve glared at him. "Raise your hand everyone who hunts humans for food."

Kauri glared back. "Raise your hand everyone who tried to murder the person we're here to rescue."

I sighed. "Raise your hand everyone here who needs to shut up right now."

They shut up.

"Do you want my help or not?" Maeve climbed off the swing and wiped her hands on her dress.

"Is bloodletting in a sewer really a good idea?" I asked.

"No." She gave an ironic half smile. "But none of this is a good idea."

"Okay, what do we have to do?"

"Give me your hands."

"Don't make me regret this."

She drew a knife from her belt and pricked my fingertip. Then she did the same to Kauri's, and finally to her own. She pressed our hands together and said something in a language I didn't understand and probably didn't want to.

Kauri blinked at his finger. "Is that it?"

She nodded, raising a hand and gently sweeping it through the air as if she was feeling its texture. "It's this way." And she led us straight into a wall of brickwork, wire, and climbing roses.

I felt a bit dubious about walking into solid objects, but this was magecraft, so I kept my mouth shut. And sure enough, the wall parted as we passed through it.

Of course, then we were back in the fucking maze.

Maeve went first, stopping every now and then to let a drop of her blood fall on the floor.

"Oh," I said, "by the way. There are indestructible killer zombie nuns running around in here."

"I know, I can sense them."

"Any idea where they are now?"

Maeve gave me a look.

"Oh, fuck."

"Two of them. Behind us."

I looked up and down the very long, very straight tunnel.

A couple of nuns stepped into the corridor, crossbows ready. We had nowhere to hide, and if we ran we'd just get shot in the back. I was starting to see why swords had gone out of fashion.

"Go." Kauri waved us away. "This is my big number."

I hesitated. "We stick together."

"Honey, you're cramping my style. Now get out of here."

I heard the soft whoosh of a crossbow bolt. I looked down to see that Kauri had caught it just before it hit me in the chest. He opened his fingers, and it clattered harmlessly onto the floor. Then he bamfed down the corridor faster than I could track.

Maeve and I turned and ran for it.

"The others aren't far," said Maeve.

"Corners. We need corners, dammit."

We got off the main tunnel and found some corners. I normally hate these kinds of twisty, narrow passages but then again, I'm not usually fighting medieval sniper nuns. I pressed myself to the wall, barbs and briars snagging at my clothes, edged my way along, poked my head round the corner, and ducked back just as a crossbow bolt whizzed through the space where my left eye had been.

You had one shot, lady, and that was it.

I broke cover and went tearing for the nun. She was as quick as the last one and had another of those little spring-loaded wrist blade things, but I was ready this time. Stab me once, shame on you. Stab me twice, shame on me. I kept her on the retreat, hammered her into a wall, and ran her through.

I whirled round, and, of course, there was another nun back there, with a crossbow pointed right at me.

I had just enough time to realise how totally fucked I was (again), before thorns and wires lashed out from the wall and entangled her. I Rule Twelved her, in the hope it would keep her down long enough for us to get away, and moved cautiously down the corridor to where I'd left Maeve. She was standing by the wall with one hand impaled on a thorn, blood and ooze tracking down her wrist.

"What the fuck are you doing?"

She gave me a look. "Magic."

"I got that bit."

"I've taken control of the maze. Not much of it, and not for long, but enough."

There was another nun wrapped in roses and barbs a little further down the corridor. I stabbed her as well. Just in case. Tied up and skewered is probably safer than just tied up.

"That's all of them," I said. "We met the other four earlier."

"We should hurry, then. My control won't last."

"Can we do anything for them?"

Maeve eased her hand off the thorn. "For who?"

I pointed at one of the nuns.

"For the woman you just stabbed in the chest?"

"Only because she was trying to kill me. I don't want to leave them trapped here forever."

"The world is vast and cruel." Maeve pressed her palms together to slow the bleeding. "Sometimes bad things happen, and sometimes they last forever."

"Wow, that's harsh."

"Of the two of us here, who tried to rip the other one's throat out?"

"Not the point. Can you help these women or not?"

"I could, but it would take time we don't have. And I've angered my Gods enough on your account."

"Fine," I sighed, "let's go."

I didn't like it, but it didn't seem as if there was any other choice. We hurried on, and, when I felt we were far enough away, I tore a couple of strips off my shirt and bound up Maeve's palms.

"Your hands are wrecked. Why do you do this to yourself?"

"Why does anyone do anything? Power. And my Gods demand it."

"Your Gods are psychos."

She smiled. "They are wild and ancient and dangerous. But they're also terrible and beautiful beyond imagining, and there are few left in this world who remember them. They matter to me."

"They're still psychos."

She gave me another one of those looks. "And who are we here to rescue again?"

"You liked her too."

"I worship crazy blood Gods, what's your excuse?"

Huh.

We continued through the maze. And at last—fucking finally—we came to the bower of the King of the Court of Love. Four of the familiar arches met in the middle of a great vaulted chamber strewn with mouldering rose petals and trickling sewer water. Vines and roses criss-crossed the walls and wound about heart-shaped windows that opened onto blank brickwork. The King was sitting on a delicate throne of gold-veined marble, decked with lilies. Julian hung from golden chains behind him. She looked scarily like a corpse, and I hoped we weren't too late. But if she was properly dead, she'd have turned to dust, right?

The King of the Court of Love stood and came towards us, his hair trailing gracefully behind him in a train of petals, lilies, and maggots.

"*Knyght.*" His voice was sweet and light as champagne. "*Welcum iwys to þis place.*"

"I've come for my girlfriend," I said. "Cockstain."

"*Ye haf your lemman.*" He gave a gracious sweep of his arm. "*Þis lady is myn awen.*"

"She fucking well isn't."

"And I'm no one's lemman," added Maeve.

"What's a lemon?" I asked.

"Girlfriend."

Well, this was awkward. "Look, dude." I pointed at Julian, who still hadn't stirred. "That's my girlfriend, she's not your lemon, and I want her back."

"*I bere hire druerie.*" He held out his arm with the beads wrapped around it, and I recognised the rest of Julian's rosary.

I sighed. "Oh, you're just fucking insane."

"*I bid yow pees and no plyght seche.*" He smiled serenely at me and pressed his palms together in a gesture of humility. "*Wolde yow be myn knyght, I wouldst gif yow þe comlokest to discrye.*"

I turned to Maeve. "What's he on about?"

"He says chill out and don't be starting anything. Work for me and I'll give you all the pretty lasses."

I'd had enough of this. I went for him. My sword swept harmlessly through the air as he danced back and caught up his twin blades from beside the throne. Just like Julian had said. "*Pyn fare is veyn, Sir Knyght.*" I was pretty sure he was taking the piss.

"Not a sir." I charged.

After he effortlessly parried my first three or four attacks, I realised I was hopelessly outmatched. Eve had always told me that nobody seriously fought with two weapons. I guess she was wrong. The fucker wasn't even trying, just batting my blade aside like a cat with a piece of string.

"Little help here, lemon," I shouted.

Maeve had unbound her hands and was tracing symbols on her arms and face with her own blood. "Give me some time, this is fiddly."

I kept on hacking at him. I wasn't really getting anywhere, but if he wanted to fanny about, that was okay by me. Suddenly he spun his whole body a quarter circle and his hair lashed around my sword arm.

Oh, you have to be *fucking* kidding me.

Maggots crawled up my sleeve, and he pulled me off balance, bringing his blades level with my throat and heart.

"*Wolde yow batayl for luf,*" he said, with a mocking smile, "*þenne yowre luf is ful wayke.*"

I didn't know what medieval smack he was talking, but he was really getting on my wick. I made another attempt to reach my mother's power. I caught a taste of blood and spite, but nothing came. Well, thanks, Mum. I was starting to get the feeling that this had been a bad deal. My mum was in a huff, and Nim wasn't pulling her weight.

A silver mist stirred the petals on the floor. Very pretty, but not exactly helpful.

And then I felt a hand on mine.

I twisted my sword in a C-shaped arc and sliced through his hair, spilling maggots and filth onto the floor. He stabbed at me, and I sprang back out of reach. He came at me, whirling both swords in overlapping figure eights. I could hear them cutting the air like helicopter blades. I really wanted to get the fuck out of the way, but something made me hold my ground. I realised with a sudden clarity that while the mincing machine technique looked scary as hell, the pattern itself was rigid and predictable. I picked my moment and thrust. To my amazement, my sword passed between his blades and plunged into his side. I flew out, parrying his counterattack on the way.

He paused, looking down at the wound. Pale, pus-white fluid was slicking down his skin. He flicked back what was left of his hair and laughed. It was a joyous, seductive sound, and I didn't like it one bit.

He came at me again, even faster this time. And, instead of the windmill of death, his blades whirled through the air, without rhythm or pattern. It was a merciless onslaught, a flurry of steel and chaos. I searched for an opening, but he was moving so quickly and so unpredictably that by the time I'd found one, he was somewhere else.

It wasn't long before I was backed into a corner, frantically warding off a hail of blows. I reckoned I could keep that up for all of eight seconds. It turned out I didn't even have that option. As I brought my sword up to defend myself, he hooked one of his blades behind mine and pushed the other forwards like he was turning a winch. My wrist twisted back, my hand opened, and the sword fell out of my grip.

He laid the edge of one sword across my throat and drew the other back with its point lowered towards my eyes. Poser.

"*Now farez wel.*" He was still smiling.

Then Maeve shouted something in the ancient language I'd heard her use before. The King of the Court of Love was dragged across the room and pinned to his own throne, his swords clattering to the floor at my feet. Maeve was standing with one arm raised as if she was holding him back, the bloody patterns on her skin writhing and reforming as she chanted. Sweat was pouring down her face and mingling with the markings. I probably didn't have much time.

I grabbed my sword, ran across the room, and swung for his neck. Gasping with effort, he raised an arm to protect himself, and I severed his hand at the wrist. This unfortunately left his head intact. He gave a cry of fury, maggots and filth oozing from the ragged stump. I brought my sword back for a second try, but he tore himself free and punched me in the face with his good hand.

I stumbled backwards, pain and the shock of impact thudding through my head. For a moment, I couldn't focus. When I could see again, he'd recovered one of his swords and was turning to Maeve. Roses reached down from the walls and twined around her wrists and ankles. She gave a shriek as they drew tight.

I dashed forwards and swung my sword straight at his head. He brought his blade over his shoulder and parried without even looking.

Maeve screamed again.

Okay. New plan. New plan.

I really didn't want to see someone torn apart by roses.

The King of the Court of Love turned to face me.

Shit. Shit. Shit. What was I supposed to do? If I ran at him, he'd stab me. But if I stayed here fighting, Maeve would get ripped to bits. She'd closed her eyes and started chanting. I had no idea what that meant, but I hoped it was good.

I feinted, just a bit impressed I knew how, and while that had his attention, I darted sideways. He countered hard, trying to drive me back, so I stood my ground, knocked his blade aside and punched him in the ribs. He tried to pummel me in the face, so I dodged back and around, closing the distance between me and Maeve. I hacked into the roses that were holding her right arm, and then I had an angry faery lord to handle.

We traded blows, but I was tiring. Magic swords and mystical crash courses were all very well, but I was still a mortal, and I was going to fall over long before I got through his guard.

Maeve worked her knife free and starting cutting into the roses. Shallow wounds opened and closed across the King's arms. Then she managed to free herself and made a bolt for the door.

"What the fuck are you doing?" I yelled.

"I'm bringing reinforcements."

She stood in the doorway with arms outstretched, murmuring something in the language I didn't speak, and the thorns reached down to embrace her, sinking hungrily into her flesh.

"I just got you out of that," I protested.

The King swung a heavy blow at my head, and when I dragged my sword up to block, the fucker kicked me in the gut. I stumbled backwards, gasping for breath, and he turned to Maeve.

"Oh no, you don't," I wheezed, staggering after him. "Fight me, you immortal tosser."

And just in case he wasn't getting the message, I grabbed a handful of his hair and yanked him backwards. He spun round and tried to stab me, but we were too close and the angle was all wrong. I knocked his sword aside and got the fuck out of the way.

"*Ich wax wroth,*" he announced.

He wasn't kidding. He wrothed me all the way across the room with a relentless barrage of strikes I just managed to fend off. My arms had pretty much had it, and the rest of me wasn't too happy, either. Backing me against the throne, he rained blows down on me until my legs gave up and I collapsed onto it. Well, at least I was going to die in state. He brought his sword crashing down, and I threw myself sideways. The blade split the throne in half, showering me in lilies and marble dust.

The King of the Court of Love walked up the ruins of the throne and balanced on the arm like some crazy bird. I tried to stand, but couldn't. He slipped down, grabbed my collar, and drew his blade back to strike.

There was a whirl of shadows, and Kauri pulled me clear. Then Aeglica's hand closed round the King's sword, ripped it from his grasp, and cast it aside. He seized the faery lord and threw him across the room. Kauri helped me to my feet and bamfed off into the fight. Since they seemed to have it covered, I made a dash—okay, a hobble—for Julian.

She was bound to the wall with a series of fine golden chains, pretty to look at, but not exactly that secure. I broke them one at a time, and Julian fell into my arms.

She stirred very slightly. "My hero. You look hot with a sword."

"Are you all right?"

"It's fine . . . you got here in time."

I gathered her up and turned. Maeve was hanging in the doorway, dead or unconscious—I hoped unconscious. Aeglica, Kauri, and the King of the Court of Love were beating seven kinds of hell out of each other in the middle of the room. The King was fast, but not as fast as Kauri, and strong, but not as strong as Aeglica. He had technique, but Aeglica had a thousand years of kicking the living shit out of things. It would have been fascinating to watch if I hadn't been exhausted, at risk of death, and ankle deep in sewer water.

The King of the Court of Love was facing off against Aeglica, throwing out strikes that the Prince of Swords was casually batting aside with his forearm. Kauri rushed him from behind in a blur of claws and darkness. Without even looking, the King spun his sword in his hand and thrust under his own arm, driving the blade deep between Kauri's ribs with flawless precision. You almost had to admire the poncy fuck.

Kauri slumped to the ground like an extremely well-dressed sack of potatoes, and Aeglica grabbed the King by the throat and hurled him against his own broken throne.

What happened next was really not pretty, and I had a front-row seat.

Aeglica strode across the room, caught the King by the hair, and pounded his head repeatedly into the shattered marble, while the King clawed, scrabbled, and kicked.

I was never drinking a smoothie again.

Finally, the King of the Court of Love went limp, and Aeglica stood, his hand dripping with glistening fluid, and slowly backed away.

"Is it dead?" Kauri tottered to his feet like Bambi.

"I do not know," said Aeglica.

There was a sudden flash of movement, and the King of the Court of Love twisted like some kind of horrible lizard, shot across the room, and rose to his feet. He shook out his hair. Apart from his severed hand and the cut I'd left in his side, which was still weeping, he looked completely unharmed. Though still pretty wroth.

Aeglica blinked. "Hmm."

The King looked up and smiled. And then the ceiling fell in.

Chunks of jagged masonry tumbled down on top of us. Kauri slowly unravelled into shadow, and Aeglica just stood there and took it, but I didn't have that luxury. I picked up Julian and zigzagged for the archway where Maeve was hanging. It was a close thing. I was tired and carrying a semi-conscious vampire, and the floor was still slick with mushed petals and greyish water. Rocks crashed down on either side of me, almost shaking me off my feet, and the more that fell, the harder it was to find a way across. At last, I pressed myself into the doorway and clung on while the room shook. Maeve, at least, was still breathing. I cut her down, and laid her and Julian in a pile on the floor. They'd have looked almost cute if they weren't both nearly dead.

When it was over, we were in a tattered, half-flooded rose garden strewn with filth and debris. A glittering alien starscape stretched above us. I think I preferred the sewers.

The King of the Court of Love turned slowly to face Aeglica, sweeping his one remaining hand in a regal gesture. "*Of þis regne*"—his voice seemed to come from everywhere at once—"*I am þe kynge, blod-þef.*"

Aeglica met his gaze, expressionless. "I have stood against the glory of kings."

Light pierced the distant horizon as the sun began to rise.

Well, fuck.

Kauri tumbled out of the air and collapsed next to me. He looked up at the sky. "Now that's just cheating."

The King of the Court of Love snatched up his sword and advanced on Aeglica, laughing. Aeglica brought his arm up to block, and the blade went straight through his hand. He staggered back and the King redoubled and ran him through. Aeglica caught the King behind the head and wrestled him to the ground, but the faery lord yanked his sword lose and wriggled free. Aeglica pursued him, but he was slowing.

The sun was almost at its peak, shining on the dirty water and the rotting roses that filled the vast open sewer that was the new Court of Love. Midday was coming unnaturally fast. I had a feeling that when it got here, it'd be here to stay. And this was why you didn't fight faery lords on their home turf.

The King drew his blade across Aeglica's cheek with contemptuous grace, leaving a deep gash that didn't heal. Aeglica slammed his fist into his opponent, knocked him to the ground again, and stamped heavily on his face. The King of the Court of Love rose unharmed.

Fuck, I was going to have to do something.

I gathered the last of my strength, waited for the King to turn his back on me, and charged. He pirouetted, flicked my sword away, raised his point, and stabbed me.

Oh, dear.

It didn't hurt nearly as much as I thought it should, which was how I knew it was really really bad.

I sank to my knees. The King of the Court of Love smiled down at me.

"*Ye fighte wyth hert, Sir Knyght.*"

Aeglica rose up behind him, grabbed his sword arm, and yanked it back across his neck, holding the faery lord immobile against his body. The King struggled but, for the moment, Aeglica had him.

"Strike."

I didn't hesitate. I took up my sword and plunged it hilt-deep into the heart of the King of the Court of Love.

A look of complete horror crossed his face.

And then he dissolved around the sword into a slurry of rotting petals and pus. His remains drifted away in the water, which ran suddenly clear. That left Aeglica, bleeding from a dozen cuts, my sword buried in his chest.

I pulled my blade free, and he sank slowly to the ground.

"Oh, shit." I didn't know what else to say. I was pretty sure I'd just killed him.

He bowed his head. "I am world-weary." His skin had grown tight over his bones and was crumbling to ash. "Ungleaming is the golden hall. The warriors are lost to the shadows." He closed his eyes. "The exile cannot withstand his fate."

And then there was nothing left of Aeglica Thrice-Risen but dust.

I crawled over to where I'd left Kauri, Julian, and Maeve.

Kauri sat up and stared me. "Fucking hell, you killed . . . everyone."

"And probably me. And all of us if we don't get out of here."

I didn't know what was happening to the Court of Love, but it seemed to be falling apart around us. The roses were rotting away to nothing and the Victorian brickwork was crumbling and being swept away with the sewage. Grass and trees were pushing up through the shattering flagstones.

Maeve's eyes flickered open. "Did we win? Or am I dead?"

"Hard to tell at the moment."

Since I seemed to be wasting such a lot of my blood, I wet my fingers in it and pressed them against Julian's lips. She lapped them clean and opened her eyes. She still looked uncomfortably like a corpse, but at least she was moving. "Did we win?"

"Yes and no."

She sniffed the air. "You're bleeding. Heavily."

"That's part of the 'and no.' The King's dead, Aeglica's dead, I'm probably dead, and we're trapped in a crumbling faery realm with no way to get back to London. So we won, but it was on a technicality."

She twined her fingers with mine. "Don't die on me, Kate." She glared at Maeve. "You're a witch, do something."

"Fine," snapped Maeve. "Bring me a virgin, a silver bowl, and a copper dagger, and I'll see what I can do."

"I'm serious."

"So am I."

"If you're no use to me alive," drawled Julian, "I'm sorely tempted to eat you."

"Can we not do this now, please?" I interrupted. "Maeve saved your life and you're not eating anybody." I looked hopefully around. "Now, does anybody have any magical healing powers that don't require a virgin sacrifice? Or failing that, a way to get home?"

Maeve shook her head. "I don't know where we are anymore, or how we got here."

"Aren't we in the Court of Love?"

"I don't think so."

Kauri looked round at the wild forest we were sitting in. "Not unless your idea of love is strictly *al fresco*, honey."

"Oh, fuck." This place looked too familiar. "We're in the Deepwild."

Maeve gazed at me for a second. "Ah. You're a fecking changeling, aren't you? I should've guessed when you tried to rip my fecking throat out."

"I'm not a changeling, more of a dumpling. My mother dumped me on my father's doorstep and buggered off back to Faerie. But that still doesn't explain what we're doing here."

"You staged a coup, Princess," explained Maeve. "I'm pretty sure we're still where we were, it's just part of the Deepwild now."

"If people don't starting using words I understand," said Julian, "I'm definitely going to eat someone."

Maeve sighed. "As far as Faerie is concerned, Kate *is* her mother. So when she killed the King of the Court of Love, she got his power and his kingdom."

"That's messed up and I wish I hadn't asked." Julian rose unsteadily to her feet. "Now how do we get out?"

"We ask her." Maeve pointed.

I turned, and there was my mother. She was barefoot, wrapped in animal skins, and wearing a crown of teeth and bones. Frankly, she looked a lot like me, only scarier. In one hand, she was holding her stone dagger, and in the other, a dripping, still-beating heart. She smiled.

"You have done well, daughter." Her voice was strong and clear— wild things and forgotten places.

"You know I'm probably going to die now, right?"

"Perhaps."

"Thanks for your concern." I didn't like to ask, because owing my mother a favour was unlikely to end well, but I didn't see that I had any other option. "Can you at least get us home?"

She thought about it for a moment. Then she held out her arm and a sharp-beaked, yellow-eyed bird swooped down and alighted on her wrist.

"Follow the hawk." She cast it aloft and walked away, the forest closing behind her.

"Let's go," I said, and fell over.

When I opened my eyes again, Kauri was carrying me and my sword, and Julian was holding my hand. I was in too much pain to protest. The forest went by in a blur of green. I could hear the splash of footsteps in water, and then came the chill of walking between worlds. Dark sky, familiar stars, the reek of the Thames, and the chill of a London night.

"Ring Elise." I flapped weakly at my phone. It had been in my jacket pocket this whole time, and while I'd been knocked on my arse, smacked in the head, and stabbed in the gut, my top half had come out okay.

"Who's Elise?" asked Julian.

"New assistant. You'll like her. She's hot." I blacked out again.

When I opened my eyes, I was lying in Julian's arms, staring at the inside of my car. I hurt. I hurt a lot. I turned my head to look at Julian's face. She seemed to be crying.

She squeezed my hand. "Don't try to move and don't die."

"Where are we going?"

Elise spoke from the driver's seat. "Hampstead Heath, Miss Kane."

"I think I'd like to go to hospital."

"That was initially my suggestion, but Miss Maeve believed it would be more efficacious if you were taken to Miss Nimue."

I turned my head a bit and saw that Maeve was crumpled in the passenger seat, smeared in blood and filth. All in all, Operation Confront a Faery Lord in His Lair could have gone better.

"I'd really like to go to hospital."

Julian lifted the hand she was holding and kissed it. "It's going to be all right. I promise."

I wasn't convinced, but then I passed out.

Eventually, I drifted back to wakefulness. Elise was carrying me across a field, and Julian was still holding my hand.

"Hospital?" I asked.

Elise put me down on a bench.

"Not bench. Hospital."

And then Nim was leaning over me. "Shut up, Kate." She began undoing my shirt.

"I'm not really in the mood," I told her. "And my girlfriend's right there."

"Shut up, Kate," said Nim and Julian together.

Nimue put her hand right over the place I'd been stabbed, sending a fresh wave of pain through me. Then I felt a warmth radiating from her palm and flowing into me, taking all the pain away.

I passed out. Again.

And when I came to, I felt absolutely fine.

Huh.

I sat up on the bench. I was on Hampstead Heath, overlooking a slightly crappy lake with a horizon of bushes and high-rises. My girlfriend, my ex-girlfriend, my girlfriend's ex-girlfriend, and my new assistant were all staring at me. I closed my shirt urgently. It was soaked with blood, but the skin underneath looked like it had never had any sharp bits of metal rammed through it. My thigh felt better too, and the cuts on my arms had gone.

Huh.

I pulled down the brim of my hat. "So this is awkward."

"On the contrary, Miss Kane," said Elise, "the operation appears to have been a complete success."

"Uh?"

"I would not have imagined your body could have been fixed so easily. I am greatly relieved that I was mistaken."

"Uh?"

"Miss Nimue was able to repair you by means of some sorcery I did not understand."

I turned carefully towards Nim, and then realised I didn't have to be careful because I was fine. "Since when can you do that?"

"Since you pledged fealty to my court."

"By the way," Julian scowled at me, "I'm really not happy about that."

"If I hadn't," I pointed out, "we'd both be dead."

"Look," said Maeve. "I've done my bit and then some. I'm going to leave you ladies to sort this out. Because I really need to take a bath and sacrifice a goat so I don't get hepatitis."

I decided to just let that one slide. "Thanks for your help."

"Normally I'd say anytime, but if you ever have to fight another deranged sewer god, call somebody else."

She turned and strode off over the Heath, her hair rippling like red ribbons in the early morning breeze.

"So are you two still at war?" I asked.

Julian glanced away. "We've come to an arrangement."

"What does that mean?"

"It means, we've come to an arrangement."

Nim touched my shoulder gently. "I'm glad you're all right, but I should go."

"Thanks for, y'know, saving my life and everything."

"Don't thank me, Kate. I'll see you soon."

Nim tucked her hands into the pockets of her hoodie and walked away.

That just left me, my vampire girlfriend, and the animated statue who I was looking after for a giant rat gestalt.

"Elise," I said, "can you give us a minute?"

"Certainly, Miss Kane." She stood there obligingly.

"Um, I meant can you go somewhere else? For longer than a minute. In fact, do you want to go back to the flat? Take the car, I'll grab a taxi."

"Certainly, Miss Kane. And welcome home."

Elise went back to the car, leaving me alone with my vampire girlfriend.

Julian watched Elise walk away. "So, she seems nice."

"She's interesting."

"Honestly. To breathe life into inert matter is one of the deepest, most ancient, and most sacred mysteries known to theurgy. And I swear people only ever use it to make sexbots."

Julian sat down next to me and slipped her hand in mine. The first suggestion of light was starting to creep across the night sky. "You know," she said, "you scared the shit out of me."

"Sorry."

"Don't be silly, you saved me." She paused. "Though not without cost, I fear. Poor Aeglica. Still, I think it's the way he would have wanted to go."

"What, in a sewer?"

"In battle against an ancient and powerful enemy."

Well, it wasn't really what you'd call an ancient and powerful enemy. It was more, sort of, me. That was when I realised Julian had been unconscious for most of the fight and hadn't seen what actually happened. Shit. How do you 'fess up to something like that?

She sighed. "I'll miss him, though. In a way. We'd known each other for the best part of a millennium. It seems strange to think of a world without him in it."

Shit. Shit. Shit. "Uh, sorry."

"Aeglica wasn't afraid of death. It was the only thing he truly understood. Though electing a new Prince of Swords is going to be a pain in the arse. I might have a lot to answer for."

Okay, Kate. If you're going to tell your girlfriend that you stabbed one of her oldest mates, this is the time to do it. "Look . . . Julian. I . . . I . . . I'm sorry if this causes problems for you."

Well, that could have gone better.

Julian gave me a sweet little smile. "I'm sure it'll all blow over. At the end of the day, it's just politics, and I'm afraid that never ends. It's one of the downsides to being immortal." She put a wrist to her forehead. "Along with the utter meaninglessness of existence, the unbearable ennui, and the soul-crushing loneliness."

"That's all bollocks, isn't it?"

Her teeth glinted. "Yes, it is. Being immortal is fabulous. Just think, if I hadn't been transformed into a bloodsucking abomination against God and nature, we might never have met."

I couldn't help it. I laughed. Truthfully, Julian Saint-Germain was the cutest bloodsucking abomination I'd met for a long time.

"So do all your relationships start like this?" I asked. "Murders, faeries, near-death experiences, massive political upheavals, whacky hijinks in sewers . . ."

"I did warn you, sweeting. I'm a motherfucking vampire prince."

She was. But at least I wasn't staring at an empty flat through the bottom of a whiskey glass. Yes, I'd nearly been killed, yes, people were dead, yes, we'd blown up Tottenham, and no, it probably wouldn't last but . . . fuck it, I was feeling great.

I leaned in to kiss her. "It's one of the things I like best about you."

She tasted of wine and roseleaves. The sun rose slowly over the Heath, the lake, and the grey concrete towers.

Don't miss the next exciting adventures in the
Kate Kane, Paranormal Investigator series:

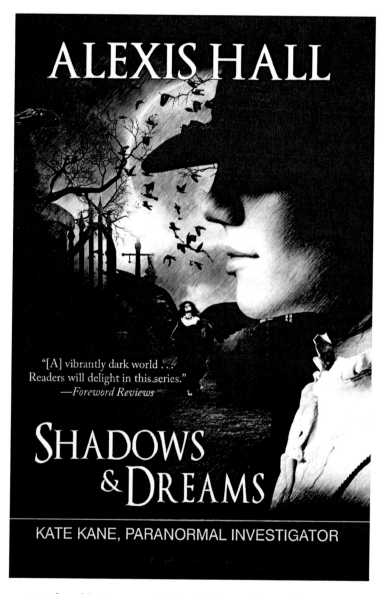

ALEXIS HALL

"[A] vibrantly dark world . . .
Readers will delight in this series."
—*Foreword Reviews*

SHADOWS
& DREAMS

KATE KANE, PARANORMAL INVESTIGATOR

Dear Reader,

Thank you for reading Alexis Hall's *Iron and Velvet*!

We know your time is precious and you have many, many entertainment options, so it means a lot that you've chosen to spend your time reading. We really hope you enjoyed it.

We'd be honored if you'd consider posting a review—good or bad—on sites like **Amazon, Barnes & Noble, Kobo, Goodreads, Twitter, Facebook, Tumblr,** and your blog or website. We'd also be honored if you told your friends and family about this book. Word of mouth is a book's lifeblood!

For more information on upcoming releases, author interviews, blog tours, contests, giveaways, and more, please sign up for our weekly, spam-free newsletter and visit us around the web:

Newsletter: tinyurl.com/RiptideSignup
Twitter: twitter.com/RiptideBooks
Facebook: facebook.com/RiptidePublishing
Goodreads: tinyurl.com/RiptideOnGoodreads
Tumblr: riptidepublishing.tumblr.com

Thank you so much for Reading the Rainbow!

RiptidePublishing.com

AUTHOR'S
NOTE

The stylised heart would not, in fact, have been used as a symbol of romantic love at the time of Julian's confrontation with the King of the Court of Love. And, indeed, the King of the Court of Love himself is a little anachronistic in that he embodies a concept of courtly love, which never actually existed. But given that we're talking about a magic faery who was taken out by a secret army of demon-hunting ninja nuns, one of whom is now a vampire, I decided anachronism was the least of my problems.

ACKNOWLEDGEMENTS

As ever, thanks to my friends and, for want of a less saccharine phrase, loved ones for putting up with me. And to the wonderful Sarah Frantz for, once again, correcting my abuses of innocent commas and making everything better. And, finally, to Riptide for being amazing and, yet again, taking a chance on me.

ALSO BY
ALEXIS HALL

ABOUT THE
AUTHOR

Alexis Hall was born in the early 1980s and still thinks the twenty-first century is the future. To this day, he feels cheated that he lived through a fin de siècle but inexplicably failed to drink a single glass of absinthe, dance with a single courtesan, or stay in a single garret.

He did the Oxbridge thing sometime in the 2000s and failed to learn anything of substance. He has had many jobs, including ice cream maker, fortune-teller, lab technician, and professional gambler. He was fired from most of them.

He can neither cook nor sing, but he can handle a seventeenth-century smallsword, punts from the proper end, and knows how to hotwire a car.

He lives in southeast England, with no cats and no children, and fully intends to keep it that way.

Website: quicunquevult.com
Twitter: @quicunquevult
Goodreads: goodreads.com/alexishall
Newsletter: quicunquevult.com/newsletter

Enjoy more stories like *Iron & Velvet* at RiptidePublishing.com!

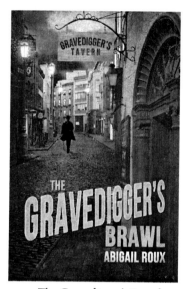

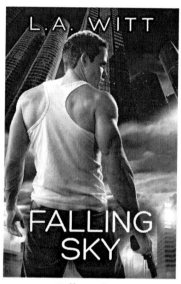

The Gravedigger's Brawl
ISBN: 978-1-937551-53-7

Falling Sky:
The Complete Collection
ISBN: 978-1-62649-040-6

Earn Bonus Bucks!

Earn 1 Bonus Buck for each dollar you spend. Find out how at RiptidePublishing.com/news/bonus-bucks.

Win Free Ebooks for a Year!

Pre-order coming soon titles directly through our site and you'll receive one entry into a drawing to win free books for a year! Get the details at RiptidePublishing.com/contests.

9-16

CPSIA information can be obtained at www.ICGtesting.com
Printed in the USA
LVOW07s1200110916

504132LV00007B/661/P